The QUEER PRINCIPLES of KIT WEBB

ALSO BY CAT SEBASTIAN

The QUEER PRINCIPLES of KIT WEBB

A NOVEL

CAT SEBASTIAN

AVON

An Imprint of HarperCollinsPublishers

THE QUEER PRINCIPLES OF KIT WEBB. Copyright © 2021 by Cat Sebastian. All rights reserved. Printed in the United States of America. No part of this book may be used or reproduced in any manner whatsoever without written permission except in the case of brief quotations embodied in critical articles and reviews. For information, address HarperCollins Publishers, 195 Broadway, New York, NY 10007.

HarperCollins books may be purchased for educational, business, or sales promotional use. For information, please email the Special Markets Department at SPsales@harpercollins.com.

FIRST EDITION

Designed by Diahann Sturge

Library of Congress Cataloging-in-Publication Data has been applied for.

ISBN 978-0-06-302621-6

21 22 23 24 25   LSC   10 9 8 7 6 5 4 3 2 1

Since laws were made for every degree,
To curb vice in others, as well as me,
I wonder we han't better company,
Upon Tyburn Tree;
But gold from law can take out the sting,
And if rich men like us were to swing,
'Twould thin the land, such numbers to string,
Upon Tyburn Tree.

—John Gay, *The Beggars' Opera*, 1728

The QUEER PRINCIPLES of KIT WEBB

Chapter 1

*K*it Webb had principles. He was certain of it. Even at his worst, which had reliably been found at the bottom of a bottle, he hadn't hurt anyone, at least not too badly. Well, at least not on purpose. Better, perhaps, to say that he never threw the first punch. As far as daggers and pistols, he found waving them about to be so effective that he never needed to resort to using them. Better not to dwell on whether this owed more to luck than to any skill or moral refinement on his part.

Yes, he had lightened a few purses in his day, but nobody whose purse wasn't altogether too heavy to begin with. He wasn't going to keep himself up at night worrying about what some or another lady was going to do with one fewer ruby diadem. Besides, that diadem had been murder to fence, nearly put him off the entire enterprise of jewel theft altogether. Betty hadn't spoken to him for weeks. He much preferred coin, please and thank you.

He did feel badly about the coachmen and outriders and other fools who got dragged into fights that were, properly, between Kit and the great and good of the land. But he figured that any poor sod who was fool enough to come between a highwayman and a gilt-encrusted traveling coach got whatever they had coming to them. Which, as it turned out, tended to be nothing more than a couple of well-placed punches.

But that was all in the past now anyway. He had turned over a new leaf, started fresh—or as close to fresh as a man could when he was nearly thirty and all his acquaintances were criminals and the back room of his place of business was little more than a house of assignation. As close to starting fresh as a man could get when three times a day some bastard walked past the coffeehouse singing that bloody fucking ballad about that one time he had escaped from prison—yes, the escape had been dashing but it wasn't even in the top 10 percent of his most impressive feats, and it was a sin and a shame that jail rhymed with so many words. Besides, his shoulder still hurt from where he had injured it in squeezing through the barred window, and the less said about the gunshot wound that had been allowed to fester during his week in prison, the better. And that ill-fated escape had followed hard upon Rob's death, which was not the sort of thing he wanted to be reminded of in lazily rhymed couplets.

No, he probably didn't have principles at all, sorry to say. But he could act like he did. In fact, he had to act like it, seeing as how with his leg in this state he could hardly continue to merrily thieve his way across England. He was the very model of what the preacher in Hyde Park was pleased to call A Virtuous Life and the boredom of it would probably kill him.

For twelve months now Kit had lived the life of an honest and respectable shopkeeper. He turned his attention to running the coffeehouse, which he had bought some years ago on a drunken whim and then operated as little more than a convenient staging ground, a literal den of thieves. But these days, when a customer came in with a purse full of gold and a head full of cotton wool, they left with both head and purse intact.

And if the past year of trying to live a decent sort of life had only resulted in Kit getting more foul tempered by the day, it was probably his own fault for being so very bad at being good. He had to try harder, that was all. Still, sometimes after walking Betty home after closing up at night, he almost wished footpads would come after him. He'd leap at the flimsiest excuse to fight back.

Maybe that was why when something that looked like first-rate trouble walked into Kit's coffeehouse, Kit felt like a bloodhound who had finally scented its quarry.

Chapter 2

$\mathscr{F}$or the rest of his life, Percy would associate the smell of oil paint with criminal conspiracy. It was fitting, he thought, that these meetings at which he and Marian plotted together would be preserved forever on canvas, displayed in the portrait gallery at Cheveril Castle.

Except—of course that wouldn't happen. This portrait would never be hung in the Cheveril Castle portrait gallery, because its subjects were not, after all, the Duchess of Clare and the future tenth Duke of Clare. Instead, they were plain Marian Hayes and Edward Percy Talbot—well, Edward Percy, he supposed, which was his mother's maiden name. His mother's only name. It was a small mercy she hadn't lived to see this. She'd have murdered the duke in his bed, without a single compunction, despite how immeasurably vulgar it would have been to be hanged as a common murderess.

"I think you have the wrong man," Percy told Marian when they were seated in the temporary studio the portraitist had set up in Clare House.

"He's the right man," Marian said. "My informant was quite certain."

Percy placed the fact that Marian had people she referred to as informants into the growing pile of things that would not have made the least bit of sense a mere month earlier. "He's not a"—Percy lowered his voice so the portraitist, situated a few feet away behind his easel, wouldn't overhear—"a highwayman. He's a shopkeeper. And just about the most boring man I've ever laid eyes on."

As far as Percy could tell, Webb seldom left the premises of his coffeehouse. He lived upstairs and worked downstairs. The only time he ventured farther than the limits of Russell Street was when he walked the serving girl home after dusk, sometimes stopping on the way back for supper. Webb frequented neither church nor tavern nor anywhere even remotely interesting. Percy had become momentarily intrigued when he realized how often Webb went to the baths, but the man seemed to spend his time there actually bathing, so Percy resumed being unimpressed.

If Webb had any friends, they came to him, never the other way around. He exchanged pleasantries—if semi-grunted greetings could be considered pleasant—with some of his more regular patrons but left the actual chatter to the tawny-skinned, gap-toothed girl who worked for him. A person less like a dashing highwayman Percy could not even begin to imagine. Percy had hoped that consorting with the criminal classes would at least be interesting, and was quite depressed by the reality.

"That's him," Marian said. "The coffeehouse is just a front."

A *front*? Percy would very much have liked to know when and where the Duchess of Clare had the opportunity to pick up criminal argot, but before he could open his mouth to ask the question, he noticed that Marian's maid had looked up from her mending.

The duke, perhaps sensing that Percy and Marian had aligned against him, or perhaps simply because he was committed to sowing unpleasantness everywhere he went, had taken to keeping a hawklike eye on his young wife. At all times she was either in his company or chaperoned by the maid he employed, and it had proven all but impossible for Percy to catch Marian alone for more than a few seconds.

"Your hair is crooked again," Percy said. "It keeps listing to the side." Marian had evidently decided that sitting for a portrait required about two pounds of wig powder, not to mention a profusion of feathers; the coiffure probably couldn't remain upright without the aid of flying buttresses, but Marian could at least put forth some effort.

Percy had, at great expense and personal inconvenience, imported this artist from Venice as a wedding present for Marian and, he supposed, his father. The duke, making his move in the game of chess he and Percy had been playing for years, had that morning declared himself to be too busy to sit for a portrait. Percy decided that he would sit for the portrait alongside Marian. The duke would be painted in later, likely wearing something that clashed grossly with Percy and Marian, spoiling the entire portrait.

Perhaps Percy could spirit the canvas away before his father was added in. How very quickly one could go from being a law-abiding citizen, the scion of a noble family, to consorting with highwaymen and then contemplating stealing one's own portrait. There was a lesson in there, he supposed, but he preferred not to think about it.

Instead, he allowed himself a moment of self-congratulation for having insisted on the sky-blue satin; it flattered Marian's complexion while complementing the slightly darker blue of his own coat. The effect was pleasantly harmonious, without making Percy look like a lapdog tied with a ribbon to match his mistress's costume.

"It's the latest fashion from Paris," Marian said, nonetheless raising a hand to straighten her hair.

"It's nothing of the sort. I'm not going to be immortalized on canvas as Unknown Gentleman and Lady with Crooked Periwig."

"Dearest, if you think we're going to be remembered by posterity for our coiffures, you really haven't been paying attention. We should be so lucky."

"*Your* coiffure," Percy corrected, although Marian was quite right. "Speak for yourself. My periwig is unexceptionable."

Percy kept an eye on Marian's maid, waiting until she appeared bored by the conversation and returned her attention to the hem she was mending. "Your highwayman is crippled," he murmured. "He uses a cane."

"Hmm," Marian hummed. "They don't mention that in any of the broadsides or ballads."

"Probably because it's a new injury, which would also explain his retirement. He can't possibly be capable of much in the way of robbery with a limp like that. We need someone else."

"We don't have anyone else," she snapped. "It was hard enough to turn up the name and address of one highwayman. For heaven's sake, Percy. We don't have that much time. Go back and get another name from *him*."

She was right, of course. The first letter had arrived a month ago, relating the bare facts of Percy's father's bigamy and demanding five hundred pounds before the first of January. Now they were left with a scant two months to come up with a plan. "Can you get rid of everyone so we can speak privately?" he whispered. "Even if it's only for a moment?"

Marian gave an imperceptible nod, then shifted in her seat, moving the doll that served as a placeholder for her daughter from one arm to the other.

"Your Grace," the portraitist said, his heavily accented voice carefully polite. "If you could be still, I beg you. The light, it moves. And, Lord Holland, if you could be so kind as to keep your attention on your infant sister, if you please?"

"I'm afraid I can't," Percy said, playing his role. "First of all, that poppet is—" He broke off with a shudder. Marian had found the godforsaken thing in the attics. What she had been doing in the attics was something Percy strongly preferred not to think about. "I believe repellent is not too strong a word." The doll's head was carved from wood and painted with pink cheeks, blue eyes, and a rosebud mouth. Glued to its head were strands of yellow silk embroidery thread, which made Percy think that the ghastly thing had been made to resemble a Talbot for the amusement of some long-dead aunt. But between the combined efforts of damp, time, and quite possibly rats, it was more suited to ritual witchcraft than belonging in a civilized nursery. "The poor thing has either leprosy or an advanced case of the pox."

"Don't listen to him, my darling," Marian cooed, covering the doll's moldering ears and pressing a loud kiss to its decayed forehead. Percy wanted to gag.

"Secondly," Percy went on, "if I fix my gaze on the doll, it'll look like I'm staring at the duchess's bosom." Marian's gown revealed an expanse of décolletage the approximate dimensions of a cricket pitch. "And while I daresay it's a pleasant enough bosom,"

Percy went on, "as far as those things go, I'm afraid I'd rather not be accused of leering at my stepmother."

"You've given me the most brilliant idea," Marian said in a tone of voice Percy knew from long experience meant nothing but trouble. She tugged down the bodice of her gown and determinedly applied the doll's head to her exposed breast.

"Why?" Percy cried, flinging a hand over his eyes. "Put it away!"

"I feel certain this is what the duke would want," Marian announced.

"Nobody wants this!" Percy protested.

"Like the holy mother," Marian said grandly. "I'm even wearing blue. Who would you like to be, Percy? I believe Saint Elizabeth is the traditional choice, but a young John the Baptist would be a bold alternative."

"You do have a point," Percy observed. "I've seen paintings of the Madonna and child in which our savior is even uglier than that poppet."

"That's Lady Eliza to you," Marian said, holding the wretched doll up as if for Percy to make its acquaintance.

"I feel certain this is blasphemous," Percy remarked. "Poor Signore Bramante wasn't expecting to have his principles compromised this afternoon," he said, indicating the artist.

"I do beg your pardon," Marian said, addressing the painter, who, Percy noted, had put down his brush and adopted an expression of mortified suffering, which he directed toward the ceiling, resolutely avoiding Marian's bosom. "Perhaps we ought to rest now and resume in an hour's time. Jane, will you fetch some hairpins so we can do something about my hair? No, that's quite all right, I'll survive on my own for a few minutes. Hurry, or Signore Bramante's paints will go dry. Signore, you'll find cakes in the kitchen."

"Nicely done," Percy said when they were alone. Marian had taken rather frighteningly well to this life of deception and intrigue they were apparently now leading. She had certainly managed it better than Percy, who still expected to wake up and find things restored to the way they were supposed to be.

"Thank you," Marian said primly, rearranging her bodice and casting the doll to the floor. "We don't have more than five minutes before Jane returns."

"We need to decide whether we're going to pay the blackmailer," Percy said bluntly.

"I've already told you what I think. Paying the blackmailer is letting your father get away with it. I want to make him suffer," Marian added with a degree of relish Percy found entirely understandable. "But I'll go along with paying the blackmailer if that's what you prefer."

What Percy would have preferred was not to have to make this choice. They had spent the past month investigating the blackmailer's claim. Percy had gone to Boulogne himself and seen the parish register with his own eyes: his father's name, his father's unmistakable signature, and a date twelve months before the duke married Percy's own mother. Marian's brother tracked down old companions of the duke and plied them with brandy until they admitted to knowing about what they had assumed to be a sham wedding. Percy's only hope was that the French strumpet had managed to die before the duke married Percy's mother. The blackmailer insisted that the woman was alive and well, and said he was prepared to prove it as publicly as possible on the first of January. Marian's brother was trying to track down the woman or her family, but Percy didn't have much hope he'd turn up a clearly marked grave or a witness to her death.

That was the crux of the problem: even a whisper of a rumor of his own legitimacy ruined the Clare legacy, and ruined it permanently. It would be passed on to his sons, and their sons, and linger like a miasma over Cheveril Castle for eternity. The more Percy fought, the worse the rumors would be.

"It would only delay the inevitable," Percy said. "Unless we mean to burn down this church in Boulogne and murder the blackmailer as well as half my father's old cronies, we can't hope to keep it a secret forever."

Marian remained silent rather longer than Percy thought it ought to take to agree that murder and arson were undesirable courses of action, however dreadful their present crisis. "That does sound impractical," she conceded.

"Instead, if we can get the duke's book, we can use it to force him to pay us enough to live quite comfortably. Since you have Eliza, he might not cast you off without a penny, but I'm afraid he'll only too gladly put me out on the street. We need that book for leverage."

"And then we let the blackmailer tell the world the truth about what a despicable man your father is," Marian supplied.

Percy swallowed. "I think, rather, we ought to tell the world ourselves. That way we stay in control." The idea of bringing about their own ruin was terrifying but so much better than living a lifetime in fear of having the truth exposed. "Does that sound agreeable?" he asked, as if proposing a promenade rather than a farewell to everything they had ever known.

Marian narrowed her eyes. "I plan to drain the estate of every penny we can. And, Percy," she added, "I'm going to see your father brought as low as humanly possible. When he married me, he made a bargain. I kept my end, but he didn't keep his. I will not be cheated, Percy."

He took one of her hands. Neither of them were particularly affectionate by nature, but she squeezed his hand with both of hers. It was the first time since returning to England that he had truly seen a trace of his childhood playmate. When he left for the Continent, she had still been barely out of pinafores, and now she was coiffed and powdered and the mother to his three-month-old sister; she had become as cold and shrewd as all the duchesses of Clare who had preceded her.

Sometimes he wondered exactly how his father had managed to convince Marian to marry him. The union had been presented to him as a fait accompli, the news arriving at Percy's lodgings in Florence troublingly soon after the news of his mother's death. It plainly wasn't a love match. Marian remained tight-lipped on the subject, and Percy and his father were hardly on cordial enough terms for such a conversation.

"Do you want to talk about it?" he asked, pitching his voice as gently as he could.

She shook her head, and before he could say anything else, Marian's maid returned, and they let go of one another's hands.

Chapter 3

*A*ll sorts of people came to Kit's. That was the point of the place, the point of coffeehouses in general. Ink-stained Grub Street hacks could get out of their cramped hired rooms, shopkeepers could pretend to be intellectuals, and well-shod gentlemen could get their hands dirty—but not too dirty.

What Kit sold was the fiction of democracy, accompanied by the aroma of coffee and tobacco and the company of a pretty serving girl. An afternoon in a coffeehouse was a chance for everyone to pretend the rules were less important than conversation. It was Twelfth Night, it was Carnival, but it took place in broad daylight, with everybody involved dead sober and wide-awake, with newspapers and hot drinks to lend everything the faint sheen of respectability.

Still, they didn't get too many gentlemen like the one Kit noticed in the corner. He was wigged and powdered, a birthmark too dark to be real affixed above one lip. Even from across the room, Kit could tell that the man's coat—wool of a violet so dark it was nearly blue, adorned with gold braid and brass buttons—must have cost a small fortune. The buttons alone would be worth nicking, as would the expanse of lace that spilled over the man's wrists. He had one leg crossed over the other, revealing, beneath the hem of his violet knee breeches, thin stockings of the palest lavender, embellished with a pattern of white flowers that crept up the side of his calf. On his feet he wore shiny black shoes with silver buckles and a small but obvious heel. At his hip he wore one of those shiny, ornamental swords that gentlemen insisted on swanning about with.

The man didn't have a newspaper open before him, nor a book, nor even a broadside. Apart from his cup of coffee—untouched, Kit noticed—his table was empty. Instead of sitting at the long table at the center of the room, which was where most unaccompanied patrons chose to sit, this man lounged at one of the smaller tables that lined the walls. It was off to the side but not in the shadows. It was almost as if he wanted to be looked at. It stood to reason, Kit supposed—one didn't wear purple coats or high-heeled shoes if one wished to remain unobtrusive.

Odder still, the man wasn't talking or reading or taking snuff. He wasn't even drinking his coffee. Instead, he was doing one thing, and he was doing it incessantly—he was watching Kit.

"Don't look now," he murmured to Betty the next time she came out from the kitchen, "but the man at table four is up to something."

She took her tray and made a circuit of the room, removing empty cups and exchanging remarks with a handful of regular patrons. "I could snatch his watch, his handkerchief, and his coin purse before he even reached the door," she said when she returned. "Not that I will. Keep your hair on, I know the rules," she added hastily and with audible regret. "My point is that the poor lamb's about to have a very bad day. As soon as he steps one pretty foot outside, somebody'll lighten his pockets. Maybe even before then, if I know Johnny Fowler."

They both cast a sideways glance at Fowler, who was indeed watching the gentleman almost as intently—but more covertly—than the gentleman was watching Kit. Fowler's mouth was practically watering. Kit sighed: he doubted Fowler would manage to wait until the gentleman crossed the threshold.

That was another thing coffeehouses were good for; an observant pickpocket could browse patrons for a likely target, follow them outside, and ply their craft. Hell, that was why Kit had thought to buy a coffeehouse in the first place—after spending hundreds of hours and countless pounds in such establishments, he figured he might as well try life on the opposite side of the till. And now it turned out operating a coffeehouse of his own was one of the few types of work—honest or otherwise—that he was fit for.

"But what's he doing?" Kit asked. "The gentleman, not Fowler. Why is he here? Gentlemen usually come in groups of twos or threes, not on their own."

"Maybe he's looking to pick somebody else's pocket," Betty said.

"Maybe," Kit mused. This man wouldn't be the first thief who dressed as a gentleman in order to throw off suspicion. He wouldn't even be the first thief to actually *be* a gentleman. "But he's only looking at me, not the room."

"You sure you don't know him?"

Kit raised his eyebrows at her. "I think I'd remember meeting the likes of that."

He chanced another look at the man. Kit was good at remembering faces—he had to be, both in his present line of work and his former one. And he knew he had never seen that man before.

Beneath the powder, the man's face was unremarkable—straight nose, a jaw that was neither weak nor strong, eyes of some color that was neither dark nor light. His eyebrows were a pale wheat, meaning that the hair beneath his wig was likely even lighter. It was hard to tell, what with all the stuff he had on his face, but he was probably not an unpleasant-looking man. Maybe even handsome, in a bland sort of way.

With the powder, patch, and rouge, not to mention that very stupid wig and a frankly unethical quantity of purple silk, though, he was exquisite. There was, unfortunately, no other word that did the man justice. Kit found it hard to look away. Within an hour of the man's arrival, he could have described the precise number and variation of flowers on the bastard's stockings.

There was always the possibility that he knew who Kit was, but Kit had covered up his tracks pretty well. Only a handful of people knew Kit in both his identities, and nearly all of those were past confederates in whose interest it was that Kit never be exposed. Still, he had always suspected that revenge would come to find him one day, but he hadn't expected it to arrive in a purple coat and with lavender ribbons in its wig.

But no, this man wasn't looking at Kit with anything like malice. If anything, he looked . . . curious. Maybe even appreciative. Kit was just letting his imagination get the better of him.

So Kit ignored the man, or at least he tried to. He filled and re-filled the kettles that hung over the hearth. The sun began to set behind the gray stone buildings across the street. The patrons at the long central table gradually filtered out and were replaced by new customers. Kit brewed pot after pot of coffee, and whenever he looked out of the corner of his eye, he saw dark velvet, a shiny shoe, and a pair of keen eyes.

His mind, he decided, had been finally driven over the brink by too much boredom, and now it looked for intrigue where in reality there was only a reasonably attractive man paying him too much attention.

Finally, Kit left Betty to manage the shop and stomped upstairs to punish himself by balancing the books.

He always left the door to his office not only unlocked but open. Across the landing, the door to his bedchamber was fastened by a heavy bolt, but he wanted Betty to be able to reach him—and his dagger, his pistol, and the rest of the modest arsenal he kept about his person—with a single shout. He also wanted to be able to hear the hum of voices from down below. He wanted to hear the clatter of cups, the sound of chair legs scraping across the wood floor, all almost loud enough to drown out the sounds of the street outside his window. Anything was better than silence.

And in through that unlocked door walked the powdered, beribboned gentleman.

Kit didn't say anything, nor did he get to his feet. It would be not only useless, but an admission that he didn't have the upper hand, if he asked what this man thought he was doing. Instead, he calmly rested his dagger on the table before him, his hand relaxed on the hilt. For some reason, the sight of this made the stranger break into a broad, slow smile, revealing a row of small white teeth that transformed what might have been a pleasant face into something altogether vulpine.

"Oh, marvelous," the stranger said. "Really, well done. You are Kit Webb, are you not? Short for Christopher, middle name Richard, alias Gladhand Jack?" He pulled a chair out from the wall and brought it to face Kit's desk, and then he sat, one leg delicately crossed over the other as he had done downstairs. That surprised Kit, even more than the fact that this man knew who Kit was. This man was rendering himself vulnerable, open to any attack Kit might choose to make, and surely he knew that Kit had every motive to attack him. "I'm Edward Percy."

At the name, Kit's fingers involuntarily closed around the hilt of his dagger. Not because he recognized it, but because he didn't. He had never had any dealings with a man of that name, and if this stranger were acquainted with a friend of Kit's, he would have led with that information. Instead, he had announced that he knew exactly who Kit was and what Kit had done. Briefly Kit considered telling this Percy that he had the wrong man. But this stranger *knew*. Kit could see it in his eyes. Somehow—and Kit would dearly like to know who had informed on him—Percy had found out, and denying the truth would only make getting rid of him more tedious.

Percy's gaze traveled to Kit's hand, still wrapped around the hilt of the weapon, and then back to Kit's face. Nothing in his posture changed, nothing to indicate that he knew he was in danger, not the slightest trace of fear or even vigilance. That, in Kit's experience, meant one of two things: either the man was enormously stupid and overconfident, which were certainly common enough traits among the wigged and powdered set, or he thought knowing who Kit really was would be enough to keep him safe, in which case he was very stupid indeed.

"To what do I owe the pleasure, Mr. Percy?" Kit said, trying to imbue his words with as much boredom as he could, barely bothering to turn his voice up at the end.

"I have a proposition for you," Percy said, crossing his legs in the opposite direction. His silver shoe buckle caught a beam of light from Kit's candle, drawing Kit's attention to Percy's ankle. It was thin, almost delicate, and those clocks on his stocking seemed almost to writhe before Kit's eyes. For one mad moment, he wondered if he might like whatever proposal Percy had to offer, however insulting.

"Eyes up here, Mr. Webb," Percy murmured softly, and Kit felt his cheeks heat at having been caught out, but also at the lack of rebuke in the man's voice. There were times when a lack of rebuke was almost an invitation, certainly a concession, and Kit did not know what to do now that he found himself in one of those situations.

"You enjoyed looking at me downstairs, too," Percy went on. And, damn it, Kit knew he ought to have been more discreet. He hoped the dimness of the room concealed his flushed cheeks but had the sense that he was rapidly losing whatever upper hand he might have had at the start of this interview.

"I wasn't the only one looking," Kit replied.

"Indeed, you were not," Percy said promptly. "Can you blame me?" He slowly raked his gaze down Kit's body, and Kit had the inane idea that this man's penetrating eyes had rendered the heavy oak desk as transparent as glass. "But work before play, Mr. Webb," he said, a note of arch reprimand in his voice, as if Kit had started this, whatever it was. "Not to put too fine a point on it, I'd like to engage your services." He paused, as if deliberately giving Kit a chance to get ideas about what those services might be, and whether he would like them. Kit let his thoughts trail down this path for a moment. Patrons were forever attempting to purchase Betty's favors, so perhaps it wasn't so very odd for one to attempt to do the same with Kit.

The fact was that Kit didn't let himself look at men the way he was looking at Percy, at least not often, and certainly not so obviously as to get caught. He wondered what it was that had tipped his hand to this gentleman. Kit's closest friends, such as they were, didn't even know. He had the uncomfortable sense that this man saw everything Kit wished to conceal.

"I'd like to hire you to remove some papers from the possession of a man of my acquaintance," Percy said, a trace of laughter in his voice, as if he knew precisely what Kit was thinking and that it wasn't about stealing papers.

It took a moment for Kit's brain to catch up with Percy's meaning. "No," he said, any thoughts of well-turned ankles and slender calves evaporating into the air. "I don't do that."

It would have been easy for Percy to point out that Kit didn't do that *anymore*. But Kit had already learned that this man never said the obvious thing. Instead, the gentleman nodded. "Quite. I'm hoping you'll make an exception for the right price." He uncrossed and recrossed his legs, as if he knew what that did to Kit's ability to think straight—and he probably did, damn it. "And for the right person," he added, as if to drive home the point.

"I said I don't—"

"Is it because of your leg? Are you not able to ride?"

Kit searched the man's face for a sign of insult or insolence, but found only the same amused curiosity. "I can ride," he said, which wasn't quite a lie. He could ride, and he could walk, and he could climb stairs, as long as he didn't mind pain and if one employed a fairly generous definition of ride, walk, and climb.

"Interesting. I thought there had to be a reason for a man with your storied past to live the way you do now."

"Well, you're wrong."

Percy rose to his feet but didn't turn toward the door. "Pity," he said. "Could have been fun. You can't tell me that a man with your skills and your history is content to stand in one place all day, warm and safe and terribly, terribly bored." He adjusted the lace at his cuffs. "Could have been quite fun."

Kit picked up the knife, allowing its blade to catch the candlelight, so Percy could be under no misapprehension as to what Kit meant. "No," he repeated, putting his free hand flat on the desk, as if preparing to stand. "Get out."

Percy left, and as Kit heard his near-silent progress down the stairs, he wondered how the stranger had known things he had hardly admitted to himself.

Chapter 4

$\mathcal{P}$ercy certainly hadn't anticipated using his questionable powers of seduction to persuade the man, but if he could get that book from his father and also get into that highwayman's breeches, he'd consider it time well spent. Not only did Webb have that jawline and those shoulders, but he spoke with a pleasantly rough growl of a voice. He would probably be as boring in bed as he was out of it, but when a man looked like that, one could lower one's standards.

Buoyed along by this pleasant train of thought, he decided to perform a task he had been delaying.

"The book your father won't let out of his sight," Marian had murmured that morning while she and Percy once again sat for their portrait, "is bound in dark green morocco and has faded gold lettering embossed on the cover."

Percy's heart had given a thump, and he'd forced himself to remain very still and very calm so as to conceal any trace of his excitement. "So, it *is* my mother's book," he responded, equally low. Until this point, all Percy had known was that his father was taking great pains to guard and conceal a book he kept about his person at all times. That alone told Percy of the book's value to the duke. If Percy could steal it, then he could force his father to pay for its return; that was reason enough to want the blasted thing. If the book had been his mother's, however, that opened up a rather intriguing vista of possibilities.

Percy remembered his mother removing her little green book from the folds of her gown, sometimes running her finger down a page as if to remind herself of something, other times writing something inside. He had never seen its contents but was certain that she had used the book as a means to amass power, and that his father was now doing the same: gathering and hoarding power was the one thing Percy's parents had in common.

Percy had known from his earliest days that his parents were engaged in a protracted domestic war that seemed to have originated some time before their marriage, and over a cause no more complicated than their long-standing hatred for one another. Percy often only learned of the individual skirmishes long after the fact, and from overheard whispers among servants; this was how he learned the duke locked the duchess in her rooms after the duchess caused the duke's morning chocolate to be laced with what was either an emetic or arsenic, depending on who one believed. It was also how he learned the duke had his mistress housed in the east wing of Cheveril Castle, and also that the duchess, either in retaliation or in provocation, had sold a coronet and used the proceeds to build a Roman Catholic chapel on the grounds of that same estate.

During these years of civil war, Percy was well aware that his parents were equally matched adversaries, and that the only people who imagined the duchess to be an innocent victim were the same people who could not imagine a woman as conniving as his mother even existing. But none of that mattered: Percy was a partisan of the duchess, a fact as immutable as his yellow hair or his gray eyes.

The duchess had other partisans, of course, and Percy needed to visit one of them to confirm his suspicions about the book.

Lionel Redmond was a distant maternal cousin. He had been sent to seminary in France and was now a Roman Catholic priest in London. His mother's family, the Percys, were an old family of Catholics. His father's family, the Talbots, were emphatically Church of England. After decades upon decades of persecution, English Catholics could now, at least, be relatively certain that they could huddle in an alehouse or a cockpit for a makeshift mass without finding themselves burned at the stake, but that didn't prevent Percy from looking repeatedly over his shoulder as he made his way from the carriage to the narrow little house where his cousin lived.

"Cousin Edward," Lionel said when he saw Percy waiting in the parlor.

"Father," Percy responded, getting to his feet and bowing his head.

"Have you come to tell me of your travels?" Lionel asked, and Percy realized his cousin probably imagined that Percy had dined with the pope or some such.

"You're a kind man to invite me to bore you with my stories," Percy said. "But in fact, I have a more sorrowful reason for my visit."

"Oh dear," Lionel said, and gestured for Percy to sit.

"As you know, I was in Florence when news of my mother's death reached me during the summer of last year. The solicitor wrote to me about the portions of her marriage settlement that pertained to property left to me upon her death." There had been startlingly little. The property that was his mother's dowry passed into his father's hands at the time of their marriage, with a nominal amount held back for the dowries of their future daughters.

"I hoped you could tell me what became of her personal property. When I returned last month, I discovered that her rooms were now occupied by the new duchess, and my mother's little things—books and combs and so forth—were gone. My father claims to have distributed them among the servants, but I hope he sent you something as well."

Lionel frowned. "Indeed, he did not. But, as you know, your father is hardly sympathetic to the true faith."

Percy hummed in understanding. "I wish I had something of hers to remember her by," he said. Which was the kind of truth he didn't like to think about, so he uttered the words without letting them seep into his thoughts. "Do you remember that little green book she carried about? I'd pay a king's ransom for the chance to even see it one more time."

Percy didn't know if it was his imagination or if something shifted in his cousin's posture—a tilt of the head, a narrowing of the eyes, but suddenly the old man looked as shrewd as Percy's mother.

"The only book I ever saw your mother with was her Bible," Lionel said.

As far as lies went, that was a bad one, because there was no possibility Lionel had somehow escaped noticing that little book. *An easily disproven falsehood is no better than a confession* was one of the duchess's lessons.

"That's a pity," Percy said lightly. "If you remember anything about it, please do tell me. Meanwhile, I've brought a bank draft for you to use as you see fit in the tending of your flock." He took the paper from his pocket and left it casually on the chimneypiece, and hoped that his cousin would correctly interpret that as a promise to pay for future information.

When he returned to Clare House, Percy found his valet waiting in his apartments.

"If you'll forgive my forwardness, my lord," Collins said as he helped Percy out of his coat, "but my lord is satisfied with my service, I hope."

Startled, Percy regarded his manservant in the looking glass. "Of course I am. We've been to Italy and back. You got me through that beastly sickness in the Alps. When you do something daft, like try to get me to wear crimson, I tell you so."

"That is a relief, my lord."

"What prompted this crisis of confidence?"

"The duke has dismissed Mr. Denny."

"He's done what?" Percy asked, astonished. Denny had been the duke's manservant since before Percy was born.

"Indeed, my lord. Mr. Denny's replacements are two large and scruffy ruffians, neither of whom seems capable of brushing a coat or dressing a periwig. They take turns sleeping in the duke's antechamber."

"Ah." Percy wondered if Collins knew he was describing guards. "And where is Denny?" If the duke's former manservant had been sacked and cast out without a farthing, Percy could possibly employ him to help access his father's inner chamber.

"He mentioned to the underhousemaid that he planned to open a public house in Tavistock, where his people are from."

Percy raised an eyebrow. That didn't sound like the man was dismissed so much as paid off. He wondered if Marian's brother could be persuaded to make a trip into Devon to have a chat with the fellow.

"Thank you," Percy said to his valet. "You are, as ever, invaluable." He wanted to say more, wanted to assure Collins that whatever was happening in the rest of the household, Percy would see that Collins was treated fairly. But he did not, first because he knew he was in no position to make promises, and second because he knew better than to be effusive in his praise or excessive in his reassurances—both were sure signs of a desperate man, according to the duchess, and the duchess had seldom been wrong about these things.

Chapter 5

*P*ercy was surprised to find that he was an adequate spy. After twenty-odd years of assuming that attention and notice were his due, it was rather humbling to see how quickly he became invisible. Without all the usual accoutrements of fashion—wig, powder, patch, rouge, and so forth—and wearing a forgettable brown coat and a similarly forlorn pair of breeches Collins grudgingly acquired at the secondhand stalls, he was able to spy on Webb unnoticed. For a week, he sat at the central table of the coffeehouse, sometimes armed with a newspaper but always keeping a keen eye on the proprietor. Nobody cast him a second glance, not even Webb, who had hardly been able to take his eyes off Percy when he had been dressed to attract attention.

After a week, Percy realized that he had badly missed his mark by offering Webb money. While Percy was certain that everybody had his price, Webb's price would not be strictly monetary. He was plainly living within his means. He kept the premises in good repair, let the girl—Betty—keep any tips the patrons left, and often swept and polished the tables and fittings himself. When a drunken street brawl became a regular melee and a broom handle got put through one of Webb's windows, Webb

had the glazier repair the broken pane that very day and paid him
on the spot without even attempting to haggle over the cost.

While Webb's upstairs office was furnished in a spare, almost
spartan, manner, Percy had noticed a wax candle burning in
the simple pewter candlestick, not cheap and smelly tallow or
a humble rushlight. Percy didn't know much about poverty, but
he knew what it looked like when a man wasn't in the least bit
worried about where his next meal was coming from—mainly
because he could compare what he and Marian had looked like
before their present crisis with what they looked like now. Perhaps Webb had just been that good at his former trade and now
had ample savings.

If Webb couldn't be enticed with money, then Percy would
have to find another way to persuade him to join in his scheme.
He watched Webb, looking for a weakness he could exploit. A
weakness, according to his mother, was anything at all that Percy
could use to his advantage. He'd find Webb's weakness; it was
only a matter of time. Meanwhile, it was no hardship watching
the man.

Webb was tall, possibly even taller than Percy. He filled out
his ill-tailored breeches admirably and, even while using his
cane, carried his weight with the ease of a man who had always
been strong. His hair was the same dark brown as the coffee he
brewed, falling past his shoulders in heavy waves. He made some
minimal attempt to keep it confined to a respectable queue, but
whenever Percy saw him, some strands around his face had broken free. He seldom smiled at anyone other than the serving girl,
but when he did, he exposed a chipped incisor, and Percy's heart
flipped around in his chest for no good reason at all.

But Webb had lines around his eyes that hinted at some old,

forgotten readiness to smile. He also had other lines, the kind that never came from laughing.

Percy watched to see who Webb paid attention to. He didn't look twice at any of the handful of women who ventured into his coffeehouse, but he didn't look at men, either. The only person he seemed to care about was Betty, and he treated her like a daughter. In fact, Percy had thought she might actually be his daughter, but Webb couldn't yet be thirty and the girl had to be nearly twenty.

After a week of close observation, Percy concluded that Kit Webb was grouchy, sullen, and palpably bored, and no wonder. Percy was bored just watching him, and nobody would accuse Percy of having a taste for adventure. Webb had to be chafing at the bit for some excitement. Percy had seen the man's expression when he gripped his dagger the other evening. He had seemed almost relieved, as if he had been waiting for an excuse to wield the thing, as if a spot of violence would be a welcome reprieve.

His entire life was a picture of almost soporific boredom, and if Marian's informant hadn't been certain, Percy wouldn't have believed that this man had ever done anything as thrilling as go for a walk without an umbrella, let alone engage in any criminal activity. It seemed unfathomable that he was a highwayman of such famous charm and bravado that a ballad, multiple handbills, and no small number of engravings paid tribute to his feats of daring and his cunning escapes from the law.

Percy could use that; he knew he could. Webb would want to join in their scheme if only Percy could come up with a pretext that would allow him to gracefully agree. Percy had to give him a reason why saying yes would be easier than saying no.

In preparation for their second meeting, Percy dressed in

much the same way he had for their first: coat and breeches of duck-egg blue, waistcoat just a few shades darker, stockings a few shades lighter with clocks the same hue as his waistcoat. He wore a freshly curled wig that was powdered to the requisite shade of alabaster, generously powdered his face, applied a velvet birthmark over the corner of his mouth, and then added just enough rouge to make it clear that he was wearing it. If his valet noticed that Percy's toilette was as elaborate as it would be for a dinner party whose guests included members of the royal family, he did not mention it.

Percy descended carefully from his carriage, stepping gingerly over one of the more egregious puddles that stood between himself and the door to Webb's coffeehouse. He could not do what he was about to do with muddy stockings.

He took his time opening the door and stepping through it, giving Webb the opportunity to notice him. Out of the corner of his eye, he saw Webb turn his head, stiffen momentarily, then bring a hand to his hip. That, Percy assumed, was where Webb kept his dagger, or perhaps a pistol. Whatever it was, Webb didn't remove it, didn't even put his hand inside his coat to grip it. Percy supposed that was partly because he wasn't afraid, and partly because he didn't want to frighten his patrons. Either way, Percy was counting on that weapon remaining inside Webb's coat.

Percy went directly to the table where Webb brewed his coffee. "Mr. Webb," he said, smiling in the way he would before asking someone to dance. "My apologies. I realized after leaving last week that I left vital information out of my proposition." Before Webb could object, Percy went on, leaning in. "I'm going to tell you a story. There's a man who is, shall we say . . ."—he drummed his fingers on the table—"a stunning piece of shit. I could enumerate his misdeeds, but you have a business to run and my shoes aren't meant for standing around in. Suffice it to say, he's a negligent landowner and in general a brute."

This was so far from a comprehensive list of his father's worst misdeeds that it was almost incorrect, the understatement so severe as to verge on dishonesty. But he could hardly explain the whole truth. Webb looked at him, flat and unimpressed. Remembering how Webb saw the serving girl home on dark nights, Percy added as if in afterthought, "He's also one of the worst husbands a woman could ask for."

Something shifted in Webb's expression, a hardening of his jaw and a flintiness that crept into his dark eyes, and Percy suppressed a victorious smile. One corner of Webb's mouth hitched up in the beginnings of a smile—but not, Percy noticed, the kind smile he shared with the serving girl. "But what kind of father is he, Mr. Percy?" Webb asked, his voice low and scratchy. His voice was, Percy reflected inanely, the verbal equivalent of the stubble on his jaw—rough, careless, inconveniently attractive. Percy was trying to determine which trait he found more distressing, when the full import of Webb's question struck him. Percy had carefully avoided disclosing his relation to the man he wished to rob and wasn't sure what he had said that gave it away. Stupidly, he allowed himself to become flustered for a moment, and he knew that one moment of letting his thoughts show on his face was enough to confirm Webb's suspicions.

"What is it you wish to steal from your father, Mr. Percy?" Webb asked in that same sandpaper voice. "Is your allowance insufficient? Do you have gaming debts? Did you get a girl in trouble?" He spoke as if each of these predicaments was boring, as if anything that might afflict Percy was beneath Webb's notice.

Percy might have been offended if he didn't entirely agree that those problems were laughable compared to the truth.

Then he remembered that Webb had repeatedly addressed him as Mr. Percy rather than Lord Holland, which meant he didn't know who Percy was or who his father was. That was a relief. It meant that Webb was nothing more than a good guesser. He allowed a flicker of amusement to pass over his face. "If you think I'm interested in personal gain, Mr. Webb, you're badly mistaken. In fact, you're welcome to help yourself to anything of value you find during the robbery," he said, his voice nothing more than a murmur. Webb would have to strain his ears to hear. "All I want is a book."

"A highway robbery is the most dangerous, least reliable method you could possibly have come up with if all you want is a book," Webb said, his voice hardly above a whisper. "Hire a housebreaker, Mr. Percy. Hire a burglar and a lockpick. There are many who would jump at the chance. You don't need a man of my skills."

"He sleeps in a room guarded by two armed men. The book is always on his person."

And that, of all the things, was what made something like interest flicker in Webb's eyes. Percy wanted to crow in victory. Webb opened his mouth and snapped it shut, as if he was dying to know what exactly this book was but didn't want to ask. Well, Percy wasn't going to help him out.

"Pity you can't help," Percy said. He turned on his heel and walked through the coffeehouse and out the door, feeling Webb's gaze on him all the while.

Chapter 6

*T*ry as he might, Kit couldn't stop thinking about Percy. No, not about Percy, he told himself, but about Percy's proposition. Percy's target, moreover. A man who needed two guards was interesting in and of himself; a man who had a book he never let go of was even more interesting, especially if Percy valued the book over whatever jewels or gold this man had on him. And Kit would wager that a man who could afford two guards and a son who dressed like the worst kind of popinjay carried around plenty of valuables.

Kit was certain the mark was indeed Percy's father. The man had seemed caught out, and he had the sort of face that didn't look like it was in the habit of giving away any secrets. Kit was inclined to trust that fleeting hint of surprise.

"You look lively," Betty said as they were closing up the shop. "Nice change not to see you sulking about. I don't think you snapped at a single customer all afternoon."

"I don't sulk," Kit said, depressed by the realization that contemplating a return to crime had put him in a sunny mood. "Christ, I'm an unprincipled bastard."

"Of course, you are, pet," said Betty, handing him a clean rag to polish his half of the table. "Famous for it, you are."

"It wasn't meant to be a boast and you know it," he protested, dutifully attempting to scrub off a stain left by a dripping cup of coffee. "It was meant to be a confession."

"If you want to confess to something, confess to being sad as shit and a thorn in my side. Never in my life have I seen a man carry on the way you are. You're like a lady in a play, pining." She clutched the polishing cloth to her chest in a way he gathered was meant to be theatrical.

"I am not pining," Kit said, torn between outrage and amusement. "My face doesn't do that."

"You keep telling yourself that. Lord, do I wish you'd just go and nick somebody's handkerchief and be done with it. Get it out of your system. Nick a handkerchief, receive stolen goods, clip some coins. I have a lot of ideas, just ask," she said helpfully.

"You're a real mate, Betty."

She gave him a shrewd sideways glance, the one that always made Kit suspect her of mind reading. "Plenty of mischief you can get up to even with a bad leg."

That fucking leg. Every time he almost got used to it, it found a way to get worse. Every time he thought he figured out how far it would carry him, it decided to give out completely, and Kit would need to hire a bloody chair to get home. It was better to just stay put.

And now his leg was ruining his chance to either take part in a very interesting robbery or prove to himself that he was capable of being decent for once in his life. Because either way, he was going to turn Percy down. He couldn't stay in his saddle at anything over a trot. Hell, he couldn't even dismount his horse without falling on his face. He certainly couldn't hold anyone up, not if he wanted to get away with his life. It would have been nice to have the choice, though.

Bugger that. It would have been nice to just do one last job. To once more see the look on a gentleman's face when he realized there were some things out of his control, and to feel, however briefly, the dark satisfaction of revenge. He missed the rest of it, too—the thrill of making an escape, lying low, disposing of their haul.

"I see we're back to sulking," Betty said. "I hope you're enjoying your penance, because I'm not."

Kit let out a frustrated huff. "Only you, Betty, would see a man trying to do his best for once in his life and think there had to be some twisted explanation for it."

"Only you, Christopher, would have his head so far up his arse to think that this"—she gestured around the shop with the rag—"was the first time you did your best."

He pointedly ignored her and resumed tidying up the shop, all the while wondering how he had been brought to a point where he was so thoroughly bossed around by a woman ten years his junior, and also wondering how he'd even begin to get on without her.

After walking Betty home, his leg was in a right state. He turned down her mother's invitation to stay for supper, then ignored her brother's shouted invitation to meet at the corner tavern for a pint. Instead, he turned into a lane, as he always did, and leaned against the wall to rest. After a year of this routine, he thought there might be a Kit-shaped indentation in the bricks. He knocked his fist into the side of his right leg, which sometimes made his hip remember that it had a purpose. Gingerly he put some weight on it and, when he didn't crumple to the ground, called it a success and returned to the street.

Sometimes on his way home he stopped at the baths and soaked his miserable leg, and sometimes he stopped at an eating house, and sometimes he ran into someone he knew and had a chat. Sometimes, when he was really in the mood for misery, he stopped by the stables where he put Bridget up and gave her an apple. But most of the time he went home, hauled himself up the stairs, and read by the light of a candle until he fell asleep.

At some point in the last year, Kit's world had compressed to the span between his coffeehouse and Betty's house, with increasingly infrequent forays into the wider world. After spending most of his adulthood stalking his quarry and running from the law, flying back and forth across the countryside as he saw fit, he felt every inch of his imprisonment.

Maybe Betty was right and he was punishing himself—for Rob's death, for years of unrepentant theft, for not being able to thieve anymore. It didn't make sense, but in Kit's experience, not a lot of things that happened in a person's mind really did. Maybe he was hobbling around one tiny corner of London because he wanted to feel like rubbish; if so, he was doing a fine job of it.

He tried to remember the last time he had gone anywhere outside his usual circuit—two weeks ago he visited the cobbler to have his boots mended, then returned a few days later to pick them up. Before that? In September he went to the apothecary when a spate of damp weather aggravated his leg and he needed a new tin of salve.

When he got home, he hauled himself up the stairs and collapsed into bed, not even bothering to take off his boots. The boots could wait until it hurt a little less to move. So could supper. So could everything that wasn't staring at the ceiling and watching a spider weave a cobweb in the corner.

He wondered what Percy did of an evening. Surely, he didn't mope around whatever fine house he lived in. Kit bet that Percy dressed even more absurdly than he did during the daytime, and then spent the night dancing and flirting with ladies. And probably doing a fair bit more than flirting with men. Those remarks he had made, those looks he had given Kit—they didn't leave much room for doubt about Percy's preferences. He didn't make any kind of secret about it.

That thought was enough to ruin what had been shaping up to be a fine little fantasy. The only reason Percy was able to ogle other men in broad daylight without getting hit, arrested, or flat-out murdered was that he was rich. He wondered if rich men took their wigs off while fucking, and then got very annoyed with his prick for not finding wigs sufficiently unattractive. His prick didn't understand anything. Bringing himself off to an aristocrat in a goddamn wig would be a humiliating end to a foul day.

He dragged himself out of bed, lest his thoughts and hands wander, and crossed the landing to his office to balance his books.

Chapter 7

*P*ercy decided that it was high time to put the screws to the highwayman. It had been days since their last encounter, and besides, the errand would get him out of Clare House, fill a few hours, and bring his father one step closer to public ruination, so all in all, a morning well spent.

He took extra care with his toilette. It was a bleak and dismal day, so he chose yellow. It was not, he would concede, his best color, but one of the many advantages of beauty was that he could wear the ugliest conceivable color and still look better than almost everybody. He had Collins button him into his jonquil silk waistcoat and the saffron-colored coat that was positively stiff with gold embroidery. A lesser man might find yellow breeches to be a bridge too far, but Percy was not a lesser man.

He sailed into the coffeehouse with the maximum possible to-do only to find the place bursting with patrons. The weather was grim, so it stood to reason that these commoners would wish for a more hospitable environment than whatever hovels they undoubtedly hailed from. But he was disappointed to realize the table he occupied on his previous visits—at least those visits he had made as himself, rather than in his boring spy clothes—now seated four men in depressing black coats.

But he could hardly leave, not after sweeping into the place as he had done, so he settled himself at the end of a bench at the long central table, adjusting his coat around him. He could feel Webb's gaze. He looked up, meeting the highwayman's eye.

"You'll be wanting coffee, then," Webb grumbled.

"Yes, I am here for coffee," Percy said. "How observant of you. No wonder this place is such a bustling success."

Webb wordlessly plonked a cup of coffee onto the table, causing a not insubstantial quantity to spill over the rim of the cup. Percy ignored both the spill and the coffee.

"Good God, Kit," said the man who sat beside Percy. "You'll soak my book if you don't mop that up. Give me a rag, why don't you." Then, turning to Percy, "The place goes to ruin without Betty here to see to things. Ruin, I tell you."

"Ruin," Percy agreed, and apparently that was all one needed to do at a place like this to begin a conversation, because then they were off. The man told him what a grave tragedy it would have been if Kit had managed to destroy his book when here he was, mere pages from the end. And that prompted Percy to confess that he hadn't read the book.

"You must take it!" the man cried. His name was Harper, or Harmon, or possibly even Hardcastle. He spoke with a rustic accent that sounded like so much nonsense to Percy's ears. Also, Percy did not much care what the fellow's name was. "Here," said Harper or whoever he was, pressing the book into Percy's hands.

"I couldn't possibly," Percy said. If Percy wished to read this book about a Tom Jones, or some such common-sounding fellow, he would order a copy bound in the same green leather as the rest of his library. He would certainly not read a book that belonged to an utter stranger and which looked like it had been read by several people with hands in various stages of dirtiness. "I don't wish to impose on your kindness."

"And you wouldn't be, my good man. It's not my book. It's Kit's." Harper gestured at a wall on the far side of the room, lined with bookcases and hardly visible through the tobacco smoke.

"Is Mr. Webb running a lending library as well as a coffee-house?" Percy asked. The mind boggled at the career choices of retired highwaymen.

"That," said a man across the table, not looking up from a paper on which he had been furiously scribbling, "would imply that he charged."

"I do charge!" interjected Webb, who was stomping around the table collecting empty cups.

"No, you don't," said the man across the table.

"You're supposed to put an extra penny in the bowl."

"Nobody does that," Harper told Percy in confiding tones. "You just take the book and put it back when you're done."

"And put a fucking penny in the bowl," said Webb. "What are you all still doing here? Don't you have homes to go to?"

Harper left soon after, shoving the book in front of Percy as he went. Percy ignored it, preferring instead to watch Webb poke at the fire and grumble at the pot of coffee that brewed near the hearth.

Around supper time, the crowd at the coffeehouse began to thin. Percy really ought to be going as well. When he checked his watch, he discovered he had been sitting on a hard wooden bench for three hours. He had read four pages of the novel, idly listened to a debate that sounded shockingly seditious on both sides, and spent the rest of the time watching Webb.

He watched Webb sweep, add what seemed to be utterly indiscriminate and unmeasured quantities of herbs to the coffeepot, pour coffee in a way that could only be described as reluctant, shelve a pile of books in a manner that could have nothing to do with the alphabet, and tell about three dozen patrons that "Betty isn't here, God damn you, just drink your coffee and get out."

Percy knew nothing about shop keeping and would have been gravely insulted by anyone who suggested otherwise, but he had spent enough money at enough places to know that Webb's manner of running his business was both eccentric and not especially likely to encourage customers to return. But still, the place had been full every time Percy had seen it.

Maybe they were all there to admire the proprietor. There was certainly a lot of him to admire. Even his scowl didn't ruin his looks. He had the jaw to carry it off, making the scowl into a proper manly glower.

Now there were only three people left, including Percy himself, and surely it was past time for Percy to be going. He had only meant to show his face and remind Webb of what fun and intriguing criminous activities he could be engaging in instead of brewing coffee. But somehow he had whiled away the entire afternoon.

One of the remaining patrons got to his feet and made not for the door, but for the stairs. "That garret still empty, Kit?" he called when he was already on the bottom step, so he must have been fairly sure of the answer in advance.

"It's yours." Webb glanced up from the counter, where he was counting out the day's earnings into neat stacks of coins.

"Mrs. Kemble is on the floor below, so mind that you tread lightly. You know how she gets."

That was the most Percy had heard Kit say that day or any other day, and it was the first time he had heard the man speak in anything other than a grumble. He had a nice voice, too—low and a bit rough. His accent was hardly polished, but neither was it rustic. He didn't sound illiterate, and indeed, now that Percy thought about it, he had seen Webb reading books from his own library. One could put him in a respectable coat, introduce him to the concept of a hairbrush, and scrape off that stubble and he would pass for a prosperous shopkeeper, a respectable member of the middling sort—which was, Percy supposed, exactly what Webb was, felonious past notwithstanding.

"Stop staring at me like that," Webb said when the two of them were alone in the shop. He didn't look up from his coins.

"No, I don't think I shall," Percy said.

"You'll get yourself arrested if you carry on acting like that."

Percy raised his eyebrows. "I have to say, I wasn't expecting to receive counsel on being a law-abiding citizen from *you*."

Webb made a noise that it took Percy a moment to realize was a laugh. Webb recovered himself immediately and scowled at Percy, as if he were cross with Percy for being amusing.

"You're not going to tell me that a man like you minds a brush with the law," Percy said.

Webb gave him an odd look, but still there were no offended dramatics about him not being that sort of man, how dare Percy, et cetera and so forth. The man wasn't even blushing.

"Did you take my advice?" Webb asked.

"To stop staring at you?"

Webb looked up, exasperated. "To hire a thief."

"I already told you why that wouldn't work."

"Ah, yes, because your father has guards."

If Webb thought he could so easily get Percy to admit that his target was his father, he could guess again. "What a fool you must think me to fall for such a trick," Percy said. "How demoralizing." He got to his feet and walked out the door, taking the tattered first volume of *Tom Jones* with him and pointedly dropping a penny into the bowl, feeling Webb's eyes on him all the while.

Chapter 8

*K*it leaned heavily on his cane, looking at the familiar building. The same lace curtains fluttered in the evening air as fiddle music drifted out to the street on a breeze. He thought he might even be able to smell the women's perfume all the way from the pavements, but that was probably his imagination.

He knocked, and the door was opened by a girl Kit hadn't seen before. She had red hair and beneath her powder he could see a smattering of freckles on her cheeks.

"Good evening," she said in what sounded like it was supposed to be a seductive lilt but actually came out with a bit of a nervous stammer. Kit knew the girls who were truly nervous didn't work the door. This one, with her half-concealed freckles and her shyness and the way she moved a hand to her chest as if in an arrested effort to tug her bodice higher, was there to appeal to the sort of man who wanted to take care of a girl. Scarlett knew what she was doing, and so did this girl. He'd bet that within six months she would be set up in a cozy house by some man who was set on rescuing her. And bully for her. Kit hoped she fleeced the fellow.

"Would you tell your mistress that Kit Webb is here to see her?"

She opened her eyes wide, and he couldn't tell whether she recognized his name or whether she did that to all the men who called at the house. He took off his hat and she showed him through a series of rooms papered in shades of rose and ivory. They passed a salon in which a handful of men clustered around a woman who played a lively tune on the harpsichord, then a room in which men and women played cards, some of the women perched on the laps of their companions.

At the end of the corridor, the girl gestured to an empty parlor and instructed Kit to wait. He sat near the fire, gingerly lowering himself onto a delicate settee. The furniture on the ground floor of Scarlett's establishment was all constructed along similar lines—chairs that seemed just a shade too fragile, tables that were maybe half an inch too low, all designed to make men feel like huge strangers in a feminine place. When Kit had first asked Scarlett about it, he had questioned her logic—wouldn't it make more sense to fill the house with furniture built on a more masculine scale, so as to welcome paying customers? She had simply told him that the beds were sturdy and her pockets were full.

"It really is you," came a throaty voice from the door. "I thought Flora had to be mistaken."

"In the flesh," he said, rising to his feet and turning to the door.

Scarlett crossed the room and took his hands, looking up into his face. "Twelve months, Kit." He wondered if she could see the passage of time on his skin. He thought she might have new lines on her face, maybe another strand or two of gray hair among the auburn.

"The girl who answered the door," he said. "Flora, I think you called her. Is she your sister?"

She smiled and shook her head. "Flatterer."

"Daughter?"

"Clean living has made your mind go soft if you think I'll admit to having a daughter old enough to own her keep." Which, he noticed, was not a denial. "But what brings you here? I don't dare hope it was for the pleasure of my company."

"Intelligence," he said.

"The usual arrangement, then?" She sat in one of the armchairs and gestured for Kit to do the same.

"Not exactly," he said, sitting. In the past, she had worked as something of a scout for Kit and Rob. If one wanted to hold up a gentleman's conveyance, one had to be sure the man carried enough on his person to make the job worthwhile. A highwayman also needed to know what roads the man was likely to travel, and when. Men, while in their cups and well satisfied, were liable to let this sort of information slip. Scarlett's girls knew they'd be well compensated if they relayed useful details to their mistress.

"Pity," she said. "I've a list as long as my arm of men I wouldn't mind coming to harm."

"Don't we all," Kit said.

"Sometimes when I hear about an especially bad one," Scarlett said, "I think, Well, Rob would like to hear about that."

Kit tamped down the swell of grief he felt at hearing Rob's name. It felt unexpectedly fresh. He was used to grief, couldn't even remember a time when he hadn't been grieving somebody. But his parents' deaths were half a lifetime ago, long enough for that wound to have long since scabbed over. And as for Jenny and—and everything that had followed from that, he had been too angry and tired and out of his mind with drink to remember now what it had felt like.

But he had grieved Rob while sober, and with plenty of time to go over the events of that last day again and again until the memory was frayed at the edges, blurry like a print in a book that had been handled too many times. He could hardly remember it without also seeing every moment he could have acted differently, turned back, picked a different mark, a different route, a different life entirely.

It wasn't as if he and Rob had set out to become highwaymen, for God's sake. Rob's father had been a gardener at the manor; Kit's parents owned a small tavern. They could each have followed in their fathers' footsteps, and indeed they would have if it hadn't been for the whims and caprices of the Duke of Clare.

"I should have visited you earlier," Kit said, tearing his thoughts from events of a decade earlier and looking at the woman before him. It was a shabby thing to leave a woman alone with her grief.

A peal of laughter came from a room upstairs. Not that Scarlett was alone, of course. But a brothel keeper could hardly put on black crepe and draw the curtains.

"We've both been busy." Scarlett glanced at his cane. "I heard you were injured but hoped it was a rumor."

"If you heard the version of the tale that had me shot with a poisoned arrow in defense of Bonnie Prince Charlie, then I'm afraid it's fiction. It was a very ordinary pistol and a very frightened coachman. But I didn't come here to bore you with tales of my injuries. Somebody came to me for help," he said. "A stranger."

She raised her eyebrows. "After nearly a year, it's a stranger who gets you to come to me? She must be pretty."

"He," Kit said absently, and Scarlett's eyebrows rose even higher. "But no, that isn't why I'm tempted."

"Then why?" She toed off her slippers and stretched her legs toward the fire.

"Because," he said carefully, "he knows who I am." He had debated whether to tell her this. He didn't want it to sound like an accusation. "He knows my name, and who I—who Rob and I, rather—used to be." There were only a handful of people who knew enough to make the connection. He and Rob had been prudent about that, if about nothing else. And Scarlett was one of them.

He thought she'd protest her innocence, but instead she frowned. "That's troubling. I don't like it."

"Neither do I," he admitted. "I'd like to know how he found me. He wants me to do a job for him. Wants me to hold up"—he stopped himself before he could say *his father*—"some aristo. The job, to be frank, sounds like the sort of thing I'd have done in a heartbeat, but I've never worked on my own and now I couldn't even if I wanted to." He gestured vaguely at his leg and hoped she understood. "But I want to know who he is and why he came to me. It would help me put the matter to rest," he said. "He says his name is Edward Percy."

"Edward Percy," she repeated. "I'll find out whatever I can."

He walked home and let himself into his dark shop, feeling something he told himself wasn't anticipation.

Chapter 9

The girl entered Kit's with the same air of bashful self-consciousness with which she had answered the door to the brothel a few days earlier. A hush fell over the coffeehouse at the sight of her, as not many women ventured into coffeehouses, and never alone unless they were selling their favors. Kit watched in amusement as his patrons tried to figure out if this pretty, meek girl could possibly be a prostitute.

"Mistress Flora," Kit said when she approached the counter.

"Mr. Webb," she answered, her cheeks flushing, and Kit longed to ask whether she was able to do that at will. "I have a message for you from my mistress." From between the folds of her cloak, she withdrew a sealed letter and held it out to Kit in an immaculately gloved hand.

As Kit broke the seal, he could smell the scent of rosewater that always surrounded Scarlett, and he wondered if she deliberately scented her stationery or if it simply picked up the scent from being near her. He'd bet on the former: nothing Scarlett ever did was by accident. The missive was brief and direct.

"There is no Edward Percy," the letter read. "Nobody by that name has attended any of the usual schools. No Edward Percy has ever been presented at court. No Edward Percy is known to any of the servants at any of the great houses. He could, of course, be the son of a merchant or some other personage who has taken to dressing like his betters, but in that case, I'd be even more certain to have heard about him. Yours, S."

Kit frowned. He had hoped that Scarlett would have been able to tell him something that would lessen his curiosity, not stoke it even higher. Kit had always liked a riddle, a puzzle, a challenge. Even robbery—hell, especially robbery—had been a sort of puzzle. Does this baronet travel with a purse full of coin? Are his outriders armed? At what time would he be likely to reach that ever-so-convenient bend in the Brighton road? How many men would Kit need in order to see the job safely done? How should they get away once the job was over? Avoiding the hangman satisfied some part of Kit's brain in the way unpicking a stubborn knot might. Now, a year after planning his last robbery, it occurred to Kit that some of the challenge may have come from how persistently drunk he had been in those days. It was more than possible that sober he'd need more than a simple holdup to occupy his mind. He might need more of a mystery.

He was interrupted by the sound of Flora delicately clearing her throat. Now, why had Scarlett sent this girl to him? She had boys she used as couriers. There was no reason to send one of her prettiest and greenest girls out on an errand, unattended. Except—of course. The whole point of this was to display Flora in front of as many men as possible. Scarlett was all but having an auction.

"We're putting our best merchandise in the shop window today, are we?" Kit murmured. In answer, Flora ducked her head and looked up with a sly wink. Well, she was in on it, then, and that put his mind at ease. "I'm meant to walk you home, aren't I?" Scarlett would know that Kit would never let this girl out into the street on her own. While he thought it more than likely that she could take care of herself, walking her home was a small enough favor.

"If you please, sir," she answered. "But you needn't do so until you're ready to close up the shop. I have a book to occupy myself."

"Of course you do," he said. "Take a seat and I'll bring you coffee and some cake."

He watched as she sat near the window, where she would be seen by everybody walking past and everybody within. When he brought her coffee and a plate of seedcakes, he huffed out a laugh when he realized that the book she had brought with her was the Bible. He couldn't help but grin. He hoped she landed herself a lord and took him for every penny she could.

He was still smiling when he heard footsteps approach the table where he brewed the coffee. Looking up, he saw a now-familiar wigged head and powdered face. The theme of the day, he noticed, was rose: rose silk waistcoat, rose ribbon at the nape of his neck, and he knew that if he looked down, he'd see stockings with rose clocks adorning the sides. He was predictable, orderly, this man who had taken the decidedly outlandish step of attempting to hire a highwayman to rob his father.

Only when he saw Percy's mouth quirk up at the sides into a grin matching his own did Kit realize he was still smiling like a fool. He also remembered that Percy wasn't Percy at all.

"You lied about your name," Kit said, pointing a finger at the other man's rose-clad chest.

"Did I?" the man asked. "I can't recall." He spoke the words as if he were sharing a private joke, rather than defending an accusation of lying. Kit had the strangest wish to be in on the jest, to know what had stolen away the man's arrogance and replaced it with a smile that managed to be both wry and soft.

"Why are you here?" Kit asked.

"So suspicious, Mr. Webb. I've become rather fond of your coffee. Isn't that reason enough to visit your establishment?"

"It's very inconvenient, you know," Kit said, the words leaving his mouth before he could think better of it, "not to know with what name to think of you."

"Is it? You must think of me often if that poses such an inconvenience." His arrogance was back in force now, written in the lift of his eyebrow and the way he leaned forward toward Kit, his hands on the table, pushing into Kit's space ever so slightly. Kit didn't lean away—this was his coffeehouse and he had all the power in this situation, no matter how he felt. But he could smell lavender and powder, could see that the man's eyes were the dark gray of wet cobblestones, could tell that the patch he had affixed over his lip wasn't a circle, as Kit had assumed, but rather a tiny heart. It was, perhaps, the heart that did Kit in—the utter ridiculousness of a heart-shaped fake birthmark ought to have made Kit loathe the man but it achieved quite a different result.

It was too much to hope that Percy (Kit had resigned himself to thinking of him as Percy, as the alternative was a mysterious blankness that posed the danger of becoming as peculiarly compelling as every other detail about the man, whereas Percy was a very boring and ordinary name) hadn't noticed Kit's reaction. "I knew it," Percy said, leaning forward even further. Kit still refused to retreat, telling himself that it was because he would not cede a single inch of ground, but even as he formulated the thought, he knew it to be a lie.

"I don't do that," Kit said, because, evidently, he was an idiot.

"Do what, Mr. Webb? I hadn't realized we had reached that stage of the proceedings."

"Uh," Kit said, eloquently. "I don't—"

"But you want to," Percy said, undeterred and unabashed. He helped himself to a seedcake from the basket that Kit had forgotten to put away. He took a small bite, chewed thoughtfully, and then brought a lace-trimmed handkerchief to his mouth. "Quite good. Why haven't I had any cakes on my previous visits? I spent hours here without seeing so much as a crumb."

Kit snatched the basket away and put it under the table. "I save them for the customers I like."

"I think I'm shaping up to be your favorite customer ever," Percy said, leaning close and taking another bite of cake. A crumb lingered on the swell of his lower lip, and Kit couldn't tear his gaze from it. When Percy swiped the crumb away with one flick of his pink tongue, Kit thought his heart might stop.

"What's your name?" Kit asked in a desperate bid to regain control of this conversation. "The truth this time."

"I'm afraid I can't tell you that," Percy said, looking genuinely remorseful, which Kit could not begin to make sense of. "Sorrier than you can know." He was whispering now, his words little more than a breath on Kit's cheek. Kit could have turned his head an inch to the left and—and kissed him, he would have thought if he were having an even somewhat normal reaction, if wanting to kiss strange men in broad daylight in a crowded coffeehouse could be considered in any way normal. But no, Kit's impulses were entirely run to mayhem, so what he actually imagined was running his teeth over the black velvet of that stupid heart-shaped patch. He was manifestly losing his mind.

Kit was usually very good at controlling this sort of urge. Hopping into bed with attractive strangers had never appealed to him very much anyway. It always seemed like a lot of hassle and risk for pleasure that never quite lived up to one's expectations. And that was with women; with men, things were even more complicated because a heaping great dose of danger was thrown into the bargain. And while Kit was far from averse to danger, he didn't want it in his bed. The fact was that he was spoiled by knowing what it was like to love someone and be loved in return; he knew what it felt like to want to be with someone in bed but also build a future with them. Anything other than that seemed too dismal to consider.

Although, strictly speaking, he still wasn't considering it. What he had in mind didn't involve any bed at all, just this counter and a bit of ingenuity. It would be easy—all he had to do was clear the shop, bolt the door, and draw the curtains. Percy seemed like he'd be game—had spent the last fortnight making as much clear to anyone with eyes and ears. Now his lips were parted, and at this close distance Kit could see his pulse coming hot and fast beneath the lace of his collar.

"Pardon me, Mr. Webb," said a small voice. Kit looked up to see Flora holding a coffee cup in one hand and her Bible in the other. "May I trouble you for a cloth? I'm afraid I spilled my coffee all over the table and now the book is quite soaked. It was my mother's," she said, opening the sodden flyleaf to expose a page of smeared ink. There were tears in her eyes, and her voice had a dangerous wobble.

It was as if the girl's words freed Kit from whatever godforsaken spell he was under. He handed her a clean cloth and showed her how to press it between the damp pages to absorb the worst of the spill. The book wasn't badly damaged after all, and Kit more than suspected that Flora's tears—and possibly the spill itself— had been engineered for Percy's benefit. When he looked up, he expected to see Percy and wondered whether the man would have caught on to what was happening. But when he raised his head, Percy was gone.

Chapter 10

*W*ith a great deal of effort and the unfortunate necessity of breaking into an unbecoming sweat, Percy managed to get back to Clare House, wash his face, change into drab clothes, and return to Webb's coffeehouse before it closed for the evening. The serving girl hadn't been there that afternoon, and Percy wanted to see if her absence changed Webb's routine at all. Without Betty to walk home, might Mr. Webb actually do something interesting?

Percy knew he was close to getting Webb to agree. He had to be. Percy had seen it in his eyes that afternoon. All he needed was a push, and maybe tonight Percy could get an idea about exactly what might make that happen.

Percy watched from the shadows across the street as Webb stepped outside and locked the door, accompanied by the pretty red-haired woman who had been in the shop earlier that day. Percy hadn't been paying her any attention at the time, and his memory supplied only a lacy white cap, a demurely cut gown, and a coffee-soaked Bible. A prostitute, no doubt, but the way Webb led her through the streets was how Percy imagined a man might walk with a niece—faintly gallant but no hint of anything sexual.

Gladhand Jack had a reputation for gallantry, in fact. At least two stanzas of that idiotic ballad were devoted to his chivalry, not that Percy had seen any evidence of it in person, unless grumbles were considered particularly charming. But the ladies he robbed returned home safe and sound with tales of how Gladhand Jack allowed them to keep some favorite bauble. The husbands, needless to say, had no such tales to tell, only empty purses and a disrupted journey. Even a highwayman who fancied men—as Webb plainly did—would likely not flirt with the men he robbed, although Percy was quite certain he could while away a pleasant afternoon daydreaming about getting held up by Kit Webb, with those dark eyes and big hands.

Before he could get too carried away, Webb and the girl stopped before a building Percy recognized but had never entered. The place was a famous brothel, easily one of London's most expensive and exclusive. Webb saw the girl inside, and no sooner had Percy congratulated himself on correctly identifying her as a prostitute than Webb descended the steps, returning in the direction from whence he came and heading straight for Percy.

It was too late to avoid Webb, so Percy ducked his head, relying on the down-turned brim of his hat, his plain attire, and the nearly moonless night to conceal his identity. He thought he had succeeded when Webb seemed prepared to walk right past him. Just as he was about to breathe a sigh of relief, Webb looped his arm through Percy's, spinning him so they were walking in the same direction, and led him into a side street with so little fuss that no passersby would have noticed anything amiss. Percy was almost impressed.

"This isn't the first time you've followed me. Who the hell are you?" Webb demanded. The street they stood in was little more than a lane, one of those narrow passageways that seemed to exist only to confuse strangers and to provide natives a series of expedient shortcuts. It was hardly wide enough for a single cart, with the result that it was mostly shadows. It had the air—and odor—of a place seldom frequented by anyone other than feral cats.

"Haven't we already had this conversation once today?" Percy answered. "Let's not be tedious, Mr. Webb."

Webb's eyes widened, and Percy realized his error. Webb hadn't recognized Percy as the man from the coffeehouse; he had recognized Percy as the person who had already followed him several times. But now Percy watched as realization dawned in Webb's eyes. He stared searchingly into Percy's face, as if looking for traces of the man from the coffeehouse, then dropped his gaze, taking in Percy's plain and utilitarian attire.

"Which is the disguise?" he asked flatly, and of all the questions in the world, Percy couldn't have expected that one.

"This is," Percy answered.

Webb shook his head. "Unless my source is wrong, and she never is, there isn't any Edward Percy among the quality." He pronounced the last word with an acid irony that was not lost on Percy. He was, of course, correct: there was no Edward Percy among the quality. There was an Edward Talbot, but when Talbot was stripped away, he'd be left with his mother's maiden name. Percy shrugged.

"Who is your father?" Webb continued.

This, fortunately, was a much more straightforward matter. "The Duke of Clare."

Percy had expected Webb to scoff, to express skepticism or to demand proof. He hadn't expected Webb to go so pale that his colorlessness was obvious even in the scant moonlight. "The Duke of Clare," he repeated, raking his gaze over Percy's face again. But now he looked not curious so much as horrified. "What's your given name?" he asked. "And don't fucking lie to me."

"I told you already. It's Edward, but nobody calls me that because my family is lousy with Edwards. And honestly, everyone calls me Holland anyway—"

Percy might have kept babbling indefinitely if he weren't silenced by the blow of a fist colliding with his jaw.

Chapter 11

*P*ercy—no, Lord Holland, damn him—spit out a mouthful of blood with astounding delicacy. "I take it you're not one of my father's more ardent supporters, then," he said, voice too steady and too wry for a man who had just been assaulted in a dark alley by a known criminal. "Well, neither am I, come to that. See, we're going to get along splendidly."

"Shut up, you," Kit said, because he couldn't decide what to do next, and the sound of Holland's voice and the sight of blood on his split lip was making it impossible for him to hear himself think.

"Or is it that you respect and admire my father so greatly, and were so grievously offended by my plan to rob him, that you simply had to hit me? That must be it," Holland said, idly tapping one long index finger against his lower lip.

"Shut *up*," Kit growled, clenching his bruised knuckles into a fist.

"Why, are you going to hit me again?" Holland asked, not seeming particularly worried about that prospect. "Because if you are, please get on with it. I'm expected at supper in an hour and it'll take an age to cover what will surely be an impressive bruise. And if you aren't going to hit me, will you kindly bugger off, as I believe is the custom in these situations? Not, I hasten to add, that I've ever been accosted in an alley or anywhere else before this evening, so my intelligence may be lacking. It's mainly from the theater," he added confidentially.

"Do you ever shut up?" Kit asked, now fully exasperated.

"I'm afraid not," Holland said apologetically with a faint smile. He oughtn't to have been able to smile. Kit hadn't pulled that punch in the slightest and had aimed right at the sweet spot of Holland's jaw. His jaw wasn't nearly as red as it ought to have been, either. Even without powder, his skin was the sort of white that bruised instantly and reddened easily. If his jaw wasn't as red as a beet, it could only mean that either Kit had aimed badly, which he hadn't, or Holland had managed to dodge at the last instant, so Kit's fist only landed a glancing blow.

He grabbed Holland's jaw and tilted it to the side so he could see the bruise. "You have good reflexes," he said.

"Why, thank you," Holland said graciously. "The theater really didn't prepare me for this in the least. I shall write a letter about the slanderous treatment of footpads and miscreants in modern drama."

"Are you able to get home safely?"

"Am I— Yes, you lackwit, I can get home safely. You really are gallant. I wonder how much of the rest of that ballad is accurate."

That jolted Kit back to his senses. "Then get the hell out of here."

"Or what? You'll give me another extremely mild bruise?" But Holland was already at the mouth of the alley. "Have a lovely evening. I'll call on you later this week!" he shouted before disappearing around the corner.

Kit leaned back against the damp stone of the nearest wall. The Duke of fucking Clare. It was that name, that man, and every man like him, who had led Kit to become what he had been. Rage at Clare had fueled a decade of retribution against his entire class. But Kit had never been able to lay hands on Clare himself. His outriders were too well armed, his journeys too unpredictable, and his path usually limited to well-traveled roads. More than once, Kit had thought Clare lived like a man in constant expectation of being attacked. And well might he be, if he made a practice of treating people as cruelly and needlessly as he had treated—

But Kit could get him now. After nearly ten years, he could have his revenge. He'd have not only revenge, but the satisfaction of knowing that Clare's own son had helped him get it. He'd have a chance to do one last job and with the only target he had ever really wanted.

He pressed his palms against the stone wall behind him and pushed off. He made his way through streets lit only by a sliver of the moon and the candlelight flickering through the windows of the buildings lining the street.

Kit had seen the Duke of Clare only once, when he had sentenced Jenny. At the time, Kit had thought he had the man's appearance seared into his memory, but now he could hardly conjure up a picture of the man. When Holland had said who his father was, though, Kit had seen traces of the duke on his son's face. They had the same cold eyes, the same aquiline nose, the same air of a man used to moving through a world without obstacles.

Unchecked power gave a man a certain look; it set him apart from normal people. Something terrible was unleashed when a person knew that not only could he tear down homes, take away a family's livelihood, and send people to the far corners of the earth, but he would be praised for it. There were rich men who didn't use their money and power as cudgels, but they still always knew that they had a cudgel ready at hand. They got so used to it, they probably thought they were doing a grand thing by not wielding it.

And Kit hated them all for it. People might say that what he really hated was the system that put too much power in too few hands. But Kit knew he also hated the men.

That hatred had been the engine of his life for the better part of a decade, and at the center of it was the Duke of Clare.

Led by instinct or old habit or just the darker recesses of his nature, Kit turned one corner, then another, until he found himself in the sort of neighborhood where every old lady sold gin out of her front window. He found one of these shops, knocked, paid his money, and before he could think better of it, had a tin cup in his hand. He knocked back its contents in a single gulp, the spirits burning their way down his throat and making his eyes water.

"Blimey," said the old woman. "Needed it, did you?" Her hair was white and thin, her back stooped, and her face deeply lined. She spoke with the blurred syllables of a woman with very few teeth. She reminded Kit of Jenny's grandmother, and in the middle of a Saint Giles street he was assailed by the memory of a brace of pheasants roasting in the hearth of a crumbling cottage in Oxfordshire.

He hated to think that far back, in the same way that he refused to go back to the little corner of Oxfordshire where he had been born and lived out the first eighteen years of his life. He didn't want to think about that younger version of himself, and above all didn't want to wonder what that younger man would think of his present-day self.

The gin had already started to work its magic, and the memories came hard upon one another. He could see his father pulling pints and his mother polishing the brass fittings she was so proud of. He could all but smell the wood fire that burned bright all year round in the taproom.

He remembered another cottage, a cradle he had built with his own hands, a child wrapped in fresh linens—

And he remembered how it felt after it was all gone.

"You all right, dearie?" the old woman asked, and Kit had to be in a truly bad state when the purveyor of an illegal gin shop was worried about him.

"It's just been a while," he said, handing her the empty cup through the window along with another coin for her to fill it again.

Chapter 12

*P*ercy knew that vanity was not only a sin, but possibly his besetting sin. Or at least it had been before the revelations of the past month introduced him to the various temptations of theft, cruelty, and the general consignment of the entire fifth commandment to the midden pile. But he was vain, and he knew it, and he was not appearing in public with a bruise on his jaw.

Still, he did not relish the prospect of pressing a raw piece of meat to any part of his person. Collins assured him that this was the received practice for treating new bruises, but that didn't make it any less disgusting. Averting his eyes, he applied the slab of meat to his face. He breathed through his mouth to avoid gagging at the smell of fresh blood. His vision swam, the walls of his bedchamber seeming to dissolve before his eyes; the distant sounds of the household settling down for the night receded as if muffled by cotton wool, so at first he did not hear the tapping at his window.

When the sound came a second time, he shakily got to his feet and pushed aside the curtain with the hand that was not holding the revolting meat. He expected to see a loose piece of ivy or a creeper that had come away from the trellis, or, at worst, an especially large moth.

What he did not expect to see was Marian, three stories aboveground, her face a pale, almost spectral, oval against the darkness of the night. He managed not to jump, but only barely. She gestured impatiently for him to open the window. He gestured for her to move aside so he didn't open the window directly into her face, causing her to plummet to her death. Finally, he managed to get the window open with one hand, and she stepped inside with an almost acrobatic grace, as if she climbed in and out of windows every day of her life. Her dark hair was pulled into a long plait and she wore black silk knee breeches that he recognized as a pair that had gone missing from his wardrobe shortly after his return home.

"Those are my breeches," he said by way of greeting.

"They're your shirt and waistcoat, too. Pity your boots don't fit." She gestured to her feet, which were clad in black stockings and her own black dancing slippers.

"A true shame that my wardrobe couldn't supply all your needs for outfitting yourself as a housebreaker. To what do I owe the honor?"

"You had a bruise on your face at supper," she said. "I could hardly ask you about it in front of the duke."

He frowned, the movement tugging at the injury. Percy didn't need to ask why Marian had sneaked in through his window instead of knocking at his door or approaching him in the drawing room. The duke was suspicious of all men Marian spoke to, even his own son, despite the fact that Percy had never in his life done anything to make anyone think he might be interested in going to bed with a woman. Indeed, during his teenage years, he had been something less than discreet, relying on his name and position to get him out of any trouble he might find himself in. There had been a few boys at school, then the village blacksmith and one of the grooms. And also one of Marian's grooms. And also Marian's brother.

"How *is* Marcus these days?" Percy asked.

She shot him an exasperated look. "Yes, I tiptoed along a ledge for twenty yards to gossip about Marcus. He's still in France, trying to find Louise Thierry, or whatever that scribble in the parish register was meant to spell. More to the point, he's trying to find out if she has a son." Marian pressed her lips together. "We need to know who will be the next Duke of Clare."

For a moment, Percy was certain the wind outside stopped blowing, the fire in the hearth stopped crackling, and his own heart stopped beating. Until then, he had assumed that the title and estate would go to a third cousin, a cadet branch of the Talbot family to be sure, and hardly worthy of Percy's notice, but respectable people. Percy was going to be disinherited, Percy's mother's memory and Marian would both be dishonored, and for that his father would pay, but at least Cheveril and the rest of the estate would go to someone who would look after it. The idea that instead it might fall into the hands of a French peasant, the son of some woman his father had taken to a foreign church and secretly wed, probably for no reason other than to smooth his path into her bed—Percy found himself choked with something horribly like grief.

He was dimly aware of Marian speaking. Her lips were moving but he couldn't make out what she said. Absently he let his hand drop from his face, the raw meat falling to the floor. When he looked at his hand, he saw smears of blood on his fingertips. Then things got hazy, a sort of mist descending on him, and the last thing he was sure of was that he was falling.

When he came to, the first thing he was aware of was acute embarrassment. The second was that his head was in Marian's lap, her fingers carding through his hair in a manner that was almost gentle and caring. This was so disconcerting that he sat bolt upright.

"Easy," Marian chided. "I caught you once. The next time you're on your own."

"Entirely reasonable," he managed, his tongue thick and lazy in his mouth.

"I forgot how you used to do that," Marian said. "Still do, I suppose. Remember when I fell from the apple tree and bloodied my nose? You were out for five full minutes. I thought you had died."

"You bled all over me!" Percy protested. At the time he had been entirely certain that passing out was the only reasonable course of action when someone had bled all over one's waistcoat, and he still believed this to be the case.

"I don't know how you can play around with swords if you faint at the sight of blood."

"I don't *play around* with swords, and I'm entirely too skilled to let myself be cut to bits, thank you."

"Shut your eyes so I can wipe the blood from your hands and face," she said, rising to her feet.

He complied, hearing her soft footsteps cross the room, then the sound of water being poured from an ewer. She took his hand and briskly wiped each finger. "Now your face," she said. He tilted his chin up, wincing only slightly as she passed the damp cloth over his jaw. "Now are you going to tell me who hurt you?"

"It was your highwayman."

"Ah. I take it he won't be lending us a helpful hand, then?"

"Oh, he'll be lending us a hand. I guarantee it. Marian, who is he? He did not react well to the sound of my father's name." Percy gestured at his bruise.

"I imagine the country, if not the entire hemisphere, is filled with people who become consumed with a murderous rage when they hear of the Duke of Clare."

"True," he said. But Marian's response hadn't really been an answer to the question he had asked. "Does this man have a special reason to hate the duke?"

"You should ask him," she said lightly.

That still wasn't a proper answer. He knew Marian well enough to understand he'd never get any information from her she didn't choose to divulge, so he let the topic drop. Still, he had the uncomfortable sense that she was playing a deeper game than he was, and was playing for stakes he didn't yet understand. "Who told you about him? When I left England, you certainly didn't have any connections to London's criminal demimonde."

Her jaw tightened. "A lot happened after you left." She shook her head briskly, her eyes sparkling with what he at first thought were tears but then recognized as anger. Then she got to her feet, the bloody piece of meat in her hand.

"What are you doing with that thing?" he asked.

"I have an idea," she said.

Before he could ask what she meant, she stepped out the window. He held his breath as she descended the trellis instead of edging along the ledge back to her room. When her feet hit the ground, the old hound who patrolled the gardens of Clare House came up to her. But before the dog could bark, Marian dropped the meat, then sprinted toward the gate.

Chapter 13

*Y*ou're an idiot," Betty said the next morning when Kit stumbled downstairs, his clothes rumpled and his face unshaven. "I can smell the gin on you from across the room. I hope your head hurts."

It did, but he wasn't going to give her the satisfaction of his saying so. "Remember the man in the brightly colored coats?" he asked, the sound of his voice ricocheting off the insides of his skull like seeds in a dried-out gourd.

"The one who stares at you all day?" She dragged a chair across the floor to the table where it belonged with more clatter than could possibly be necessary.

"He's the Duke of Clare's son."

She raised her eyebrows. "Well, bugger me."

"Hence, the gin."

"Fair," she said, her expression softening marginally. For a moment he thought she was going to hug him or attempt to say something soothing, and he braced himself, but she recovered her senses and resumed rearranging the chairs.

"He wants to hire me to rob his father. I'm going to agree."

She stared at him for a long moment, her lips pressed together into a tight line. "You really are a fucking idiot," she finally said. "Go get yourself cleaned up and don't show your face until you've eaten something."

Kit rinsed off at the pump, then carried an ewer of water upstairs to wash more thoroughly. He thought about shaving, even going so far as to pick up his razor and look meaningfully at it, before remembering that Betty wasn't the boss of him or his incipient beard, and decided to leave well enough alone. He brushed his hair and made an attempt to smooth it into a queue before giving it up as a lost cause and letting it fall around his shoulders. He cast his linens into the pile of things to be sent to the laundry and dressed in a crisp clean shirt and a fresh pair of breeches. He was still buttoning his waistcoat when he went downstairs and emerged into the shop.

"There you go," Betty said. "It's always easier to think like a reasonable person when you don't look like something dragged in from a sewer."

"I've already made up my mind."

"Your mind is scrambled, then. Stop using it. Let me do the thinking for you. That's why you keep me around, isn't it? Listen to me, Kit. We both know you can't run or ride fast enough to be safe during a robbery. You'll put yourself and everyone you're with at risk."

"I'll figure out a way around that," he said. "I have to."

"The feelings you have where Clare is concerned have no business in a robbery."

"He's the whole reason I have any business doing robbery in the first place," Kit said. "If it weren't for him, I'd be—" He didn't dare finish that thought, not after yesterday's gin-fueled trip down memory lane. "I started all this because I wanted revenge."

"That's because you were young and foolish and grieving your wife and child."

He held up his hand to stop her. "Hush."

"No, you hush. You got by on gin and luck. Now you're older and you know better, and you have me to tell you what to do. I've seen what happens when people go into a robbery seeing red. They wind up losing their heads and taking stupid risks. I'm not putting my neck on the line just because you're too angry to think straight."

Kit let out a breath. Betty was a fence, and came from a family of fences, and maybe because she dealt only with goods and coin, she didn't understand anyone who approached life without the levelheadedness of an actuary. "Every job I've done, I've been angry."

"Bollocks. This job would be personal. Not to mention the fact that you shouldn't want to ally yourself with the Duke of Clare's son. You ought to know a trap when you see one. I won't be a part of it."

"Then don't."

"Go to hell." She closed her eyes and seemed to gather herself. "What good is revenge if he doesn't know that you're the one serving it to him? I know you, Kit, and you'll want to let him know exactly which of his sins he's paying for. And once he knows it was you, it'll come back to you, here." She gestured around the shop, as if he didn't already know what was at stake. "And to me. And to *my* family. Unless you plan to kill him." When Kit didn't answer right away, she sucked in a breath. "Christ. Do you plan to kill him?"

"No," he said. "I'm not going to kill him." If anyone deserved a knife in the heart it was Clare, but Kit wouldn't be the one to put it there. "As for the rest of it, I don't need him to know who I am. It's enough that I know."

Betty looked at him long and searchingly. "Then you'll do this sober, Christopher." She crossed her arms, looking as displeased with him as she ever had, including during the ruby diadem incident.

"Yes, Elizabeth," he said, trying to tease her back to their usual good relations. He needed her, not as a fence, certainly not as a serving girl, but as his friend. He had known her since she was a child, running around London in her brother's clothes, delivering messages and arranging meetings for her father. She had arrived in his life when he thought he'd never again be able to give a damn for anyone ever again, least of all a child, and certainly not a surly, ill-tempered child, but here they were. He had watched her grow up, and she had seen him at his worst and stuck around anyway. In Rob's absence, she was his closest friend, and even before Rob disappeared, Betty had been indispensable. He didn't have any illusions about this indispensability going both ways: Betty didn't need anyone. When her father died, she had quietly taken over the family business and was, in Kit's professional opinion, the best fence in London. She could get a good price for anything and make sure it was never traced back to its original owner. The only thing Kit contributed was the coffeehouse, which provided a convenient meeting place with the people she called her customers.

If this robbery was going to cause a rift with Betty, he needed to do something to reassure her. He couldn't and wouldn't pass up the opportunity to get revenge against Clare, but he could keep his involvement as minimal as possible. He could plan the thing at arm's length. After all, planning had always been his particular talent, a well-organized plan being nine-tenths of a successful robbery, and the other tenth consisting of sheer bravado, a bit of luck, and a cheerful willingness to stare down the barrel of a pistol. And gin, probably, but Kit could do without that, especially if—

"Betty," he said as the plan coalesced in his mind. "Sit down." He pulled out a chair for her.

"Some of us have work to do," she said, evidently determined to sulk for the rest of the day. "It's past nine, and you'll have people at the door soon. You might want to, oh, I don't know, brew some coffee."

"They can wait," he said. "Come. Sit down. I have a plan."

Chapter 14

*P*ercy thumbed through the invitations that sat on his writing desk. It seemed his return to England had not gone entirely unnoticed, despite his best intentions.

When Marian had sprung the news of his father's bigamy on him, Percy had been in England for a matter of hours. He had hardly had time to get used to being home, after an absence of over two years, before he was uprooted again, this time a distance further than the span of the channel.

All the invitations were addressed to Lord Holland, and he—Edward Percy, or whoever he was—had no claim on them. He had no claim to the company of the friends with whom he used to visit gaming halls and pleasure gardens. He had no claim on any aspect of the life he had once lived as Lord Holland, and he had too much pride to help himself to something that wasn't rightly his.

He supposed an entirely different sort of man might have counted on the support of his friends, might have assumed they would stand by him regardless of his changed circumstances. But Percy knew that if one of his friends had turned out to be the subject of a scandal and the fodder for gossip the likes of which

England hadn't seen in a generation, Percy would have bitterly resented the man for bringing Percy's name into association with his own. As a matter of dignity, he couldn't expect more from his former friends than he would have given them himself.

And so he found himself at something of a loose end, loath to spend any more time in Clare House than strictly necessary but without anywhere else to go or anyone to see.

He dressed in his plainest clothes and set off on foot in the direction of Webb's, for lack of anything better to do—not because he was beginning to enjoy the place, not because he found himself at the end of the first volume of *Tom Jones* and eager to begin the next. Almost as an afterthought, he recalled that it had been a few days since the punching incident, and Webb might be ready to accept his proposition.

On his way, he passed a boisterous throng surrounding a raised platform in Covent Garden and slowed his pace. Amid the shouts of the crowd and the jingle of coin he heard another, infinitely more intriguing sound: the clatter of blade upon blade.

Percy's hand went to his hip, in an almost longing reach for a weapon that wasn't there. Since returning to England, he had yearned for a chance to fence. Ordinarily, he sparred with those of his peers who were similarly interested in the pastime, but that was presently out of the question. Sometimes he even visited a fencing studio—low sorts of places, but needs must—but it seemed that during his absence, something of a fashion for fencing had sprung up among the more daring sons of the aristocracy. And so Percy had spent the weeks since his return eyeing his weapons, occasionally taking them out to sharpen or polish, but with no prospect of putting them to good use.

It had been his mother who insisted that he learn to fence,

on the theory that Percy, who had been so small as to be nearly delicate, needed to develop some talent at intimidation. He was the last of the Percys; his mother had hoped for more, but she got a thin, pale, invisible, charmless child and made the most of him. And for that, Percy was grateful.

Nobody would have considered the late Duchess of Clare to be a doting mother, but she had detected in her son the early signs of a fatal weakness and done her best to teach him to conquer this failing. She had seen that he was eager to please, generous of mind, and disinclined to cause pain. In a person born into ordinary circumstances, a person who need concern himself with nothing more than his acres and his family, these qualities might even merit praise. For the future Duke of Clare, they would get him trampled on, stolen from, and possibly killed. His very gentleness would make him putty in the hands of the wrong person.

She taught him that because he was the heir to an uncommon degree of wealth, power, and pedigree, people would try to use him. She taught him to trust nobody but herself and people who he paid enough to need him.

She taught him that there was no such thing as peace and that any struggle or skirmish would involve the Duke of Clare; for a man in his position there was no such thing as neutrality. She taught him to look for the seeds of unrest, and it wasn't until much later that he realized she never told him what to do once he found those seeds—whether to stomp on the tender shoots or to water them.

Percy was to be aware of the hidden currents of power and strife that flowed beneath the surface of ordinary life, and he was to channel them for his own preservation. For preservation had been the duchess's goal, and all her lessons had been for the purpose of teaching her only child self-defense against a world that she believed would eat him alive.

Percy insisted that he didn't need to use a weapon in order to survive in this frightening world his mother described; he said that surely a sharp tongue and a title were all he needed, citing the duchess herself as all the precedent he required to support his argument. But she had prevailed, and a fencing tutor had duly been imported from France.

That had been ten years ago, and since then Percy had grown tall enough that he hardly needed a sword to intimidate. But now he thought he understood his mother's motivation—she had probably been trying to improve Percy's confidence more than his ability to physically defend himself. After all, life as the heir to the Clare dukedom and loyal son of his father's principal enemy hardly required much in the way of physical combat. It did, however, require quite a bit of brazenness.

And it required even more, now that he knew he wasn't the heir at all. It would be a great deal easier if he could simply go after his father and his hirelings with a sword.

Percy watched the prizefight with increasing interest, the delicate clash of swords soothing him in the way he supposed a hot cup of tea might work on someone with more reasonable sensibilities. He had witnessed prizefights as a child and abroad as a young man. The combatants were usually ruffians of a very low order who attempted to hack one another to pieces with badly honed weapons and no pretense to any skill whatsoever. And at first glance these swordsmen were little better than vagabonds: one of them had a long gash bisecting an eyebrow, and he didn't think the two men had more than a dozen teeth between them.

But just as he was about to decide that this spectacle wasn't worth his time, the fight ended and the loser left the platform to a chorus of jeers. Another man climbed up, there was some exchange of words that Percy couldn't hear, and the next thing he knew both men held swords. They bowed to one another and began sparring, with rather more clatter and elaborate footwork than strictly necessary, but Percy had to concede that they knew what they were doing. They both wore close-fitting garments and had their hair shorn close to the scalp. This, he supposed, gave their opponents fewer places to grab should the fight devolve into outright fisticuffs. His lip curled in distaste.

One of the men executed turns and flourishes to the wild enthusiasm of the crowd. Coins appeared from purses and pockets rather faster and more often than they had during the previous match. Percy wasn't certain how the fighters were paid, whether their only incentive was the final prize awarded to the last man left standing at the culmination of the day's battles, or whether they received a share of the amount wagered on the fight's outcome. They fought like a small fortune was at stake, and Percy had a hard time prying his eyes away.

As he watched, he realized that the uncertain feeling in the pit of his stomach was jealousy—he wished he were on the platform, holding a sword. He missed the feeling of a hilt in his hand, a blade obeying his commands. Of course he couldn't join in a public prizefight; the Marquess of Holland simply didn't—

Except that soon enough, he wouldn't have any standing to lose. And he could earn some coin, a prospect that he found rather thrilling in its novelty as well as probably a good idea for someone whose fortunes were, at best, uncertain. The idea of earning money through the one skill he possessed surely should not feel quite so daring, but Percy's heart raced at the thought.

He let his feet carry him the short distance to Webb's coffeehouse. When he opened the door, he was surprised to find that the overwhelming smell of tobacco and coffee was almost welcoming. He slid into a seat at the long table. Webb was nowhere to be seen, but Betty poured him a coffee. Her eyes slid right over him, and he realized that she didn't recognize him in drab clothes.

Half the table was involved in a debate about taxes, a topic Percy found about as thrilling as a dose of laudanum. Instead of joining the conversation, he sipped his coffee and found that he could tell this pot had been brewed by Betty, not Webb, because it tasted like proper coffee rather than what Webb achieved by tossing in a chaotic array of herbs and spices. He glanced around the room, noting that the bookshelves were as distressingly disorganized as usual and that a spider was weaving a cobweb across the entrance to the staircase. Strands of silk caught the light, shimmering prettily through the smoke, and Percy regretted that it would be destroyed as soon as Webb knocked his stubborn head into it.

As if Percy had summoned him, Webb stomped into the room, not from upstairs but rather from the door that led outside to an alley. He banged his walking stick into the floor in an apparent attempt to get everyone's attention. The stick didn't even make that loud a noise, but the room quickly hushed.

"All right, you lot. Somebody's been scribbling Tory nonsense on the privy walls." Every eye in the room was on Webb, as if he were a magnet. He wasn't even raising his voice above his usual scratchy growl. "You want to write Tory slogans, you do at it the coffeehouse across the way with the rest of the Tory scum." As Webb spoke, he looked at his audience, and his gaze caught on

Percy, and Percy knew he had been recognized. "Here, we serve Whigs and radicals."

Webb turned away, and the room erupted in a chorus of whistles and cheers as if the man had just delivered a speech on the floor of the House of Commons rather than a scolding about his privy walls.

Webb was even more disheveled than usual, and the scruff on his jaw was a dark shadow. He looked like he hadn't slept, and Percy didn't know whether it was his imagination or whether Webb leaned more heavily on his stick.

And despite all of that, he looked good. Maybe because of it, even. Percy didn't bother to pretend that he wasn't looking—he never did. What was new was that Webb looked back—not surreptitious little glances, but a steady gaze. Percy wanted to preen. He wasn't even in his fine clothes, just his sad brown breeches and a coat that made him look no different than anybody else in this place.

Percy deliberately got to his feet and stretched, and out of the corner of his eye saw Webb's hand still as he measured out ground coffee. He crossed the room to the bookshelves and looked for the second volume of *Tom Jones*. As the books were arranged with no regard to title, author, size, color, or any other quality Percy could determine, this took quite a while, and if he shifted his hips and stretched his arms over his head and in general posed like a bawd in the window of a cathouse, that was hardly his fault, now, was it.

It took a bare quarter of an hour for Webb to give in. "What in hell do you think you're doing?" he growled.

Percy reached into his pocket and drew out his coin purse. He took out a penny and held it between two fingers. "I'm looking to borrow a book." He reached out and grabbed Webb's hand, quick as anything, before Webb could react. He placed the coin in Webb's palm, holding it there with his own hand.

"I'm a patron of your lending library," Percy said, concealing his surprise that Webb didn't immediately pull his hand away. Instead, Webb just stood there, letting Percy all but fondle him, with a look on his face as if he had just been hit on the head. Since Percy had never learned to leave well enough alone, he stroked his thumb over the soft inside of Webb's wrist. That seemed to bring Webb out of his stupor, but all he did was roll his eyes and pull his hand out of Percy's grip.

"Right," Webb said. "What were you looking for—there it is." He pulled a book off the shelf, and Percy saw that it was the very volume he had been looking for.

When Percy reached the street, unaccountably dazed by that encounter, he realized he hadn't even asked Webb about the robbery.

Chapter 15

If Percy were honest with himself, and he desperately wished he were not, he was spending more time planning his next visit to the coffeehouse than he was planning a robbery. Well, he reasoned, it was all one and the same, was it not? Perhaps he would wear his plum silk ensemble. Perhaps that would provide the enticement Webb required to finally agree to perform the robbery.

His plans did not include being accosted in the courtyard behind Clare House when returning from his early-morning ride. He had just handed his reins to a yawning stable boy when Webb emerged from the shadows.

"How kind of you to demonstrate your criminous capabilities, Mr. Webb," Percy said, flicking a piece of straw from his sleeve and trying to sound like a man who hadn't just been frightened half out of his wits. They were in a part of the courtyard that was still untouched by dawn, hidden from the men inside the stable as well as anyone looking down from an upper window of the house. "One does like to know one's getting value for money. I do feel reassured knowing that I'm not about to squander my funds on a man who can't successfully lurk in dark corners. Well done," he said, and stepped toward the door.

Webb blocked Percy's path, bringing the two of them nearly chest to chest. They were of a height, but Webb was significantly broader, while it was only good tailoring that prevented Percy from unappealing gangliness.

Not that Percy had the benefit of any kind of tailoring this morning: the entire point of these early-morning rides was for both him and his horse to get exercise at an hour when nobody else was likely to see them, so he wore an ancient and shabby pair of buckskins and a coat that was cut large enough for him to dress without the aid of his valet. His hair was scraped plainly off his face in a way he knew to be unflattering, but he could not abide loose hair blowing into his eyes while riding. He was sweaty and disheveled and knew he probably smelled like horses.

He felt at a decided disadvantage next to Webb, who wore his own buckskins and ill-fitting coat with more grace than Percy thought strictly fair. He even smelled good, somehow, even though the only scent Percy could detect on him was yesterday's soap, tobacco, and what his mind stupidly and unhelpfully identified as *man*.

Percy ought to be appalled with himself for being attracted to Webb. Here he was, his life in shambles, his situation increasingly urgent, his closest friend and his only sibling both in a precarious position, and Percy's prick was running the show. Perhaps it was just used to running the show, or perhaps in times of hardship one finds comfort in the familiar, and in Percy's case the familiar was most definitely thinking with his prick. There had seldom been any reason not to.

Percy raised an eyebrow and cast a slow, heated glance from the top of Webb's sadly uncoiffed head to the tips of his scuffed boots, lingering at all the good spots in between, and hoping to convey a sort of bored lasciviousness, as if he engaged in criminal conspiracy every day between his morning ride and breakfast. Webb sucked in a breath and shifted his stance. It was some comfort knowing that Webb was so easily flustered by Percy's frank, if exaggerated, lust.

"I won't do what you asked me to do," Webb said, his voice quiet but firm, as if he thought the words would put a barrier in between their bodies.

"A shame," Percy said, leaning closer and almost purring into Webb's ear. Then he pulled back sharply. "And a waste of time for you to have traveled half the breadth of London to deliver a message that your absence would have conveyed just as effectively. I take it you want me to persuade you to do my evil bidding, and I'm meant to sweeten the deal by some means. I'm afraid it's too early for this tedium. I'll visit you at your place of business later this week or the next time I'm in the mood to be bored. Good day, Mr. Webb."

"No," Webb said, this time blocking Percy's progress with a hand to his chest. "You might let a man get a word in edgewise."

"I might, but why should I, when so few people have anything to say that I care to hear?" Webb hadn't dropped his hand from Percy's chest, and Percy felt the pressure from Webb's broad hand as if it were a hot iron burning through his clothes.

"You'll want to hear this." Webb's voice was low enough that Percy had to lean even closer to hear him, which meant pressing into Webb's palm. "I won't rob your father, but I'll show you how to do it."

Percy suppressed the urge to laugh and abruptly stepped back, letting Webb's hand fall. "I'm a man of many skills, Mr. Webb, but highway robbery isn't among them and I doubt it ever will be."

"As I said, I'll show you."

"You say that as if anybody could do what you did. As if highway robbery were a trick like juggling or a skill like playing the flute. I doubt it's either, or the roads would be teeming with attempted robbers."

Even in the shadows, Percy could see something uneasy flicker across Webb's face. "Ah, but there is a trick."

"Oh?"

"The trick is to not worry overmuch about being hanged."

"Oh, is that all," Percy said. "A trifling consideration. I'm afraid I don't agree to your terms, Mr. Webb. It has not escaped my notice that you'd like to see the duke get his comeuppance—ah, don't deny it, I can already see that you're a terrible liar and it pains me to watch you try. As I said, you wish to see my father suffer, which means you're a man of taste and judgment, for which I commend you. However, you must think me an utter simpleton if you believe I'm going to do your dirty work."

"I'm sure you'd prefer me to do your dirty work."

"Because I'd be paying you," Percy said, exasperated. "People don't walk into your coffeehouse expecting to be told to make their own coffee."

"I wouldn't take your money."

"Why on earth not?"

"Talbot money is filthy."

Percy was only slightly taken aback. "Well, of course it is, my good man. I defy you to find a single wealthy man whose money isn't filthy. There's even something in the Bible about it. Eyes of the needle and so forth, positive I've heard about it. All the more reason for you to take it. Good heavens, why am I trying to persuade you, a man who is positively infamous for taking other people's money?"

"Honest theft is one thing. Making a bargain with the likes of you is something else. That's filthy."

"How offensive," Percy said lightly. "If we were in civilized company, I'd have to call you out. Thankfully, we aren't at all civilized this morning." He realized he was blathering and tried to regain his composure. Obviously, it would be ludicrous for Percy to undertake a highway robbery. Among other things, he knew himself to be too much of a coward to carry out the "stand and deliver" routine without fainting from terror. He couldn't muster up the bravado to hold up perfect strangers, let alone his father, who had cowed him for the full twenty-three years of his life.

They had been standing in the shadows for several minutes, and now the sun had risen just that much further so that a beam of light landed on Percy's face. He saw Webb frown at him, then before Percy could move out of reach, Webb's hand was on Percy's chin, tilting it up to catch the light. Percy could feel blunt fingertips, calluses on the pads of Webb's fingers, but the touch was astonishingly gentle.

"It didn't bruise badly," Percy said when he gathered what Webb was looking at. He didn't relish the fact that Webb was looking at his face this closely without any powder, utterly bare.

"I don't usually throw the first punch," Webb said, not dropping his hand from Percy's jaw.

It seemed a strange thing for Webb to protest his lack of capacity for violence, given who and what he was. It was even stranger that Webb's thumb moved along Percy's jaw in a way that could, in a different circumstance, be called a caress. Percy stepped back. He was perfectly content to use sex to distract or persuade Webb, but not the other way around.

"What's to stop me from hiring someone else to do this job?" Percy asked.

"Nothing, except for how you don't know anyone else."

"How can you know that?"

Webb gave Percy a flat look, up and down his body. "You don't strike me as someone who has much to do with ordinary people."

Percy opened his mouth to protest that there was nothing ordinary about highwaymen, but snapped it shut again. That was hardly the point, and besides, Webb was correct. "Is this because of your leg?" Percy asked, pointedly looking at Webb's walking stick. "You'd like to see my father suffer, but your leg won't let you?"

Something cold and hard flashed in Webb's eyes. "I could have no legs at all, and I'd see to it that your father suffered, if that was what I wanted."

"How industrious of you," Percy said lightly. "And if you won't take my money, am I to believe that you'll do this out of the goodness of your heart? Or is it that knowing my father will suffer is reward enough?" At Webb's silence, Percy arched an eyebrow. "The latter, then. A man after my own heart. Alas, I can't agree to your terms."

Something like surprise and—could that be disappointment?—flickered across Webb's face. Percy decided he was not going to linger long enough to think about why. Without any attempt at farewell, Percy crossed the courtyard, feeling Webb's gaze on him.

As Percy entered the house, the sounds of a baby crying filtered through an open window. He knew that in one of the upper stories of the house, his sister's nurse walked the infant back and forth in front of the window. Baby Eliza invariably woke in a foul mood and could only be appeased by fresh air. At three months, the child was every bit as demanding and imperious as her forebears.

Usually, if Percy hurried upstairs after his ride, he could arrive in time to take his sister from the nurse's arms. One advantage to his unlovely riding clothes was that he didn't much care if they were further spoiled by baby spittle or worse. He stood at the base of the stairs, listening to his sister's intermittent cries and remembering that he had to consider more than his own comfort, more even than Marian's well-being. There was Eliza—her future, her fortune, her name.

He was going to have to accept Webb's offer. November was nearly over; even if he could find another man to do the job, he didn't have time.

Chapter 16

When Kit saw Holland in the coffeehouse, his heart gave a stupid extra beat. He sat at the long table, a book spread open before him.

It had been only a day since Kit had cornered Holland at his home, and he had almost given up on ever seeing the man again. He was trying very hard to persuade himself that he was relieved by this prospect, not disappointed.

"You here on business or pleasure?" Kit asked, putting a cup before the man.

"I didn't know you were capable of serving coffee without slamming it onto the table," Holland said, not looking up from his book. He licked his finger and used it to turn the page, and Kit forced himself to look away. "Business. I came to accept your offer, as I hope you already deduced."

"I might have, if you were wearing anything halfway suitable for, er, what we talked about." He gazed pointedly at Holland's coat, a fabric the color of fresh cream and which caught the light in a way that suggested there was silk in the weave. It made Holland look like a marble statue, and would be no better than a dusting cloth after five minutes of sparring.

Holland made a soft scoffing sound and gestured at his feet, where a neatly tied parcel sat. "I have a change of clothing."

"You'll have to wait," Kit said, because he had to do something other than imagine Holland stripping out of those clothes right here in the shop.

"Obviously," Holland said peevishly.

"The shop doesn't close for another two hours," Kit said.

"Then bring me something to eat," Holland said slowly and with exaggerated patience. "That is a thing you do in this establishment, is it not? You provide food in exchange for money? Or is one of us under a grave misapprehension about the nature of commerce?"

When Kit returned several minutes later with a plate of warm buns studded with currants, he found Holland pointing to a page and talking to the man beside him.

"It's very droll," Holland said. "Here, listen." And then he proceeded to read aloud a passage from what sounded like *Tom Jones*.

When Kit returned to gather the empty plate and replace the coffee with a fresh cup, he found Holland engaged in a conversation with half the table. He likely thought he was giving the other customers a thrill by allowing them to consort with their betters.

Betty sidled over to him with a dark look and murmured something about Kit's weakness for a pretty face.

"I just thought it would be a nice change to get out from behind the counter," Kit said.

"Don't lie," Betty said. "You're so bad at it, I feel embarrassed for you."

The next two hours crept by with agonizing slowness, but finally the last customer left and Kit bolted the door. When he turned around, he found Holland already on his feet, his parcel in his hands.

"Where are we to do this?" Holland asked.

Kit gestured with his chin toward the back room.

"Ah, your assignation room," Holland said knowingly.

Kit was stunned into silence. Betty stopped gathering plates and cups and stared at Holland.

"In the circles I travel in, one does know about these things," Holland said, looking back and forth between Kit and Betty. "Heaven knows I've used plenty of rooms like that, and I know what to look for."

"Is that supposed to be blackmail?" Betty asked, regarding Holland with narrowed eyes and a hand on her hip.

"My dear girl, if I meant to blackmail Mr. Webb, I'd start with his life of crime, not his amorous predilections, which I happen to share, for that matter."

"I don't do that," Kit protested, then wanted to bang his head into the wall. Both Betty and Holland knew that Kit had been looking, and protesting about it just made him look deluded. And now they were both staring at him. "Get changed," Kit grumbled. "And be quick about it." He tried not to watch as Holland walked out of the room.

"Amorous predilections?" Betty asked. "Is he just talking about fucking men or some fancy shite I don't want to know about?"

"Shut up, you," he told Betty.

"Is that what you're doing back there? Predilecting?" She waggled her eyebrows.

"Betty!"

"You should try. Do you a world of good."

He didn't go into the back room until fifteen minutes had passed, both because he didn't want to risk seeing Holland half-dressed and because he wanted to make Holland wait. When he pushed open the back door, he found Holland leaning against the wall, his ankles crossed. The room was only lit by a pair of old oil lamps, but they were bright enough to see that Holland was dressed in plain breeches and a matching coat, his hair pulled into a queue.

"Take off your coat," Kit said. "Can't do this properly in a coat. Waistcoat, too."

Holland hesitated a moment, then stripped down to his shirt.

"How are we going to do this?" Holland asked. "I've never hit anyone in my life."

"And you're not going to start now. This isn't pugilism. It's not even a brawl. What you need is to be able to disarm an adversary."

"At least four adversaries," Holland said. "My father travels with four armed outriders, and I'm certain the coachman has a pistol as well."

"You only need to trouble yourself with the coachman, because he's nearest to your mark. You'll hire people to deal with the rest."

"Oh, so now I'm hiring people, am I?"

"Were you under the impression that I worked alone?"

"I believe the ballad mentions a Fat Tom and a woman named Nell."

Kit snorted. "Her name is Janet, but that doesn't rhyme with nearly as many things as Nell. Janet's married with a baby on the way, but Tom is still working." Tom's principal talent lay in knocking people off horses with minimal fuss.

"Oh, Tom's still working, is he?" Holland asked dryly, his arms folded before him. "And is there some reason I can't give him fifty pounds to take my father's blasted book?"

"If you ever need your father's nose bloodied, Tom's your man. But you need more than that to manage an actual robbery."

"Like what? Because all I bring to the table is a propensity to chatter and exceptional good looks."

Kit opened his mouth, ready to say something about strategy, but he stopped himself. He doubted that this man, the duke of bloody Clare's son, thought that men such as Kit were capable of anything so refined as strategy.

Kit held up a wooden spoon he had carried with him for the occasion. "We're pretending this is a pistol. You're going to try to disarm me."

"All right," Holland said. "How should I start?"

"Do whatever you need to knock it out of my hand, or, better yet, take it for yourself."

Holland reached for it; he was fast but Kit was expecting it.

"They aren't going to let me saunter up to them," Holland said. "This is pointless."

"You'd be surprised. Try again."

Holland did so, and this time Kit stepped out of the way, causing Holland to trip and nearly fall.

The third time, Holland went in with his left hand, which surprised Kit, and Kit went to block him with his own right hand. That put weight on his bad leg, and Kit almost fell. He managed to recover himself but was startled by both the sudden pain and the fact that he didn't know how to fight without both legs. He ought to have realized beforehand that this would be a problem.

Worse, Holland seemed to have noticed at the same time Kit did. "Perhaps if you sat," the man said. "After all, the coachman will be sitting."

"No," Kit snapped. "Betty!" he called. When she came in, he explained to her what he was trying to do.

"I think not," Holland said. "I will not tussle on the floor with a woman."

"Good luck getting me to the floor," Betty said, kicking off her shoes.

"Why are you agreeing to this?" Holland asked the girl. "I have at least eight inches and several stone on you."

"You think I'm going to pass up a chance to kick a lord? Been dreaming of this since I was a little girl," she said.

"You have the chance to make a young woman's dreams come true," Kit said. Percy glared at him.

"Fine. Let's get this over with." Holland stepped toward the girl, and when she began to extend her arm toward him as if about to fire a pistol, he tried to grab her wrist.

"You've just been shot in the head," Kit announced. "Try again. This time grab her around the middle."

With obvious reluctance, Holland stepped behind Betty and attempted to get one of her arms trapped behind her back. She stepped on his foot and elbowed him in the stomach. "Ow!" he cried.

"Try again," said Kit.

"I'd much rather be doing this with you," Holland protested.

"I bet you would," said Betty.

"I mean that I don't relish the prospect of hurting a woman."

"I'm still waiting for proof you can even come close to hurting me," she said.

"I don't feel comfortable becoming violent with women," Holland said primly.

"Well, get comfortable with it," Kit snapped. "If you're too squeamish to grab Betty, then you'll be hopeless when you actually have to hurt someone. On the day of the robbery, it won't be a bloody spoon and the person you're trying to get it from won't be afraid to kill you. You need to act like this matters."

"It does matter," Holland insisted.

"This book that you want to get—"

Holland cleared his throat and glanced meaningfully at Betty.

"She's a part of this job. She knows everything," Kit said. "This book, either you're willing to hurt people to get it or you aren't. You need to decide now, before you waste any more of our time or your own, what it's worth to you."

"It's of the utmost importance," Holland said tightly.

"Then act like it. Try again."

He did try again, and this time Betty managed to trip him so thoroughly he landed sprawled on his back on the bare floor.

"No more," Kit said. "Go home. And don't come back until you're ready to act like you mean it."

Holland got to his feet. "You never really meant to help me at all," he said through gritted teeth. "You're simply amusing yourself by watching your friend humiliate me."

Kit narrowed his eyes. "The people you need to hire to work with you on this robbery are my friends. I'm not asking them to risk their necks to work with a man who isn't willing to put his own neck on the line. If you can't take this seriously, if you aren't willing to do what it takes, then I can't help you."

"I will not hurt a woman." Holland clenched his fists, and for a moment Kit thought this might be more than some gentlemanly rubbish about the fairer sex or some such rot. "I was raised—".

"Fuck how you were raised, and fuck your gentlemanly scruples. You can't do this if you insist on being a gentleman."

"A gentleman!" Holland repeated, unable to suppress a bitter laugh. "That has nothing to do with it. If somehow you think that gentlemen are unwilling to hurt women, I hardly know what to do with you."

"I know perfectly well what Talbot men are willing to do with women."

"That is precisely my—" Holland began, but was interrupted by a shrill whistle, and they both turned to face Betty.

"Enough. The pair of you are quarreling like fishwives. You," she said to Holland. "I got in my first fistfight when I was eight years old and I only stopped when the boys got too afraid of me to take me on. Don't come back until you're ready to treat me as your equal. And you," she said to Kit. "This was a terrible idea for all the reasons we talked about. You're not thinking straight, and you'll never think straight where these people are concerned."

When Betty left, Kit knew he ought to follow her and give Holland time to get dressed, but if given a choice between Betty's wrath and Holland's sulk, he'd take the sulk.

Out of the corner of his eye, he watched Holland dress himself with shaking hands. It took him three tries to get his waistcoat buttons lined up. When Kit gave him a proper look, he saw that the man's cheeks were flushed with what Kit suspected was helpless embarrassment. It felt wrong, seeing Holland exposed like this.

Holland opened his mouth but evidently thought better of it, and swept out of the room, leaving Kit alone and feeling unaccountably disappointed.

Chapter 17

*K*it had once been a heavy sleeper. It had been the source of much family comedy, with his brothers attempting to cut his hair or steal his pillow while he slept soundly. Later, Jenny had often needed to shake Kit awake in the morning. But by the time Jenny was gone, Kit had become the lightest of sleepers. Anger and fear had robbed him of peaceful sleep, and habit had accustomed him to waking every time Hannah stirred in her cradle. Now his nights passed almost dreamlessly, and when he woke, the covers were seldom disturbed. Sometimes he thought he didn't sleep so much as shut his eyes.

So it happened that when, in the small hours of the morning, he heard a rapping at his door, he sprang into wakefulness. Only stopping long enough to step into his trousers—he was not going to confront miscreants in a state of total nakedness—and grab his dagger and his walking stick, he was downstairs quick enough that he doubted his neighbors would even complain of the nighttime disturbance.

When he flung open the door, he didn't know whether to expect a vagrant who had lost his way home or a messenger with bad news about Betty or some other friend. He certainly did not expect Lord Holland, visibly drunk, his coat draped over his arm, his hair loose around his shoulders.

"What in the— Get inside before the neighbors see."

"I have something to tell you." Holland's usually precise tones were slurred. "S'important."

"You can tell me indoors," Kit said, taking him by the arm and tugging him into the shop. "And you can tell me while you're sitting—no, I don't trust you with stools right now. Sit in this chair." Once he had made certain Holland was safely in a chair, he built up the banked fire. "Now, what's so important that you had to wake me up in the middle of the night?"

"It's about women."

"Oh, is it?" Kit asked, amused.

"It is," Holland said with the earnestness of the very drunk. "I don't want to hurt them and it's not fair of you to make me."

The smile dropped from Kit's face. "You couldn't hurt Betty if you tried."

"S'not the point. I don't want to try. Don't want to be the sort of man who does try."

"I see," Kit said slowly. He turned his back so he could put the kettle on the fire, and so Holland couldn't see his face.

"There're not a lot of things I do right, it turns out. I mean, not a lot of things I do that are *good*. But that's one of them. And you shouldn't try to take it from me."

Kit turned around and saw Holland, one leg crossed over the other, his elbow on the arm of the chair and his chin in his hand.

"I see," Kit said, because he couldn't think of anything else. He took a jar of ground coffee off a shelf and put a spoonful in the pot. As he worked, he occasionally looked over his shoulder at Holland, partly to make sure he hadn't fallen off the chair, and partly because his face was open and vulnerable in a way Kit hadn't yet seen it. "I ought to have guessed."

"I'm six feet tall and twelve stone," Holland said. "That's a lot bigger than most women."

"That's true," Kit said.

"I don't want to be frightening."

"I promise that Betty wasn't frightened of you."

"That isn't the point!" Holland said, his voice nearly a shout. "The point is that I know who I am and what I am, and you shouldn't make me do a thing that I know is wrong." He closed his eyes and wrapped his hands tightly around the arms of the chair, and Kit guessed that inside Holland's wine-soaked brain, the room was spinning. "I do know it's wrong."

"Of course you do," Kit said, rummaging through the jars and baskets he kept behind the counter for some solid food he could get into the man. Finally, he turned up a couple of stale biscuits. He spooned some sugar into the coffee cup and put it on a saucer, then placed a couple of biscuits beside it. "Here," he said, handing saucer and cup to Holland. "Don't drop it."

"Never dropped a cup in my life," Holland said. "Breeding."

"One of the reasons I asked you to spar with Betty was that I wanted you to understand that in order to rob your father, you're going to have to do things you don't like."

"I already know that. I knew that the first time I came to you. Did you think that soliciting criminals is something I enjoy? I mean, I did enjoy it, you're very handsome, and there's—" He broke off, gesturing vaguely at Kit. Kit crossed his arms over his bare chest, desperately wishing he had thought to put on a shirt before coming downstairs. "All very pleasant to look at, bravo, but the reason I had to come to you in the first place was appalling. I don't want to steal from my father. I don't want my father to be a villain. I didn't ask for any of this. And one day when I have time to think, I'm going to be terribly angry about being forced to deal with all this."

Kit didn't ask what "all this" consisted of, just as he wasn't ever going to ask what was in that book. Whatever Holland and his father were up to, Kit didn't want to know the details. He needed to keep this entire affair at arm's length in order to keep his promise to Betty and not get caught up in a job that could easily get personal.

"I've never seen your hair down," Kit said, the words leaving his mouth before he could think better of it. "Either it's pulled back in a queue or it's hidden by your wig."

"I threw my wig in the river. At least I think it was the river. I got lost on the way here. And of course you haven't seen my hair loose. What am I, a barbarian?"

"You're definitely not a barbarian," Kit said, not bothering to suppress a smile.

"Don't ask me to spar with Betty."

"Drink some of that coffee. The other reason I wanted you to start with Betty is that I'm not sure I can spar with my leg as it is."

"I could see it threw your balance off," Holland said, surprising Kit. "In any event, I'd rather get hurt than hurt anyone else." He primly wiped biscuit crumbs from his mouth with a handkerchief.

"Would you, now."

"Part of it is strategy," Holland said. "If a decent man hurts you, he feels in your debt. If a cruel man hurts you, he thinks he's your superior, which makes him underestimate you." He spoke as if reciting a lesson learned by heart.

"I hadn't thought of it that way."

"You wouldn't have. You're honest. Honesty is incompatible with strategy." Again, his words had the cadence of a schoolroom lesson.

"Honest?" Kit laughed. "Did you forget who I am and what I did?"

"Certainly not. There's nothing dishonest about taking things that don't belong to you. You told me so yourself. It may be wrong, and it may be cruel, but it isn't necessarily dishonest. Someone who sneaks into your house may be dishonest. But you took things in broad daylight while telling people precisely what you were about to do."

Kit felt there was something fundamentally flawed about this analysis but couldn't quite figure out what. "Are you sobering up or do you talk like that even when you're drunk?"

"Oh, I talk like this all the time, can't help it," Holland said, gesturing expansively with his coffee cup but somehow not spilling a drop. His gaze dropped to Kit's bare chest, as it had several times already, not with the exaggerated leer he had deployed on previous occasions, which seemed designed to embarrass Kit more than anything else, but with a sort of interest that seemed accidental and unstudied, and which embarrassed Kit all the more. "I do talk too much, as you've pointed out, Mr. Webb."

"I never said you talk too much," Kit said, taking another biscuit out of the jar and offering it to Holland. "Just that you do talk a lot." He watched Holland chew the biscuit, a crumb clinging above his lip where he usually affixed his beauty patch. Kit had to force himself to look away. "Everybody calls me Kit."

"Is that your way of telling me to do the same? Are we to use given names? How very cozy of us. Then you ought to call me

Percy." He yawned, covering his mouth in a gesture that managed to be graceful despite his drunkenness. "People are so tiresome about names. Mine keeps changing." He yawned, delicately covering his mouth with his hand. "It's boring."

"You're about to fall asleep. I don't know how I'm going to get you home."

"I can walk," Holland—Percy—said, rising unsteadily to his feet.

"Like hell you can. You'll walk straight into the Thames."

"Pfft," Percy scoffed. He tried to step toward the door but tripped over the leg of his chair. Kit was by his side in a single stride and caught the man before he hit the floor.

"Oops," Percy said, making a half-hearted effort to right himself but instead leaning on Kit. His forehead rested on Kit's shoulder. Kit could feel Percy's ribs under the linen of his shirt, could feel his heartbeat against Kit's chest.

"Tell me again how you're going to walk home." Kit was surprised by how soft his own voice had become, but Percy's ear was right there, inches from Kit's mouth, so it was only natural to speak quietly. But still, the gentleness of his tone and the closeness of their bodies did something to make their nearness feel intimate rather than incidental. When Percy mumbled "slowly" into Kit's shoulder, and Kit could feel his lips move, it sent a shiver through Kit's body.

"All right," Kit said briskly, setting Percy back in his chair. "You'll spend the night here."

"Oh really," Percy said with a leer.

Kit snorted. "Can I trust you not to set yourself on fire or wander into the streets?"

"You can't trust me at all," Percy said, but he rested his head on the table beside him, cushioned on his folded arms, so Kit thought the odds against him going anywhere were fairly good.

Kit looked at the stairs and sighed. Leaning heavily on his walking stick, he made his way up to his bedroom. He grabbed the pillow and blanket off his own bed, as well as a shirt for himself. He supposed he could have managed to get Percy upstairs and put him into Kit's bed, but Kit balked at the idea of letting Percy into his bedroom. He didn't think he could handle knowing what the man looked like in his bed.

When he went downstairs, Percy was fast asleep. Kit laid out the blanket and pillow before the fire, then got an arm around Percy and managed to wake him up enough to lead him to the makeshift bed.

"Enough room for you," Percy said, his eyes half-shut, lazily patting the blanket next to him.

Kit couldn't say he wasn't tempted. It had felt good when he caught Percy. It had been months since he had been that near a person and even longer since he had wanted to be. But of all the people in the world he needed to share a bed with, the Duke of Clare's son was at the bottom of the list. Strictly speaking, he shouldn't even care whether this man made it home alive, let alone safely. It was bad enough that they were working together at all; Kit couldn't afford to let any emotions cloud his judgment. Anger and resentment were troublesome; softness and sentiment would be disastrous.

With his foot, Kit shoved Percy so he was resting on his side. Then he lowered himself into a chair, resting his head against the wall behind him. He doubted he'd be able to sleep upstairs with the knowledge that Percy was asleep in the shop, so he might as

well stay where he was. He tried to tell himself he wasn't standing watch in case Percy needed him, but he couldn't even believe
his own lie. The last thing he saw before his eyes drifted closed
was pale hair spread on his own pillow, catching the firelight and
glowing.

Chapter 18

*H*er Grace was most concerned when you disappeared from the drawing room last night," Collins said when Percy returned to his apartments in the small hours of the morning. Motivated by pure cowardice, Percy had crept out of the coffeehouse before Kit woke. Now he wanted nothing more than to crawl into bed and sleep off his headache.

"Tell me you didn't wait up all night," Percy said, rubbing his eyes.

Collins remained pointedly silent.

"I do apologize," Percy said. "I ought to have sent word."

"I took the liberty of mentioning to Her Grace's maid that you had spoken of your intention to visit an establishment that caters to gentlemen."

Percy was very tired and knew he wasn't thinking clearly, but it certainly sounded like Collins was suggesting he had passed a message to Marian's maid with the understanding that it would mean one thing to the duke and another thing entirely to Marian. Which perhaps meant that he understood that Percy and Marian needed to communicate secretly. And that could simply be because he understood they had been childhood friends and were now effectively under surveillance. But it could also mean that Collins understood that Percy and Marian were conspiring against the duke. Percy could not decide whether Collins was declaring himself an ally or gently hinting at blackmail.

"You're an angel and a genius," Percy said lightly. "That's possibly the only answer that would stop my father from asking questions. I'm forever in your debt. Marian won't believe that story for a minute, though."

"Precisely, my lord."

"Thank you, Collins. Now, I suppose I ought to make myself presentable and show my face at breakfast." He sighed. "I was hoping for a nap, but that will have to wait until my father's had a chance to scold me."

Collins sent him a brief, skeptical look as if to suggest that Percy shouldn't aspire to anything so grand as presentability, given his current state. But after a bath, headache powder, and the judicious application of Collins's considerable skills, Percy thought they had achieved sufficiently passable results. When he descended the stairs and found both Marian and his father at the breakfast table, he felt considerably more alive than he had upon his arrival home.

"You've been whoring," the duke said before Percy had pulled out his chair.

"Good morning, Father, Marian," Percy said, helping himself to kippers and ham. "Yes, I'm afraid I've been whoring."

"Where?"

Percy had not been expecting that question, and could not imagine why his father needed to know the particulars. He could name a handful of brothels but that would only be meeting his father on the ground of his choosing. He chose a different tack.

"You can't expect me to admit to the name of the sort of establishment I frequent," he said. "Wouldn't do to have any dear friends stuck in the pillory, now, would it?" That made the duke's cheeks redden, because he simply hated to be reminded that his son fucked men.

"You will not speak that way in front of Her Grace," the duke said.

"I beg your pardon, Marian," Percy said graciously. "I suppose I ought to follow my father's example and confine my breakfast-table conversation to the ordinary sort of whorehouse."

"Percy," Marian said, her eyes daggers. She sat pale faced and stiff backed, her plate empty and her hands in her lap, as she did nearly every meal.

Percy supposed that in the normal course of things, it would be wise to ingratiate himself to the duke so as to secure some sort of livelihood or settlement after the truth came out. But Percy didn't for a minute think that his father would willingly toss so much as a spare coin in his direction, however agreeable Percy tried to make himself. Besides, Percy reasoned that if he suddenly started acting civil to the duke, after twenty-three years of open hostility, it would make the man suspicious. It would make the entire household suspicious, come to that. Everybody knew that the duke and his heir—ha!—didn't get along; depending on one's alliance, that was either because the duke was a belligerent and controlling mean-spirited tyrant or because Percy was a lazy sybarite with a taste for unspeakable vice.

Besides, that was the point of acquiring the book—it would be foolish to depend on the duke's unlikely largesse when they had extortion as an option.

"It's time for you to find a wife," the duke said.

For one wild moment, Percy nearly laughed. With some effort, he schooled his features into something like boredom. "I rather thought that the point of this"—he gestured between his father and Marian—"was insurance in the event that I never sired a son." He could sense Marian bristle at the other end of the table, and he regretted needing to refer to her union with his father in those terms. But he had a part to play. He took an idle sip of tea. "Indeed, I thought it remarkably prudent of you, given my inclinations."

Percy had always known that he would need to marry. As his father's only son, he had a pressing need for an heir. He had never questioned it, and, if things had gone according to plan, he would at some point in the next year have married a suitable woman and done what was needful. Now, however, it would be unthinkable to marry. He could hardly wed a woman who thought she was marrying the future Duke of Clare but who instead turned out to be a penniless bastard. He already knew he couldn't offer a wife a love match; to also deprive her of title and fortune was outright villainy.

"In case you had not noticed, you are still the only son I have," the duke ground out.

Percy nearly said that he damned well hoped he was, because all this situation needed was the arrival of a French peasant on the scene claiming to be the rightful heir to the dukedom. Instead, he stirred some sugar into his tea. "Quite right," he said, and enjoyed the confusion and disappointment that passed over his father's face. Percy realized that the duke had been longing for a quarrel that morning and had picked a fight with Percy simply because he was near at hand.

For years he had regarded his father as a casual sort of nemesis, one who had no real power to harm him. But it occurred to him now that as soon as news of his illegitimacy was public and he was no longer heir apparent to the dukedom, he'd not only lose whatever protection he had as a wealthy and titled man, but he'd also open himself up to attack from his father. The duke could see to it that Percy was arrested, pilloried, locked away in the sort of asylum that existed to hide family members with inconvenient or unpleasant proclivities. Once the duke had no obligation to treat Percy as his heir, Percy would be vulnerable in a way he never had been before.

Percy rose to his feet, having lost all interest in verbal combat. "Perhaps you or your secretary could furnish me with a list of acceptable wives," he said, casting one last look at his untouched breakfast. He hadn't eaten anything since dinner the previous night and now he was famished. But even as he formed the thought, he remembered Kit giving him coffee and dry biscuits, catching him as he drunkenly tripped, covering him with a blanket. The memory was unwanted, a discordantly tender intrusion into a moment that required Percy to operate without any blunted edges. "Good day, Father, Marian."

When he climbed the stairs and reached his bedroom, he paused for a moment with his back against the closed door. Percy had never had an actual enemy and he had never before faced real danger. It felt disturbingly apt, as if he had been born to this. He recalled his Talbot forebears whose grim faces lined the portrait gallery at Cheveril Castle and thought that quite possibly he had been born to this. Talbots were made for war and enmity. They let those with weaker blood have their easy peacetime delights.

If Percy were honest with himself, easy peacetime delights sounded grand. He'd much rather be planning a garden party than a felony. He'd much rather not plan anything at all, and just while away his days drinking coffee and reading books, and if that brought to mind Webb's coffeehouse, it was just further proof that his mind was addled and his priorities askew.

He took out his whetstone and sharpened his sword.

Chapter 19

When Kit woke, stiff necked and muddle headed, in the hard chair by the fire and noticed that Percy had gone, his first thought was disappointment, followed quickly by horror that he regretted the man's absence. He ought to be pleased that Percy was out of his hands, back where he belonged. He ought to hope that Percy never showed his face again.

Instead, Kit had to admit that he had . . . not minded Percy's presence the previous night. He had even enjoyed it, enjoyed the man's drunken chatter as much as he enjoyed his sober chatter. He had found it surprisingly satisfying to put Percy to bed, to know he was keeping Percy safe. It had been a long time since Kit had taken care of anyone, since anybody had needed him, and he found that he missed it. He didn't think of himself as a particularly nurturing person; God knew taking care of Hannah hadn't come naturally, and look how badly that had turned out. After Jenny had been taken away, Kit hadn't been fit to look after a cat, let alone his sickly, motherless daughter. Looking after the adult heir to a dukedom after a night of drunkenness was hardly the same thing, even though it prodded that same old place in Kit's heart.

Kit's heart, frankly, needed to sod off.

When Betty warned him against letting his feelings get tangled up in this job, she had been talking about anger, resentment, and vengeance. She teased him about being weak for a pretty face, but neither of them really thought that he'd care about the fucker. And Kit didn't care about him—it was just that tucking him into bed and keeping him safe had tricked his mind into thinking he gave a damn. That was all.

He brought the blanket and pillow upstairs before Betty could come in and ask unwelcome questions, then made sure he rinsed out the cup Percy used and put everything to rights.

Still, when Betty walked in, she narrowed her eyes, swept her gaze across the room, and stared at Kit. "You look shifty," she said.

"No, I don't," he said immediately, and, he quickly realized, unhelpfully. "What do I have to be shifty about?" he added.

She only shook her head.

"It's not natural," he said as he set out the coffee. "You're twenty years old. You shouldn't be able to look so disappointed. There are grandmothers who would envy that expression."

"The trick is that I really am disappointed," she said with an exaggerated sigh. He threw a coffee bean at her head. "Also, I have practice being disappointed in every small-time pickpocket who thinks I'm going to be bothered to fence a single teaspoon or a pair of handkerchiefs. My face does disappointment very naturally now."

She spoke with an air of pride that belied her words. Kit knew that she liked her work—liked having taken over from her father, liked solving the puzzle of how to dispose of stolen goods without them ever being traced back to her, the thief, or the original owner, and liked being at the center of things. It made him miss his old work more than ever. Maybe it was good, he thought, that Percy had come to him when he did.

Even as he formed the thought, he knew it was nonsense. He was getting different kinds of want mixed up in his mind—the old urge for revenge, the need for excitement, the seeds of desire he felt for Percy. All those wants were met in this one job, and that was making it hard to think clearly. That was all. The stirrings of—it was distressing to realize that tenderness was the only applicable word—he had felt the previous night were only the wisps of desire that clung to everything he forbade himself.

But perhaps it was time for some insurance. That evening, after bringing Betty home, he went to Scarlett's. The door was opened this time not by Flora but by another girl. He was shown to an unoccupied parlor, where he waited several minutes for Scarlett to arrive.

"Twice in as many weeks," Scarlett said when she entered. "I'm a lucky woman."

"You'll soon change your mind, because I'm here for another favor."

She looked neither pleased nor surprised. "Well, make it fast, and I'll forgive you."

"The man I asked you about, Edward Percy?"

"The man who doesn't exist."

"He's the Duke of Clare's son and heir, Lord Holland."

Something passed over Scarlett's face. He had known her for nearly ten years, had been what he'd call friends with her for most of that time, but had seldom seen her face express anything outside the narrow range between mild consternation and mild pleasure. But now she looked shocked. It lasted only a moment, but it had happened, and Kit had seen it.

He was put in mind of Percy, who had the same outward impassivity, the same ability to hide his feelings. They were both so accustomed to deceit that they schooled their expressions as a matter of course. When the mask dropped, it meant something.

Kit's only question was whether she was surprised to learn Percy's identity, or whether she was surprised that Kit knew.

"Of course," she said. "They all do call him Percy. I ought to have made the connection. And—good God—he's the one who wants to hire you to rob someone. He knows who you are. This is all most unfortunate."

"Do you know him?" Kit asked, trying not to betray his eagerness to know the answer. He needn't have bothered, because she didn't so much as look at him.

"He's never been here," she said.

Kit almost laughed. "I gathered that he wasn't likely to be among your customers."

Now she looked at Kit shrewdly. "Did you, now?"

He swallowed. "He hardly makes a secret of it."

"I see. To answer your question, no, I don't know him. He went to one of the usual schools, then idled about town for a while before traveling through Europe for two years. He returned earlier this autumn but has seldom been seen in society since then."

Kit might have thought this an impressive amount of information for Scarlett to have at the tip of her tongue—especially about a man who wasn't even among her clientele—if he hadn't seen her perform the same feat many times over the years.

"Is he cruel to his servants? Does he fail to pay his bills?" Kit dearly wanted any information that would kill his desire for the man.

"Not to my knowledge."

"Come, Scarlett. There has to be something unpleasant you've heard."

She looked at him for a long moment. "Why do you want to know?"

"Why do you care? Maybe I want to rob him and am looking for proof that he deserves a comedown."

"You aren't, though."

"Please, Scarlett."

"He doesn't get on with his father. They're faultlessly civil in public, but they quarrel like the Furies at home. Holland's mother died while he was away on the Continent. Everyone's first thought was that the duke had finally killed her, but in fact she was carried off by a cancer. Disappointing to gossips, but reassuring to friends of Her Grace. Almost immediately, the duke married Lord Holland's childhood playmate, Lady Marian Hayes, the only daughter of a doddering old fool of a nobleman whose property abuts the Duke of Clare's Oxfordshire estate. She and her brother were educated at home with Holland until the young gentlemen went away to school. She gave birth to a daughter shortly before Lord Holland's return to England."

"The duke's marriage was not, I take it, a love match."

"It might have been." Scarlett smoothed her skirt. "The duke is still handsome and widely considered to be one of the most charming men in London, not to mention rich and a duke. I've heard that he can be very winning."

Kit could not care less whether the duke's manners were winning. "Tell me more about the son."

"Lord Holland is Edward Talbot, commonly known as Percy. His mother was Lady Isabelle Percy, the only child of the Earl of Westmore and the last of that line of Percys. She, and everyone else, called her son Percy."

Kit waved this information away. "Any notorious love affairs? Mistreated servants? Anything."

She looked at him for a long moment. "I never would have thought of you as a blackmailer."

"I'm not," Kit said a little too defensively.

"Oh," said Scarlett, drawing in a sharp breath. "I see. You want me to put you off him."

"I don't—"

"You're in danger of liking the man." She regarded him with wide, astonished eyes. "Well, I never thought you'd be in danger of becoming fond of a lord."

"It's not like that."

"It had better not be. You want me to put you off him? How's this. The heir to the Duke of Clare will be one of the most powerful men in the kingdom. How do you think things usually turn out for people like us who get involved with men like them? Hmm?"

"Scarlett, you're involved with men like them every day."

"I take their money and their secrets. They take nothing of mine. Nothing, Kit. I've known you since you were little more than a boy, and you don't have what it takes to hold back the parts of yourself that matter. Stay away from Holland and his father."

Kit opened his mouth to protest and then realized that Scarlett had given him exactly what he had asked for: a reason not to like Percy. The fact that he wanted to argue with her was not a good sign.

Chapter 20

*P*ercy frowned at his reflection in the cheval glass.

"If my lord could explain precisely where he intends to go in this . . . attire," Collins said, his voice wavering on that last word, as if he couldn't be certain that Percy was in fact wearing clothing rather than being garbed in the stuff of Collins's personal nightmares, "then perhaps I could be of some assistance."

"I'm going to a new fencing studio," Percy lied. "One that abides by slightly different, ah, *règles du combat*." If he was going to spend a few hours getting knocked onto the floor of Kit's back room, then he wanted an extra layer of fabric against his skin. His buckskin riding breeches would do, but his riding coat wouldn't allow him nearly enough range of movement in his arms. He raided the attics and came up with a short-waisted sleeveless jerkin made of soft black leather, which fastened with buttons all the way up to the neck. Worn over a plain linen shirt, it would give him more protection than an ordinary waistcoat.

"If I may say," said Collins, an edge of panic creeping into his voice, "the pairing of brown buckskin with black leather is not a choice I would have expected of your lordship."

"It's very bad," Percy agreed. "And we haven't even got to the matter of shoes." He planned to wear his oldest, softest, and least-presentable boots. Paired with the riding breeches and the old-fashioned jerkin, the effect would be bizarre.

Bizarre, but not exactly unflattering, despite the lamentable looseness of his buckskins. He tied his hair into a queue, and remembered the sound of Kit's voice the other night. *I've never seen you with your hair down*, he had said, as if Percy had been keeping a secret from him. He took the tie out of his hair. Then he put it back again. There was vanity, and then there was lunacy.

Collins whimpered in protest.

"Nobody will recognize me," Percy assured him. "It's been years since anybody who knows me has seen me with a bare head and clean face." Other than Kit, that was. "Your professional honor will not be sullied. However," he added, thinking that Collins was due a concession, "a new pair of buckskins—fitted this time—and a new pair of boots would not go amiss."

Collins seemed slightly mollified, and Percy proceeded down the stairs. Then, realizing he had forgotten something, he dashed back up to his bedchamber, where he found Collins waiting with a tricorn hat in his outstretched hand.

"Thank you," Percy said, grabbing the hat and pulling it low over his brow.

"I thought my lord would wish to wear a hat that complemented none of his other garments, so as to keep with the theme of discordance," Collins intoned.

"Yes, yes," Percy called over his shoulder as he left. "Thank you!"

He went to Kit's on foot, avoiding the main thoroughfares, and arrived an hour before the shop was due to close. He seated himself at the end of the long table he had come to think of as his own. It was Kit who spotted him first, and Percy had the satisfaction of watching Kit scan the room, pass over Percy, and then dart back to him, studying his face, dropping lower over the rest of him.

He tucked a strand of hair behind his ear, aware that its color and lack of powder made it conspicuous, and also aware that Kit was watching him.

Betty was on the other side of the shop, so Percy assumed he'd have a while to wait for his coffee. But Kit brought a cup after only a few minutes, placing it on the table without any audible resentment.

"I wasn't sure you'd come back," Kit said. "You left without a word."

Percy paused with the coffee cup halfway to his mouth. He hadn't thought the circumstances warranted a formal leave-taking. He had woken up on Kit's floor, covered by a blanket, a pillow somehow having found its way under his throbbing head. Kit himself was asleep in a nearby chair, his head resting on a table atop his folded arms. Percy had been badly hungover and even more badly embarrassed.

Percy didn't get drunk. He certainly didn't drunkenly call on people. That was not only beneath his dignity, it was vastly imprudent.

But he had shown up here, and Kit had listened to him ramble and then put him to bed right in front of the hearth.

Percy wasn't sure whether to apologize or to leave. Or, maybe, to hide under the table until he was certain he could fight off the blush that threatened to creep up his cheeks. One of the many advantages of face powder was that it concealed his lamentable tendency to blush.

He swallowed. "If today is a bad day for a lesson, I'll come back another time." He took a sip of his coffee. "Assuming your offer still stands." He dabbed at his mouth with his handkerchief. "Why do you not have proper table linens? All the better coffee-houses have serviettes and tablecloths."

"Odd that you think I give a damn about running a coffee-house for people who want tablecloths."

"How silly of me," Percy conceded. "What can I have been thinking. I hadn't realized that wiping one's mouth on one's sleeve was something radicals enjoyed."

A moment passed during which all Percy could hear was the din of conversation and the rattle of cups in saucers, and some-how, over all of it, the pointless pounding of his heart.

"Are you always like this?" Kit asked.

"That depends on what you mean by *this*," Percy said.

"Fucking difficult," Kit said so promptly that Percy forgot himself and glanced up at him. He looked disheveled and badly shaven and as if he hadn't run a comb through his hair since God was a boy. In other words, he looked as he always did. And he was glaring down at Percy, if glaring could be accomplished without any malice. Was there such a thing as an affectionate glare? Percy found that he very much hoped so, because Percy was an idiot.

"In that case I certainly am always like this," Percy said as snap-pishly as he could in the circumstances, which probably wasn't very snappish at all. "Except for when I'm worse," he added.

"Drink your coffee and then come along," Kit said.

"I beg your pardon?" Percy hadn't come all this way, hadn't ransacked the attics and given his valet nightmares, just to be thrown out on his ear.

"Drink your coffee," Kit repeated slowly, "and then go to the back room."

"There's still an hour until you close," Percy said.

"Betty will work the shop."

Which had to mean that Percy wouldn't be fighting Betty, which in turn meant that Kit had listened to Percy's objections and taken them seriously. "Oh," Percy said, and drank his coffee as slowly as possible so as not to seem too eager.

Chapter 21

Kit couldn't stop staring. It was a blasted waistcoat, or at least something along those lines. And it was made of leather, which on its own shouldn't be enough to give Kit palpitations. Maybe it was the combination of leather and all those little buttons? Maybe it was the fact that the garment fitted so closely over Percy's chest?

Maybe, if he were honest, he had this reaction to everything Percy wore.

"We'll try again, just you and me," Kit said, shoving the few pieces of furniture against the walls to clear a space for sparring. Finally, he took his walking stick and stood it up in the corner. He walked to the center of the room without it, conscious of his limp and the pain in his hip. The other night, Percy had said that Kit's balance was off, and the more Kit thought about it, the more he thought that was the problem. If he could shift his weight to his good leg and rely less on moving, he could probably hold his own. And if he couldn't, then they'd figure something else out. "We'll try to fight, and then from there work up to disarming."

He stood in the middle of the room without his cane and felt horribly exposed. His leg could give way at any moment.

"All right," Percy said, coming to stand before him. "How do you want to start this?"

"I ought to tell you that I've never taught anyone how to fight," Kit said. "And I've never fought anyone without needing to, so I'm not sure how—"

Percy punched him in the gut.

Kit used his bad leg to sweep Percy's feet out from under him, and Percy hit the floor. Percy sprang up with more speed than Kit would have thought possible and hit Kit in the jaw.

Kit grabbed Percy's wrist and used it to spin him around, then pinned it behind his back.

"Well," Percy said, his back flush against Kit's chest. "We've established that you can fight." He elbowed Kit in the belly and then got free.

"And so can you," Kit said, dodging a fist. "Your punches are weak. I can't tell if you're pulling them or if nobody's ever taught you how to properly hit someone."

"I assure you it's the latter."

Kit was out of breath, but Percy plainly wasn't. He decided that later on, he'd let himself have a good long sulk about being old and out of shape. For now, he held his hand to the side of his body, at shoulder height. "Hit my palm, as hard as you can."

He watched as Percy pulled his arm back and swung.

"Not horrible," Kit said. "Give me your hand." He took Percy's hand and folded the fingers in, one by one, then tucked the thumb. His fingers were long and fine boned and looked frail in Kit's own far larger hands. But there were calluses on his palm and the side of his thumb, which Kit hadn't expected. "Now that's a proper fist. You do the other hand." He watched as Percy copied exactly what Kit had done and then held both hands out for Kit's approval.

Kit hadn't expected that, either, hadn't thought Percy would be an eager student, or that he'd take orders from a commoner. In his experience, rich people went out of their way to avoid listening to anybody else.

"Good," Kit said, his voice a bit gruff. And then they stood there like a pair of idiots, Percy's fists in Kit's hands. "Good," he repeated, and watched Percy's eyes open a bit wider. They weren't a simple dark gray, as Kit had previously thought, but the same glittering steel as the buttons on his waistcoat.

The late afternoon sun that filtered through the high, dusty windows of the back room lit Percy so he was all porcelain skin and cheekbones and hair the color of a new guinea, all golden and bright. Kit was thinking of how very badly he did not want to hit that face, when the next thing he knew Percy was aiming a punch at his jaw.

"You can do better if you swing like so," Kit said, blocking the blow and demonstrating the desired arc of his arm. Percy tried and didn't quite manage it. "No, let me show you." He stood behind the other man, moving their right arms as one. "Like that." Kit used his left arm to wrap around Percy's chest, holding him in place. "Now you do it." Since they were so close, Kit naturally dropped his voice and found that he was all but whispering into Percy's ear. Percy tried to duplicate Kit's movement and got it on the first try. "Now try this." He showed Percy how to punch upward, then how to hook his arm in from the side.

These motions were second nature to Kit, easy as breathing, so he didn't have to pay close attention. So it was only natural that he noticed the silkiness of the pale gold hair that had escaped from Percy's plait, and the scent of soap and leather that seemed to come from the soft skin of Percy's neck, or the way their bodies fit together. He couldn't help but notice. It would be odd if he *hadn't* noticed those things, really.

Then Kit went through all those various punches again—purely in the name of thoroughness, that was all.

On their next round, Percy knocked Kit flat onto the floor. He wouldn't have fallen if it hadn't been for his leg, but it was still a good effort.

"Oh bugger," Percy said, staring down at him, aghast. He held his hand out to help Kit up. Kit took it, and for an instant he let himself enjoy the surprising strength of the other man's grip. Then he pulled hard, tumbling Percy onto the floor and using the momentum to get back to his own feet.

After that, they were off. They were almost evenly matched, what with Kit's injury and Percy's inexperience, but he could see Percy catching up, right before his eyes. Occasionally Kit would call out an instruction—"You have two hands, use them both, God damn you" or "Tuck your chin down if you can't dodge a hit"—but either Percy was a quick learner or he had more experience than he let on.

"What do you think you're doing with your feet?" Kit panted. "This isn't a gavotte. Plant them both on the floor."

Percy did as he was told, dodged a punch, attempted to trip Kit, and then laughed. "How do you know what a gavotte looks like?"

Kit tripped him. He was getting better at balancing on his good leg. "What, do you think poor people aren't allowed to dance?"

"Oh, don't even try to convince me that you're poor," Percy said, springing to his feet. "I see how much money you take in. In fact," he added, attempting to grab Kit's wrist and winding up with both his hands pinned behind his back, "it's a wonder that you ever bothered with robbery."

Just for that, Kit tightened his grip on Percy's arms. "You do realize that you need capital to start a coffeehouse, right?"

"So that's why you did it? You needed capital? And then you stopped as soon as you had enough money to open a shop, not, say, three years after opening this coffeehouse?" Percy, attempting to get free, wriggled in a way Kit tried not to find quite so interesting.

"No, I did it because I like taking things from people who have too much."

Percy stepped hard on Kit's foot, but Kit didn't let go. "Oh, so you're an altruist, then. A modern-day Robin Hood." He made a gagging noise, and Kit laughed despite himself.

Kit realized that while Percy might not have walked into this room knowing what to do with his fists, he already understood the basics of fighting, or maybe strategy. He knew the importance of anticipating his opponent's next move, and he didn't make the beginner's mistake of putting defense before offense. He didn't underestimate Kit, and on the contrary seemed delighted when Kit surprised him.

He also knew how to fall, and more importantly how to get up. He knew how to move. God, the way he moved—Kit wanted to watch Percy fight someone else, just to be able to savor every lithe movement, every turn and twist and blow.

And after what had to be half an hour, the blasted man still wasn't out of breath. Kit was panting. Not only did his leg ache, but so did the entirety of Kit's person, from his neck to his toes. When Percy got in a solid hit to Kit's jaw and followed it up with a punch to his stomach, it felt inevitable. Kit felt himself crumple, bending at the middle, and the last thing he did before falling to his knees was pull Percy down with him.

"Mercy," Kit said, breathing hard. "No more."

"Oh, thank God," Percy said, collapsing onto his back. "Christ."

"I take it you were having me on when you said you hadn't ever been in a fistfight," Kit said, tipping forward so he was on his stomach, his cheek resting on his arm.

Percy turned his head. "No," he said, sounding surprised. "I've done some fencing, but I've never fought anyone with my hands. It always seemed a very common thing to do."

Percy's face was streaked with dirt, and he had blood on his upper lip. "You look like a proper ruffian right now, so I think you might have been right," Kit observed.

"My valet will have fits," Percy said.

Kit lay still for a moment, catching his breath and watching Percy. "My mother had a garden," he said.

Percy turned toward Kit at this non sequitur, but didn't say anything.

"She mostly grew herbs, but also the usual country flowers: foxglove, larkspur, you know. When they were first married, my father brought her cuttings from a rosebush." The rosebush had been in Percy's father's rose garden, a fact Kit had forgotten but which now brought him up short. He was lying on the floor with the heir to the Duke of Clare, after tussling like a pair of schoolchildren.

"That's not a very good story," Percy remarked after Kit had gone silent. "The next time you choose to regale me with the tales of gardens or horticulture or mothers, or whatever you were doing, do strive to be more entertaining."

Kit snorted. "She hated that rosebush. She had a garden filled with flowers that bloomed without any special treatment, but that rosebush needed careful pruning and daily watering. She had to put eggshells and iron nails in the soil. I used to hear her out in the garden, muttering under her breath at it. But every summer, the wretched thing bloomed. And every summer, she acted like she had personally brought those blossoms back from hell itself." He swallowed. "That's how I feel when I get my hands on a gentleman's purse. When that purse goes from being theirs to not being theirs anymore, I feel like I've done something."

He was speaking in the present tense, as if tomorrow he might get Bridget from the stables and hold up a traveling coach.

"When it goes from being theirs to being yours, you mean," Percy said.

"Some of it, aye," Kit said, gesturing at the building around them. "But my partner—"

"Fat Tom? Whistling Nell?"

Kit laughed. "No, my friend. Rob," he said, immediately feeling the wrongness of speaking Rob's name to this man. It felt like a betrayal to share Rob's secret with a man Rob would have counted as an enemy. A man Kit, too, should have counted as an enemy, and indeed would have, if they hadn't shared an even greater enemy. "He was also Gladhand Jack. Don't trust everything you hear in a ballad."

"Never tell me you didn't hold up two carriages at once in Newcastle, and then escape from prison with your arms tied behind your back. I'm crushed."

Kit snorted. "Rob took the money and gave it away. He was— good, I suppose. I stole because I wanted revenge and I liked adventure." It was an oversimplification but not a lie—Kit had begun to steal because he couldn't have revenge against the one man he wanted to punish, so he settled for spreading his revenge thin, across the entirety of the duke's class. The Duke of Clare wasn't the only landowner who destroyed lives; Kit would just have to take his revenge on the targets he had available to him. "But Rob stole because he wanted to do right."

"He died?" Percy asked, his voice careful and quiet.

"A year ago."

"Is that why you don't do it anymore? I thought it was your leg, but is it because it doesn't feel like you'd be doing right without him?"

The truth of that statement shot through Kit's veins like ice. He felt like he had spent months trying to figure out what was wrong, what was missing in this new life he was trying to live. And this man had figured it out after hearing not three sentences about Rob.

If Rob had been alive, Kit would have figured out how to work around his bad leg. Even if he hadn't been able to ever sit on a horse again, he'd have managed to do something. But without Rob, without Rob's conviction that what they were doing was right and good, then Kit had nothing to spur him on but anger. Kit had found comfort in Rob's unshakable, albeit lunatic, belief in the righteousness of what they were doing. Not being a madman, he hadn't agreed himself, but Rob's principles washed their actions of some of their less savory qualities.

Percy propped himself up on his elbow and looked down at Kit. Kit felt his breath catch in his throat.

"Where did you learn to fight?" Percy asked.

Kit didn't remember a time when he hadn't tussled with his brothers, Jenny's brothers, and Rob. And with Jenny, too, come to think. "In the country, children learn to hold their own," he said.

"Where in the country did you grow up?"

Kit swallowed. He didn't want to tell Percy the whole story; he didn't want to talk about it to anybody, and especially not to the Duke of Clare's son. But the thought wasn't as distasteful to him as he thought it should be. "Oxfordshire," he said.

Percy didn't say anything, but his eyes searched Kit's face. He was making a choice, Kit realized—he could ask where in Oxfordshire Kit came from, and from there it was only a short distance to the truth coming out. Percy was so close that Kit could see his pulse beating in his throat. They had been even closer when they were sparring—back against chest, cheek against cheek—but this was different.

"What did you want revenge for?" Percy finally asked.

And, Christ, Kit couldn't answer that, not when he could smell the man's soap and sweat. Not when the mere inches separating them felt both too near and too far. He put a palm flat on the ground to push himself up to his feet.

Percy stopped him with a hand to Kit's chest. "Wait," he said. "I shouldn't have asked that. It's none of my business. What I should have said is that—" He hesitated, obviously struggling for words. "I should have said that I can imagine a good number of reasons why a person might want revenge, and I find myself living through one of those reasons." He didn't move his hand from Kit's chest, even though Kit had stopped trying to get up. "I used to think that revenge was about defending one's honor, but it turns out that honor is just spite dressed up for Sunday."

Kit placed his hand over Percy's, holding it in place over his chest, so the other man could feel the rapid thrumming of Kit's heart. "And are you not a spiteful man?" Kit asked.

"I'm afraid I'm very spiteful indeed," Percy murmured. "I just didn't have any reason to find that out about myself until recently. It's amazing how high-minded one can be when everything goes one's way."

"Spite is underrated," Kit said, embarrassed at how rough his voice was.

Percy slid his hand out from under Kit's, long fingers dragging across the linen of Kit's shirt and the heated skin beneath, and brushed a few sweaty strands of hair off Kit's forehead. "You're a lovely man," he said, and it sounded like a reproach.

"Haven't we just been telling one another how unlovely we are?"

Percy shook his head, his hand coming to rest on Kit's jaw, his thumb at the corner of Kit's mouth. He glanced at Kit's mouth and bit his own lip.

"I—" Kit started without any idea of what he wanted to say. All he knew was that he liked Percy's hand on him, and that this was a complication neither of them needed.

Percy took his hand away and sat back on his heels. "I know, I know. You don't do that sort of thing. Well, my loss," he said lightly, springing to his feet, leaving Kit on the floor looking up at him, unsure whether he was relieved or disappointed.

Kit struggled to his feet and made his way to the corner where his walking stick rested and felt the handle fit into his palm.

"We're done for the day," Kit said, and went through the door to the coffeehouse without looking back over his shoulder.

Chapter 22

When Percy, uncomfortably sweaty and with a pulled muscle in his shoulder, opened the door to his room, he wasn't expecting to see Marian sitting on the edge of his bed. As she had the previous time she visited Percy's room, she once again wore a pair of his dark breeches and had her hair in a plait down her back.

"It took you long enough," she said. "Where were you?" She gave him a curious look. "I hope nobody saw you coming in looking like that."

Despite himself, he blushed. He could only imagine what she saw—his hair was unbound, and he still wore the buckskins and jerkin in which he had sparred with Kit.

"I came in through the kitchens."

"You'll have given Cook palpitations, thinking brigands were after her shortcrust recipe. Really, though, where were you?"

"I'd happily spill all my secrets to you, but how long do we have until your maid notices that you've gone missing?"

Marian examined her fingernails. "I put some laudanum in her bedtime chocolate."

Percy had been undoing the dozen buttons that fastened the

jerkin but stopped and stared at Marian. Poisoning the servants seemed rather uncalled for.

"Don't look at me like that," she said. "I only gave her enough to make her sleep heavily. And if you're squeamish about that, I can't think how you mean to get through a robbery where actual weapons are involved."

"Are you going to tell me what you've been up to, dressed like that?" he asked, gesturing at her breeches, then looking pointedly at the dirt on her hands, the small tear on the shoulder of her shirt. The sole was loose on one of her slippers, and beneath her eyes were circles so dark, they were nearly purple. Whatever she had been doing, it wasn't simply sneaking around. It was dangerous.

"No. Are you?" she asked.

"I've been learning how to hold up a carriage."

She blinked at him. "I thought you said your highwayman would do the job."

Percy had not been looking forward to breaking the news to Marian. "Well, you see. Instead, he's going to teach me to do it."

"That's a terrible idea. You'll get killed."

"It seems to be our best chance."

"What if he recognizes you?"

"Highwaymen wear masks," Percy said. "Don't they? Besides, Father won't pay any attention to my face. If someone is beneath Father's notice, he literally does not notice them. He still calls the footman George, even though George died ten years ago. Anyway, don't worry about me. Think about the book."

"I've had another letter from the blackmailer." From inside her shirt, she removed a folded sheet of paper and handed it to him.

"Already?" he asked. They still had over a month before the payment was due, and Percy needed that time.

"It's not a demand for early payment," Marian said. "Read it for yourself."

Percy scanned the letter's contents. The paper was flimsy and cheap but the writing was bold, each pen stroke a flourish. "'Dear Madam,'" he read. "'I hope this missive finds you in good health and the best of spirits. Your present circumstances are of a sort that must be uniquely trying, even without the added hardship of blackmail.' Good God," he said to Marian, glancing up, "one knows things are bad when one's blackmailer sympathizes. 'Given the nature of our previous correspondence, it is unlikely that you'll put much faith in what I say, dear lady, but please believe me when I say that I would much prefer never to have come into the knowledge that has formed the basis of our communications. If I am to be frank—and, really, to whom can one be frank if not the person whose fortune and reputation one holds ransom—I would much prefer you give me the five hundred pounds and let me disappear into the night. I assure you it will be my life's work to keep your secrets. Surely, you will protest that I ought to keep your secret out of the goodness of my heart; the trouble is that my heart isn't in the least good. I am, to the core, a mercenary creature. Please consider this letter a statement of my good-faith promise to uphold my end of our bargain; while I am a rotten sort of fellow, I am not a dishonest one. I anxiously await your reply by the usual means. Your obedient servant, X.'"

Percy refolded the paper and handed it to Marian, his eyebrows raised. "The usual means? Exactly how many letters have you exchanged with this blackguard? And is his correspondence always so solicitous?"

"Yes," she sighed. "He's exhausting."

"You don't mean to take this man at his word, do you?" he asked.

She let out a laugh, harsh and sudden. "No. That I do not." Then she leaned forward to kiss him on the cheek, turned, and climbed out the window.

Chapter 23

By the end of the first week of December, both Percy and Flora were appearing nearly every day at the coffeehouse. Percy claimed he only came for lessons. But their lessons took place in the late afternoon, and he often arrived in the morning, spending hours making light conversation with other patrons. In the span of a fortnight, he had made himself a regular. He gave his name as Edward Percy, he dressed not in the richly embroidered coats of Lord Holland, nor in the leather jerkin and buckskins of their backroom sparring, but in a brown suit of clothes not unlike Kit's own.

He wore his hair unpowdered, and Kit caught himself staring more than he cared to admit. Worse still was Percy's sixth sense for knowing when he was being watched. He kept catching Kit out, and then Kit would have to either hastily look away or endure Percy's smug little smile. None of it stopped him from looking again a few minutes later.

Kit found himself anticipating the moment when Percy would walk through the door. There was always a moment when Percy would scan the room until he found Kit, and then something curious would pass over his face, as if he were as glad to see Kit as Kit was to see him, and also as perplexed by this as Kit was.

Some days, instead of directly taking a seat, Percy would saunter over to the counter, steal whatever pastries Kit had on offer that day, and strike up a conversation as Kit stoked the fire and stirred the pot. Perhaps *conversation* was overstating the matter: what he actually did was cast a relentless barrage of insults at Kit. He complained about the temperature of the coffee, the missing third volume of *Tom Jones*, the inadequate number of currants in the bun he was eating, and various failures of Kit's grooming.

"How do you do it?" Percy asked one day.

"Do what?" Kit grumbled, trying not to look too excited about it.

"I've never seen you clean-shaven, but your beard never progresses beyond a sort of dirty-looking stubble. It ought to be halfway to your knees by now."

The truth was that he shaved on Sundays, a day the shop was closed. The truth was also that he used to shave much more often, but then he noticed what happened when he stroked his jaw, rubbing the pads of his fingers over his stubble: Percy's gaze dropped, his lips parted, and his studied leer became something a little bit raw.

That was the sum total of their relationship: insults, fistfights, and sometimes, rarely, when they were both too tired to move, a tentative conversation.

Then, when Percy left, Kit would spread out maps of the roads between London and Cheveril Castle, trying to remember every convenient bend of the road and useful pothole, every inn and innkeeper, planning how and where they would ultimately do this job.

Flora's presence was harder to explain. If she hadn't caught herself a patron after the first few days, then why bother continuing to fish in a stream that hadn't so far yielded any results? When he asked Scarlett as much, she told him plainly to mind his own business.

Day after day she sat in the window, sometimes reading her Bible, sometimes embroidering. More than once she showed Percy her handiwork. Kit assumed that Flora was attempting to catch Percy's eye: he was the son of a duke and a man whose mistress would, presumably, be well compensated. Even though Percy didn't wear fine clothes or announce himself as Lord Holland, Scarlett knew the truth, and she might certainly have told the girl to go after him. That had to be the case, because otherwise Kit was hard-pressed to explain either Flora's presence in the shop or her attempts to get Percy to notice her.

"Are we doing any work today?" Betty asked, walking past him with a stack of empty cups. "Or are we lounging around and staring at customers? Just let me know."

He heard the dishes land with a clatter in the scullery sink. "It seems that we're dashing crockery to pieces," he called.

When she emerged, she leaned in close to his shoulders and spoke in a whisper he could hardly make out over the din of the room. "Are you going to actually teach that lad to hold up his da's carriage or are you just going to keep rolling around with him on the floor?"

"You're full of questions today," he observed. "What a treat you are to be around." She was right, though. Percy was perfectly competent with his fists by now and had managed to disarm not only Kit but also the errand boy. It was time to take this project to the next stage.

The problem was that the next step was complicated. He'd ordinarily go on horseback, but so far he hadn't gone on more than short, slow rides. Hampstead Heath was five miles away. The alternative was a carriage, but that posed the problem of finding a place to stow the conveyance.

In the end, Scarlett inadvertently solved the problem by asking him to escort Flora to her aunt's house in Edgware.

"Why?" Kit asked her.

"I can hardly send her on her own," was Scarlett's answer.

"You have your own carriage and your own men. And I need hardly point out that any of your men will be better equipped than I to defend her, should it come to that." He gestured at his leg, because even though he had held his own against Percy, he was a good deal slower than he'd need to be in a brawl.

"I trust you," she said, and he didn't ask why she suddenly didn't trust the men she had hired.

He agreed, of course. He could hardly refuse so direct a request without being churlish about it. Besides, in the past, she had often asked him and Rob for small favors; in Rob's absence, perhaps it was only natural for Kit to accede.

"We're going to Hampstead Heath," Kit said, dropping the coffee cup onto the table before Percy.

Percy blinked up at him. "Why?" His eyelashes were darker than his hair, lighter at the tips. Kit could have identified Percy by his eyelashes alone, which was a lowering thought.

"Because it's closer than Richmond," Kit growled, and stomped away.

Later, after they finished sparring and sat slumped against the wall of the back room, a flask of ale passed between them,

Percy turned his head to face Kit. "What will we be doing in Hampstead?"

"We're going to hide in a stand of trees and watch the carriages go past so you can learn the best time to attack." Kit took a mouthful of ale. "The truth is that there isn't much more we can do here. Your fighting is . . . adequate. It'll suffice."

"Will it, now?" Percy said, amused.

"Aye," Kit said gruffly. "You know it will."

"Is that a compliment?" Percy's voice was light, but Kit thought there was a hidden weight to his question.

"You're a good fighter. You use your brain and your body." Kit felt slightly lewd saying body, as if he weren't supposed to have noticed that Percy had a body at all. Kit wondered what would happen if he admitted that he had been half hard the entire time Percy had sparred with the errand boy the previous week.

"Huh," Percy said, faintly surprised and a touch embarrassed, like he didn't quite believe Kit. Which was ridiculous, because surely Percy, inexperienced as he was, knew he was competent. It was almost as if he wasn't used to praise.

"There isn't much more I can teach you," Kit admitted.

"Ah. We won't be doing this anymore?" Percy asked. For a moment Kit thought he heard a trace of disappointment in the other man's voice, but that couldn't be right. The Duke of Clare's son surely had many more interesting things to do with his time.

And yet—he had been coming to Kit's nearly every day, sometimes hours earlier than necessary. And when he finished here, if he was anything like Kit, then he was probably in no condition for anything more trying than a hot bath.

All of which made Kit wonder when Percy found the time to

be Lord Holland. When did he find time for dinners and trips to the theater and whatever else gentlemen did with themselves. There were lords and ladies who had to be wondering where Lord Holland was.

And all the while, Lord Holland was here, in a dirty and badly lit room, sharing cheap ale with a criminal. Kit turned his head, resting his temple on the cool wall behind him. He was facing Percy now, their noses only a few inches apart. There was no possibility that this man would miss Kit's company, was there? It was laughable. Risible. Kit should be embarrassed for even thinking of it.

Percy liked the looks of him and seemed to enjoy trying to make him blush with wry insinuations and a sort of one-sided flirtation that Kit did nothing to discourage. But wanting to ogle somebody—hell, wanting to fuck somebody—wasn't the same as deliberately spending all one's time with them.

They were so close together. Kit could hear every soft exhale from Percy's lips, could smell his scent of clean sweat, lemony soap, and leather. The hair around his face had come loose from his queue and now curled damply around his temples. Kit badly wanted to tuck it behind his ears.

It wasn't only Percy who was choosing to spend all his time with Kit—Kit was ready to drop everything as soon as Percy walked in the door. He caught himself putting aside the buns with the most currants and the cakes with the heaviest dusting of sugar, and then casually putting the dish within reach of Percy's coffee cup as if by accident. Every day he looked forward to Percy's arrival with a complicated blend of hope and confusion, which was complicated even further by the fact that when he looked at Percy, he saw Percy's father's face.

He felt like he had betrayed himself, had betrayed his family. He tried to imagine what Jenny would say if she could see him now, if she knew he was wondering what might happen if he leaned forward and ran his tongue along the plump lower lip of the Duke of Clare's son.

He thought of all the graves the Duke of Clare had put in the ground, thought of all the love and care and hope he had buried.

What did it mean that he could forget all that? Or, if not forget it, then shove it out of sight.

"Well?" Percy said. "Does that mean we're not going to be doing this anymore?" He gestured around them, as if Kit needed the reminder about what they were doing here. And maybe he did.

"Yes," Kit said. "We won't be doing this anymore."

It didn't matter whether Percy looked disappointed.

Chapter 24

*P*ercy sat on the floor of the antechamber of his apartments at Clare House, his swords on the carpet before him, the morning sun glinting off their freshly polished blades. Carefully he wrapped the weapons in soft leather and put them in the bag he had stored them in while traveling around the Continent. He slung the strap of the bag over his shoulder and caught a glimpse of himself in the cheval glass.

The problem was that he looked too much like himself. He wore the same outfit he had worn to spar with Kit. He didn't look anything like a gentleman—what gentleman would go about bareheaded, let alone even consider wearing anything so outlandish—but he didn't want to run the risk of being identified as Lord Holland.

What he really wanted was a beauty patch. A stupid little *mouche*, right under his eye, would alter the shape of his face enough. But a patch would be all wrong with all this leather—he was trying to be fearsome, not foppish.

"Collins," he said slowly, "what do actors use to create warts and scars?"

In the mirror, he saw his valet go pale and clutch his chest. He was not taking this turn of events as stoically as Percy might have hoped. "Give me an hour," he said faintly. "And I'll see what I can do."

An hour and fifteen minutes later, Percy had a scar the length of his hand, reaching from the outside corner of one eye to the edge of his mouth. It was pink and ragged and proclaimed that this was a man who didn't give a fig about getting maimed. It was perfect.

"All right," he said. "I'm off to disgrace myself."

It was, he thought as he approached the scaffold in Covent Garden, not the most foolhardy thing he had ever done. That honor went to approaching a highwayman to assist him in committing a capital crime with his own father as victim. It would take a lot to surpass himself.

He walked up to the man who looked like he was in charge—or at least the man who was in charge of money, based on the pouch of coins he held closed in his fist.

"How do I join the fun?" Percy asked, realizing too late that he ought to have disguised his voice, or at least his accent. But the false scar tugged at his mouth and gave his speech a slightly clipped quality, so there was that.

The man looked him up and down, then regarded the sword Percy wore at his hip and the dagger sheathed beside it.

"Wait over there," he said, gesturing with his chin at a group of men Percy gathered were the other combatants. "You can go first."

This, Percy knew from having watched no fewer than a dozen of these matches over the past several weeks, meant he was the sacrificial lamb. Newcomers went first and were usually knocked out of competition after only a match or two. The prize, after all, went to the last man left standing, and newcomers were made to work the hardest.

Percy had been counting on it. He knew he could best whatever badly skilled swordsmen he'd be paired with in the first matches. He knew he could do it, moreover, without even tiring himself. He could use that time to be as showy and theatrical as possible, and to give the crowd time to take out their purses and send for their friends to do the same.

He was almost certain he could also best the more competent swordsmen he'd go up against in the following matches. Over the past weeks, he had watched them fight, studied their habits, and learned their weaknesses.

"What's your name?" asked the man.

Bugger. Percy hadn't thought of this. "Edward?" he said, hating that his voice seemed to want to make it into a question.

The man rolled his eyes. "Edward," he repeated flatly. "No. You're . . ." He gazed heavenward, as if looking for inspiration. "The Baron," he said, apparently satisfied.

"No, my good man, I'm afraid not," Percy responded, displeased with the stupid moniker and vaguely annoyed at being demoted to baron.

"Aye, my good man," the fellow responded in what Percy gathered was meant to be an imitation of his accent. "Now, bugger off, Baron." He flashed Percy a smile that contained far too many broken teeth.

Percy took himself off to stand with the other men.

"Smallsword," said a man with closely cropped red hair, addressing the word more to the weapon at Percy's hip than to Percy himself. He spoke in a thick London accent and appeared to be about thirty. Percy recognized him as one of the less skilled fighters he had watched on his previous visits. "You're new, ain't you. You take the nick, then."

"I beg your pardon?"

"Oh, lud. A toff. Clancy's barmy. You. Take. The. Nick," he repeated slowly. "I scratch you, you fall, and the next time we switch."

That was not going to do at all. "Is that customary? Are all the matches prearranged?"

"The ones early in the day are. Why tire yourself out, right?"

"Right," Percy said slowly. That made sense, in a way. However, he had not gotten dressed and disguised and given his valet a heart attack only to be taken out in the first round. "I'm about to be a very bad sport, I'm afraid," he said. "I apologize in advance."

"Clancy!" the redhead bellowed. "I thought this was a quality establishment. Are you letting anybody fight, now?"

"How else would you be here?" the man with too many chipped teeth—evidently Clancy—shouted back.

"But do you really need to saddle me with gentlemen?"

"Get fucked, Brannigan," Clancy called cheerfully.

"I do apologize," Percy said. "It's just that I don't fancy getting, ah, nicked."

Brannigan stared pointedly at the scar that sliced across Percy's face. "Oh, you don't, do you?"

"A lesson learned the hard way, shall we say?"

Brannigan sighed heavily. "Fine, have it your way."

Percy watched as the crowd before the scaffold grew. He had never fought for any audience greater than the handful of people who might be gathered in a fencing studio. And some of these people had what looked like cabbages and turnips, no doubt to use as missiles in the event that the show wasn't sufficiently entertaining.

To his horror, he grew faint. This was not the time, damn it, for his latent cowardice to assert itself. He needed to keep his wits—and his consciousness—about him.

"Come on," Brannigan said with a sigh, tugging him by the sleeve. "We're up."

They went through the motions of bowing to one another. As he suspected, Brannigan wasn't up to snuff, and Percy had him disarmed within two minutes.

To his surprise and horror, the crowd booed, and a cabbage landed at his feet.

"Too fast, idiot," Brannigan hissed at him when he got to his feet and Percy restored his weapon to him. "You've got to give them their money's worth."

"They aren't paying admission," Percy argued.

"It doesn't fucking matter," Brannigan said. "Next fight, make it last."

Brannigan's words were still ringing in his ears as he started the next match, this time against a grizzled man who had to be twice his age.

The problem was that Percy didn't know how to make a fight drag out longer than strictly necessary. He knew how to be ruthless, efficient, and spare. He didn't know how to be entertaining.

Now he felt foolish for having thought he could take his one talent and use it to earn money. He was utterly unfit for earning a living. He didn't know how to take a skill that he sometimes thought might be an art and make it into something fit for the consumption of—he let his attention get drawn to the crowd—rabble. Frankly, they didn't deserve it. This was all profoundly beneath him, and he shouldn't be here in the first place.

That was when his opponent's blade got him, right in the meat of his upper arm.

Chapter 25

*K*it had long ago learned to trust his instincts. When something nameless and frightened in his gut told him to halt, he halted. He knew from experience that a vague suspicion that things were not what they ought to be was often founded in some small, hidden truth.

For weeks now, he woke in the mornings with a sense of something left undone. He went to sleep only after limping downstairs and checking for the third, fourth, fifth time that the bolts were fastened, the windows closed, the fire safely banked. He walked Betty home every night, and every morning he paced the floors until she arrived safely.

He listened in at the whispered conversations that took place in the darker corners of the shop. Outside, he watched for tails and kept a hand on his dagger.

He asked Scarlett if something was brewing, and she had looked at him with eyes that seemed older these days and sighed. "Something's always brewing," she said, impassive as ever. "You know this."

He didn't tell Betty anything, because he didn't need to. She had one eye on him all day lately. She watched him like a pot about to spill over.

"It's your gentleman," Betty said. "Something's wrong there, and always has been. Hire a highwayman to pick your da's pocket? Rubbish. Hire a highwayman who happens to have every reason to toss your da to the wolves? *Fucking* rubbish."

"I know," he said, because what else could he say? They both knew that Kit's sense of watchful unease had been steadily increasing from the first time Percy walked through the door. He wanted to tell Betty that he trusted Percy, but he didn't. How could he? He hoped Percy wasn't idiot enough to trust him, either. He didn't trust Percy, but he believed him in a narrow, fragile way. He believed that Percy needed that book; he believed the loss of the book would harm the Duke of Clare. That was all he needed. As for the rest of it, he could look out for himself.

The notion that he shouldn't trust a lord wasn't even interesting, certainly not enough to make him wary. And he didn't trust Percy, not even in those quiet moments after sparring, when they both let their guard down a little, when they sat against the wall, tired and satisfied. That wasn't trust; it simply couldn't be. The Percy who existed in those moments was a person Kit grudgingly had to admit he was more or less fond of. But that didn't mean he liked who Percy was in the rest of his life, let alone trusted him. The fact that it felt like trust, felt in his heart like something that mattered, like something he could count on—that he would just have to ignore.

It was only that he needed to keep reminding himself of that, which was something he really shouldn't need to do. It ought to be obvious, and it wasn't, and Kit didn't like what that meant.

He was getting ready to close the shop, watching the minute hand move on the tall casement clock until it was a reasonable time to kick out the few remaining stragglers, and trying to pretend to himself that he wasn't disappointed that the day had passed without Percy stopping by. The sun had set, and the only light in the shop came from the hearth and the handful of oil lamps and candles that were scattered around the room. In an effort to encourage the last customers to leave, he began snuffing the candles one by one.

When the door opened, letting in a gust of cold air, Kit turned, ready to send away whoever thought this was a decent hour to get coffee. The man was entirely in shadows, was nothing but a dark silhouette against an even darker background.

This was it, Kit thought. This was the danger he had been waiting for. One hand went to the knife at his hip; the other grasped the handle of his walking stick even more tightly.

But then the man tilted his head and a beam of light glinted off a strand of hair that was visible beneath the brim of his hat. The hair was a pale gold, and Kit took a step forward.

"I hate to impose," said a thin, precise voice.

"Percy," Kit said. He didn't recall rushing to Percy's side, didn't quite know how he got past the tables and benches that stood between him and the door, but there he was.

He couldn't have said how he knew something was wrong. Maybe it was that Percy was leaning against the door frame instead of standing with the sort of posture that more than once Kit thought must have been whipped into him. Maybe it was just that he didn't walk in as if he owned the place.

"What's the matter?" Kit asked. And then, over his shoulder, "We're closed, lads. Out you go. Faster!" He put a hand on Percy's arm, not sure if he had ever touched the man when they weren't fighting. Percy flinched, but not before Kit felt the wet warmth under his fingertips. "Fuck," he muttered.

Percy stepped aside to make way for the customers to leave, and Kit bolted the door behind them.

"What happened to you?" Kit asked.

"It's only a minor injury," Percy said, the faintness of his voice giving the lie to his statement.

With a hand at the small of his back, Kit led Percy to the chair before the fire. "Take off that coat."

When Percy complied, dropping an oddly shaped sack to the floor beside him, Kit saw that he was wearing the same clothes he wore to spar in the back room. As he was trying to puzzle out why that would be the case, he got distracted by the blood that soaked the top of Percy's sleeve.

"Were you attacked?" Kit asked, even though he didn't think Percy was foolish enough to fight off armed footpads. Although—hadn't Kit been teaching him to do almost precisely that? Perhaps Percy decided to put his lessons to the test.

"Not exactly," Percy said, his voice strained. "I think it's only a scratch. I'm just—I'm not particularly good with blood, and I thought to myself, Percy, you know a man who will know just what to do with a bit of a gash."

Kit tore the shirt at the place where the knife had slashed it, then pushed up the sleeve to get a clear view of the injury. It was a clean slash, about two inches long, not particularly deep. He had gotten worse slicing hard bread. A bit of pressure and a few days of bandaging and it would be good as new.

Kit found that he still wanted to hunt down whoever had done this and tear them apart, slowly and with great relish.

Percy glanced down at the wound Kit had exposed and visibly shuddered, then went even paler than usual. "I dare say it wouldn't have bled half so much if I had bandaged it right away, but I rather desperately needed not to look at the thing."

"So, you came here," Kit said, wetting a rag with water from the kettle.

"I thought I'd spare my valet the trouble. I've already been quite a trial to him today, you see. And also, I was a bit unsteady on my feet and doubted I could walk that far. One doesn't want to bleed all over a hackney."

"We've bloodied one another's noses," Kit pointed out. He dabbed at the wound, and Percy's only reaction was a slight hiss. "You've split your knuckles, I've bit my tongue. I never saw you go faint at the sight of blood any of those times."

"Yes, well, I was having fun, wasn't I? I assure you I was not having fun at the moment this occurred."

"Footpads?"

Percy pressed his lips together. "No. And I'm not going to talk about it, so let's not be tiresome. Will I be fit for our trip to Hampstead tomorrow?"

"As fit as a fiddle," Kit promised.

Kit took the sleeve he had torn off Percy's shirt and folded it into a bandage, then wrapped it around the wound. When he finished tucking in the loose end of the cloth, he saw that Percy was looking intently at him. Kit felt his breath catch. There wasn't any mistaking the nature of that look, and even if there had been, it would have vanished when Percy's tongue darted to wet his bottom lip. Christ. Kit's gaze skittered away, then flicked back over the swell of Percy's exposed arm, the sharp line of his jaw, the damp plumpness of his lips.

They had been looking at one another for weeks—Percy shamelessly, and Kit at first reluctantly but now hungrily, avidly, as if there were no sight in the world quite as worth looking at as Percy. Kit kept telling himself there was no harm in looking, but maybe there was no harm in more than looking.

He took his finger from where it rested on the bandage and trailed it up to the bare skin of Percy's shoulder. A cluster of freckles rested at the top of his arm, half concealed by the remnants of his shirt, and Kit slid a finger underneath the ragged edge of fabric. It was just a fingertip, just a shoulder, just a frankly tender caress to the flesh of the man whose father had all but murdered his family. God, in the half-light, Percy even looked like his father, and why in hell didn't that make Kit want to shove him far away?

He moved his hand up the long line of Percy's throat, feeling his pulse flutter beneath his fingertips, only stopping when he had the other man's jaw in his hand, his thumb resting at the corner of Percy's mouth. Percy opened his mouth slightly, and Kit could feel the promise of wet warmth inside. Kit sucked in a breath.

It would have been simpler if they could just fuck. With a little luck, maybe he could take this man to bed and then not think about it the rest of the time. They could plan their robbery, snipe at one another, and carry on pretty much as usual. But he didn't want to keep it separate: the man he wanted to take to bed was the man who fought like it was a dance only he knew the steps to, who was brazen enough to hire notorious criminals for insane jobs, and who, apparently, swooned at the sight of blood.

He brushed his thumb against Percy's cheek, feeling the gentle rasp of stubble so pale that it was invisible. Percy had gone perfectly still, and Kit knew he was waiting for Kit's next move. It was time for Kit to either lean close or step away. He had to choose. Instead, he looked some more. He thought he might never get tired of looking at this man. "Christ," Kit breathed. "You're beautiful." He hadn't meant to say it, but it was true.

Percy brought a hand to rest at Kit's hip, tugging slightly, only the lightest pressure, more of a suggestion, really.

Kit stepped back. He felt drunk on the nearness of this man, unable to think straight. And he didn't want to do this without really meaning it. He smiled ruefully at Percy and was relieved to see Percy returning more or less the same expression.

"Have your valet change your bandage in the morning, then again tomorrow night," Kit said, his voice rougher than he had expected. "It's right in the part of your arm that will split again if you move the wrong way, so keep it covered until it's nicely scabbed over."

"Thank you," Percy said. "I know that I shouldn't have imposed on you, but—"

"I'm glad you did." And that was all wrong, too much, too earnest. "I can't have you collapsing in a puddle of blood. Our scheme would go straight to hell if you were dead, right?"

Percy looked up at him with a faint flicker of amusement in his cool eyes, and Kit knew he hadn't sold that last bit, not even slightly. "I'm glad I did, too."

Chapter 26

I'm a prosperous shopkeeper and you're a gentleman," Kit had told Percy when informing him of their outing to Hampstead Heath.

"Of course I'm a gentleman," Percy had said, furrowing his brow.

"Our cover story," Kit said impatiently. "We're escorting your cousin to the visit her aunt in the country."

"What kind of gentleman?" Percy asked.

"The kind who can sit quietly in a carriage for an hour."

"How very helpful."

"I don't know, Percy. Figure out a way for the two of us to share a carriage without it looking remarkable."

Percy had gone directly to Collins. Really, he would not have guessed that a life of crime and dishonor would afford his valet such a wide scope for demonstrating his talent.

In the end, he let Collins choose a new suit of clothes to establish Percy's sham identity, and which Percy hoped went some distance toward soothing the valet's feelings over seeing one of Percy's shirts torn to shreds after the fencing incident.

Percy himself was not thinking of that. It had been humiliating, during a time when all the fates seemed to be conspiring in his humiliation. He was also not thinking of what had followed at Kit's, except for when he brought himself off. He figured that nobody could blame him, what with the way Kit had looked—all rugged and dangerous in the firelight, his enormous hands featherlight on Percy's skin, his gaze almost soft.

Percy couldn't remember the last time anybody had looked at him like he was something special, something precious. He wasn't certain anybody ever had. He didn't even know if he liked it—he felt rather like a bad penny about to be discovered as counterfeit. But he kept turning the moment over and over in his mind, imagining what would have happened if Kit hadn't stepped away when he had.

When he met Kit at the appointed place—an inn near Spitalfields—he was surprised to find Kit sitting at a table with a young woman. When he approached, Percy recognized the woman as the redhead who frequented Kit's coffeehouse. He had known that there was to be some girl they were purportedly escorting to the country but hadn't expected it to be this bird of paradise. She was done up like a parson's daughter, covered stem to stern in gray serge and topped off with a bonnet that hid her face in modest shadows unless she chose to look up. She had another, even more demure, woman with her, evidently playing the part of maid.

When they got into the coach that Kit had hired, Percy found himself steered into the forward-facing seat alongside the girl, who went by the name of Miss Flora Jennings. Kit and the maid sat facing them.

It was a good thing the village to which they were bringing Miss Jennings was only a short distance, only slightly further north than Hampstead Heath, because the conveyance that comfortably sat two men of their height had not yet been devised. Percy's and Kit's knees bumped together repeatedly, and Percy saw Kit suppressing wince after wince. He imagined that all this jostling was murder on Kit's leg.

"Mr. Percy," said Miss Jennings, "what part of the country do your people come from?"

It was an innocuous enough question, but one that Percy did not know how to answer. Cheveril Castle was in Oxfordshire. Farleigh Chase was Derbyshire. Those were the two principal properties of the Duke of Clare, with several others scattered around the country. These facts were of such common knowledge that Percy was almost certain nobody had ever bothered to ask him where he came from. It ought to be straightforward—he had been raised at Cheveril—had been born there, in fact, and had thought his sons would be born there as well. He had thought he'd die at Cheveril, and that one day his portrait would hang in the gallery with all the other dead Dukes of Clare.

But none of that was true anymore. He had known as much for months, but he felt that he had to learn it again and again. Marian seemed to have assimilated the truth into her life in one fell swoop, but Percy was repeatedly shocked to rediscover who he was, and who he wasn't.

"Oxfordshire," he said faintly, and felt Kit's eyes on him. Then he felt the gentle pressure of Kit's foot against his own. He hadn't told Kit about the precise nature of his predicament, of course, but perhaps Kit had inferred that a man who wished to rob his father at gunpoint might have a welter of confused sentiments about a good number of things, including his home. Or perhaps Kit simply knew Percy well enough to know when he was distressed.

Percy pressed back against Kit's foot, to let him know the sympathy was appreciated.

Miss Jennings turned her attention to the Bible she held open on her lap. When she caught him looking, she smiled shyly at him. "This was my mother's," she said.

Percy did not know if this passed as normal conversation for commoners, or for prostitutes, or if the girl was attempting to engage him in what she assumed was decent conversation. "How lovely for you," he said. "One does like to have a memento of one's mother."

Miss Jennings looked altogether too pleased with Percy's answer, though. Percy wondered if this was an attempt at social climbing.

When they arrived at the village, all four disembarked. Percy escorted Miss Jennings and her maid to her aunt's cottage while Kit arranged for the horses and coachman to be fed at the nearest inn. Miss Jennings safely deposited at the house of her aunt, Percy walked to the inn, where he found Kit waiting for him.

"They're saddling a pair of hacks for us," Kit said, shoving a pint of ale across the table for Percy.

Percy wiped the seat off with his handkerchief and sat. "What exactly is your relationship with Miss Jennings? I thought she was an, ah, aspiring courtesan."

"And so she is. Do you know Mistress Scarlett's establishment?"

Percy raised his eyebrows. "I followed you there, if you recall."

"It's run by an old friend. Flora works for her."

"Do you typically escort ladies of the night around the countryside?" Percy asked, knowing already that Kit was not in the habit of doing anything so interesting.

"I needed an excuse to go to Hampstead Heath in a carriage because I can't ride that distance anymore. And Scarlett was quite insistent."

"I'm certain that she's very talented at getting men to accede to her wishes," Percy remarked.

Kit snorted and took a sip of his ale. "She's just an old friend," he said, and Percy wasn't sure if it was his imagination that Kit's words were meant to allay Percy's suspicions. Not that Percy had any suspicions—Kit was free to consort with however many brothel keepers he pleased.

"I've never taken a courtesan to visit her aunt, nor have I ever surveyed potential scenes to stage robberies," Percy murmured, leaning across the table so only Kit would hear. "This is a day of many new and fascinating experiences for me."

He stayed that way, his forearms resting on the table, his forehead inches from Kit's own, and watched Kit's lips curl in a smile.

Good God, but the man was easy to look at. He clearly made no effort whatsoever with his appearance and probably never had, which made Percy both faintly jealous and peculiarly aroused. He looked like he had slept in those clothes, then rolled out of bed and into his boots, and *still* Percy wanted to crawl into his lap. There was the ever-present stubble darkening his jaw, and the hair that refused to stay in the queue where it belonged. Even Kit's shabby old tricorn, which looked like it had been run over by a stagecoach and then taken part in a shipwreck, somehow looked alluring in a disreputable way.

Percy knew he was leering. In fact, he knew he spent a shocking portion of his time around Kit ogling the man. He might have stopped if Kit didn't do it right back. Kit was doing it that very minute, in fact, shooting furtive little glances at Percy's mouth, then his hands, then his neck.

He expected Kit to throw back his drink and stand up, but instead he stayed where he was.

"I wonder," Kit said, in that rasp of a voice that made Percy want to moan, "if you're ever going to tell me what it is you're hoping to steal from your father. What kind of book is this?"

Percy frowned. Discussing his father was certainly one way to dampen his ardor. He thought of the girl's Bible, and remembered what his cousin had said about the Bible being the only book the late duchess had carried around. "Perhaps I'm only looking for a memento of my mother. Does it matter?"

"Not especially," Kit admitted. "But maybe you'll tell me anyway."

"Maybe I will," Percy said. For a moment he let himself imagine what it might be like to be the sort of man who took people into his confidence. He had been trained to keep his secrets close to his chest, though, and didn't know how to do anything else. But he let himself imagine what it would be like if he and Kit were at this inn, sharing a meal and sharing confidences, not plotting and scheming.

"Maybe you won't," Kit said, still not moving away, the half smile still present on his lips, as if he knew Percy would always be guarded and secretive and he didn't expect otherwise.

"Maybe I won't," Percy agreed, feeling his own mouth curve in response. "Maybe I won't."

Chapter 27

The road hadn't changed much in the past year, and Kit managed to get to the copse of trees he remembered without falling off his hired horse, so he was mightily pleased with himself. He would have been more pleased if he could have managed to ride the horse at a pace faster than a slow walk, and he would have been happier still if Percy hadn't noticed, but he'd take what he could get.

"Find a tree where we can hitch the horses," Kit said after Percy dismounted. As soon as Percy's back was turned, Kit began the slow and awkward process of sliding off his horse. He managed to do it without falling on his arse, so he was counting that as yet another victory.

"What we want to do," Kit said, after the horses were secured, "is find a place where we can see the road but stay hidden. Do you see that bend? That's bloody perfect. It's fucking gorgeous." He grinned at Percy and found the other man looking at him with a slightly dazed expression.

"Gorgeous," Percy echoed.

"Look at the road, not at me. Listen," Kit said, as he heard the sounds of approaching hoofbeats. He pulled Percy behind a tree. Percy was wearing clothing that looked almost startlingly normal—no high-necked leather jerkins, no silk coats the color of hothouse flowers—so they'd have some camouflage. During the actual holdup, they'd have to do something about his hair. As it was, it caught too much light.

"Now," Kit went on, leaning in so his mouth was close to Percy's ear, "as the carriage rounds the bend, you can see it for a full ten seconds before they see you. That gives you time to get into the road and into position before they can draw weapons. You and whoever we hire—Tom, most likely—will stand in the road. The sniper—I have the name of an archer who does tricks at fairs—"

"An *archer*?" Percy repeated. "Isn't that a bit theatrical? Why use a bow and arrow rather than a rifle?"

"Better aim. And quieter."

"All right," Percy said doubtfully.

"Anyway, she'll be in the tree."

"In the *tree*?" Percy repeated.

"In a tree, she can hide and also get a clear shot, and if she's in a good position, she can see down the road in both directions and let you know if another carriage is approaching." He could see it clearly in his mind and felt his blood sing with anticipation as the carriage approached. "One, two, three, and *there*. That's where you step into the road and call out. You and Tom first take the weapons, then the valuables. Half a minute, that's your goal."

The carriage rattled along the road, around the bend and out of sight.

"I thought we weren't going to be shooting at anybody," said Percy, who was evidently still caught up on the archer.

"She's insurance." Percy remained silent. "I told you not to waste my time or your own if you weren't willing to hurt people," Kit said.

"I know, I know. I'm just . . . readjusting my principles."

"You're doing what, now?"

Percy bit his lip and looked like he was searching for words. Kit had never known the man to have anything less than five dozen words at the tip of his tongue. "Well, before all this started," he began, and Kit assumed "all this" was whatever had incited him to hire Kit, "I never really thought of myself as a particularly good person or a bad person, but I assumed I had to be at least slightly good. I carried on in the way things were always done. Comme il faut, just like everybody else." He shot Kit a wry look. "In which 'everybody else' is people like me, of course. This was the natural order of things, you understand. One doesn't steal from one's father or endanger the lives of coachmen." He swallowed. "But what I'm doing is right, in its own way, or at least it isn't wholly wrong. It's doing right by the people I care about, and if I can manage to pull this off properly, I'll prevent a good deal of harm."

Kit watched him. He had rather assumed that Percy's goal was revenge, which was a good enough reason, as far as Kit cared. But he found that he wasn't terribly surprised to find that there was more to it.

"In any event," Percy went on, "what I had thought were principles were merely manners, and they're utterly insufficient for my present circumstances. I keep running into information that makes me have to sort of reorganize everything in my brain. You know when you get a new book, you have to slide everything on your shelf over to accommodate it?" He seemed to remember who he was talking to and huffed out a laugh. "Of course you don't. You just jam the new book in there helter-skelter. I've seen the state of your shelves. Sensible people, however, attempt to maintain order."

Kit had the dizzying sense that Percy would get on well with Rob, of all people. They shared the same flexible understanding of right and wrong. Kit had never really questioned that stealing was wrong; Rob had always thought it was perfectly fine, if done for the right reasons, but Rob was a madman.

Percy evidently took Kit's silence for disagreement. "I see that I've shocked you," he said slowly, his eyes searching Kit's face. "Was I supposed to say that I think we're very bad men?"

Kit laughed, some combination of amusement and relief—although relief at what, he could not quite say—bubbling up inside him. "No," he said, and then his hand was on Percy's jaw. "It's just that sometimes, you actually make sense. A man's allowed to be shocked." The words came out stupidly tender, an impression that was probably only compounded by the thing his thumb was doing to Percy's cheekbone. He was afraid it was a caress, that he was actually caressing Lord Holland. Lord Holland who had made an argument for the virtues of crime, Lord Holland who was *Percy*, who maybe thought Kit wasn't so bad—

He wasn't sure which of them moved first to close the gap, but that was a lie because it was definitely Kit, it was definitely, lamentably Kit who put his hand to the back of Percy's head and held it there very carefully when he leaned closer. He moved slowly, carefully, as if giving Percy a chance to think twice.

His hand slid into Percy's hair at the same moment their lips met. It felt familiar—not the brush of lips over lips, not the fact that he thought Percy might actually be smiling—but everything else. The way their bodies fit together. The sound of

Percy's breathing. The way he smelled like lemons and soap. The sure grasp of his hand at Kit's hip. All the fighting had made them familiar with one another's bodies, and God knew they were used to wanting one another, so the only thing that was different was the actual fact of their mouths touching, the pure sensation of it.

And Percy *was* smiling, damn him. Kit could feel it with his own lips. It was probably that smug little smile that Kit really shouldn't like half so much, and Kit was going to tell him to stop it, he really was, and that was why he opened his mouth. He got distracted by Percy's teeth closing around Kit's lower lip and biting down, not particularly gently. Kit gasped, like an idiot, like someone who needed to have the mechanics of kissing and possibly the anatomy of mouths explained to him, maybe with charts.

Percy licked into Kit's mouth, and that was when Kit realized he wasn't in charge of this kiss, not in the slightest. And that was good, but it was also like falling out a window, so he backed Percy up against a very conveniently located tree. He kept his hand at the back of Percy's head, so he didn't get hurt. Percy grabbed Kit's hat and threw it to the ground. "In the way," he muttered against Kit's mouth, as if Kit needed an explanation, as if Kit gave a damn about hats, or anything that wasn't Percy's mouth.

Their bodies were flush against one another, and Kit was simultaneously relieved and embarrassed to discover that they were both hard. He felt like he ought to be cataloging all the ways this was different from kissing a woman, but it wasn't, really. Not in any of the ways that mattered. He thought that he might be on the verge of some kind of profound revelation when Percy slid a leg between his own, and all Kit's thoughts evaporated, only to be replaced by the *finally, finally, finally* that his heart seemed to say with every thumping beat.

Kit dragged his mouth away from Percy's and began kissing his way down to the hinge of his jaw, then to the soft curve of his neck. He felt the flutter of Percy's pulse beneath the thin skin there. He bit that spot, then gentled over it with his tongue. Percy groaned.

Kit pulled back to look at him, to take in the sight of Percy with his eyes half-closed and his lips swollen and wet, his cheeks red from rubbing against Kit's stubble.

"I should stop," Kit said.

"You should fuck me," Percy countered. "You can, you know."

There was something about Percy's tone on those last words—prim, matter-of-fact—that made Kit feel slightly hysterical. He started to laugh.

"Oh, delightful," Percy said. "Precisely what a man wants to hear in the middle of a tryst." He shoved Kit half-heartedly with one palm.

"I can, can I?" Kit asked. "Christ. Everyone who's spent more than a quarter of an hour at the coffeehouse over the past month knows I can. My God, you are a lot of things, but subtle isn't one of them."

"I am plenty subtle. Just not with you, because you're clearly not a man who understands nuance. I take it you aren't interested in fucking me."

"I'm very interested," Kit said with a helpful gesture toward his prick as corroborating evidence. "But we're in the middle of the woods."

"It's really more of a stand of trees," Percy said, hooking a finger into the top edge of Kit's buckskins and tugging him close again.

"Oh, well, in that case." Kit rolled his eyes.

"You have a spider the size of a duck egg living in your stairwell. I thought you'd feel quite at home."

"We are not fucking and then getting on horseback," he said firmly. "I have a *bed*."

Percy's counterargument was a slow, filthy kiss as he ground against Kit.

They were interrupted by the sound of hoofbeats and carriage wheels. Kit had nearly forgotten what they were doing there in the first place. He broke the kiss, pausing with his forehead against Percy's as they caught their breath. "Your turn," Kit said, gesturing at the road.

Stepping away from Kit, Percy peered out toward the road. "I would step out into the road at three, two, *now*."

"Very good," Kit said. "You're a quick study."

That made Percy go still, made the tips of his ears turn pink. "I try," he said lightly but not meeting Kit's eyes. They were a few steps away from one another now, and neither of them made any attempt to close the gap.

"That was really all I wanted to show you," Kit said. "I wanted you to see for yourself, so you can get a picture of it in your head when we plan out the next stage. The actual robbery won't be here, of course, but somewhere nearer to Cheveril Castle." He swallowed, and for a moment the only sound was the rustle of dry leaves in the surrounding trees and the call of a distant bird. "But the principle is the same."

"I suppose we ought to be getting back," Percy said, still not meeting Kit's eyes.

Kit agreed and went to untie the horses. He glanced around for a tree stump or fallen log that he could use to mount the horse, annoyed that he hadn't thought of that beforehand. He still wasn't used to accounting for all the ways his abilities had changed since his injury, and was cross with himself for his lack of forethought.

"Here," Percy said, making a cup out of his joined hands, as one would do to help a woman or a child mount a horse.

"I'm too heavy," Kit said.

"Try me," Percy said. And for lack of any better ideas, Kit did. He found that he wasn't even surprised that Percy didn't crumble under his weight. After he had a leg over the saddle, he felt Percy's hands firmly grip his hips, steadying him. It ought to have been mortifying.

Maybe some of his thoughts showed on his face, because Percy squeezed his thigh. "Come on," he said, mounting his horse and heading toward the road. Kit followed.

Chapter 28

$\mathcal{T}$he sun was setting by the time the carriage rolled to a stop in front of the coffeehouse. It hadn't yet closed, and it occurred to Percy that they would have to wait some time before they did anything involving that bed Kit had promised.

At the table nearest the door was a face that almost made Percy break stride. It was Collins, and seeing him outside Percy's apartments was almost like seeing him in a masked disguise.

"What on earth," Percy started.

"Hush," the valet hissed. "Sit."

Percy, after gesturing for Kit to carry on without him, sat.

"Her Grace has a message," said Collins, softly enough that Percy almost couldn't hear him.

"I see," Percy said slowly. No message that had to be relayed in this cloak-and-dagger fashion could possibly be good news.

"She wants you to attend the Davenport ball this evening."

"I already sent my regrets. That's the message?" Percy asked, baffled.

"I believe Her Grace means to deliver the message to you in person at the ball, my lord."

"Right. Of course. I suppose that if she wrote it down like a normal person, then she'd worry that you'd be intercepted by masked brigands and have to eat the notepaper to avoid discovery. We are in a stage comedy, Collins, and I'm afraid you got dragged into it."

"I hope my lord knows he can rely on my discretion."

Kit came then with two cups of coffee, placing Percy in the unprecedented position of needing to decide whether to introduce his manservant to the coffeehouse proprietor he was hoping to take as a lover. He could not even imagine what the protocol for that situation might be, so he settled on ignoring Kit entirely and trusting that the man would understand that Percy didn't intend it as a slight.

"How did you know to find me here?" Percy asked Collins.

"Her Grace intimated as much."

"I see." Percy looked across the room and saw Kit grumbling over the pot of coffee. Percy would have to leave now if he hoped to get dressed and ready for the ball. There would be no chance to continue what he and Kit had started at Hampstead Heath. And he could hardly go to Kit and tell him as much without alerting Collins to the existence of a relationship between them.

Collins sighed. "My lord may wish to take his leave of any acquaintances he had hoped to engage in conversation this afternoon," he said. Then, when Percy narrowed his eyes, he sighed even more heavily. "It has been my honor to work for his lordship since he was seventeen. His lordship is not subtle in certain circumstances." He took a sip of his coffee. "Also, I saw you and that fellow enter the shop together."

"It seems that everybody wants to spend their afternoon telling me how unsubtle I am," Percy griped, getting to his feet. "How lowering." He left without taking leave of Kit.

As he had no interest in this ball or in anyone he might possibly see there, Percy let Collins dress him and arrange his wig however the man saw fit. In the end, he was arrayed in a great deal of aquamarine satin and a diamond brooch that Percy realized he'd probably have to sell, along with the rest of his jewels, and soon.

"How charming that you've chosen to join us," Marian said languidly when Percy handed her into the carriage. She wore approximately four acres of scarlet damask, a color that made her look positively lurid. His father was already in the carriage and hardly looked up at Percy's arrival.

At the ball, Percy was greeted with a sea of half-remembered faces—schoolmates, friends of his parents, people he vaguely knew as his father's hangers-on. He let himself be passed along on a wave of introductions. Yes, he would dance with this young lady. Yes, he would be sure to call on that matron. Yes, he most definitely would like a glass of whatever was on offer.

The ballroom glittered with candles and jewels, and the air was heavy with the scent of perfume and powder and overheated bodies. Music, played by unseen musicians stationed behind a screen, was almost inaudible over the earsplitting chatter. Percy realized exactly how solitary his life had been since returning to London. He was seldom in crowds unless he was at Kit's, which, even at its most crowded, had nothing on the Davenports' ballroom.

It wasn't unpleasant, precisely. But the sights and sounds belonged to Lord Holland, as much as the powder and the wig did. Even the flickering, sparkling quality of the light seemed to belong to another world. He remembered, without wanting to, the smoky shadows at Kit's, the only light coming from a smattering of candles and lamps and whatever daylight managed to struggle through the fog outside and the clouds of tobacco inside.

Marian waited until the orchestra played a minuet before seizing Percy's hand. "You promised me this dance, my lord," she said, sounding intensely bored by the prospect.

"You do me a great honor, Duchess," he said, equally bored.

"Do you recall Louise Thierry?" she asked without inflection when the dance took them close enough for her to speak unheard by anyone else.

"One finds her hard to forget," he murmured. Louise Thierry was the cause of all their troubles: the name scrawled onto the parish register in the French church, the woman his father married.

"That was, evidently, a professional alias, or perhaps poor spelling. Her real name is Elsie Terry."

Percy hoped he managed not to show any surprise on his face. "How very common," he drawled. He had assumed that his father took a Frenchwoman to church because that was the only means he had of getting into her bed. If he had wished to marry an Englishwoman, why on earth had he brought her to France? And if she had gone with him to France as his mistress, then why had he bothered marrying her at all?

"Indeed," she agreed. "Some people in the village still remember the *beau Anglais* and the pretty strumpet he brought with him."

"Marcus's research is very thorough," Percy observed the next time they passed close. "Since I doubt he would have put all that in a letter, am I to take it that he's in London now?"

"I believe he's playing cards somewhere around here," she said.

He was about to complain that he could have avoided this ball if Marcus had simply called at Clare House, but he supposed a conversation at a large gathering would be less remarkable and less likely to be overheard by the duke's servants than a meeting at Clare House.

The dance finally ended. Percy bowed, Marian curtsied, and Percy strode off in the direction of the card rooms. All he had to do was follow the steady stream of men escaping the dance floor.

He found Marcus in a book-lined study, at a table with three other men, engaged in what looked like whist. Percy leaned against a nearby table, waiting until Marcus noticed him. Marian had gotten all the guile in that family, so when Marcus noticed Percy, he almost spat out his brandy.

"Christ almighty, how long have you been there, Perce?" He got up from the table, still holding his cards, and embraced Percy. Then he stood back and looked Percy up and down. "Look at you, you shocking fop. What have you done to yourself?"

"More than you have," Percy said, wrinkling his nose as he took in Marcus's coat, which had to be at least two years old. He gripped Marcus's hand. "Now, darling, you're forfeiting this game. We have to make up for lost time." With that, he pulled Marcus out to the terrace.

"I don't understand," Percy said several minutes later. "If she gave a false name, then the marriage isn't binding." They were deep in the garden, where the noises from the party were remote and they could be assured of their privacy. Percy pulled his coat around his chest.

"Was it a false name, or was it a French priest's best effort at transcribing a foreign name?" Marcus asked. "And even if it were an alias, that doesn't necessarily mean the marriage is invalid. At the very least it would take some infernally long time in the courts to get settled and cast a long shadow over the future of the title. I say, what would happen if you went to your father and told him what you know? Surely he wouldn't leave you and Marian and the baby to starve."

Percy looked at his old friend in wonder. "He'd cut me off, cast me out, and spread it about town that I was mad. I'd be lucky not to end my days in a lunatic asylum."

Marcus sighed. "In that case, I think you and Marian need to save as much money as possible. Sell your jewels and replace them with paste, invest the proceeds, and live off the income. Save your allowance for a few years and buy a modest house. That way, when the truth comes out, you'll have something of your own to live on."

This would be prudent, Percy had to concede. This was probably the counsel he would offer a friend, so he wasn't going to hold it against Marcus. "And while I'm saving my pennies, I live with the sword of Damocles over my head. I let my father and the blackmailer control my destiny."

"That's rather dramatic, don't you think?" Marcus gave a little laugh that made Percy want to scream. "It's a title and some money—granted, a significant title and an enormous fortune. But you'd live quite well on the money you could put aside over the course of a few years. In fact, you'd live better than nearly everyone in this country. You wouldn't be here"—he gestured at the distant ballroom—"but you'd be well-off, and safe."

Percy grit his teeth, knowing that Marcus was right but also not able to communicate that this was inadequate, not because Percy was greedy, but because it was letting his father win. "I don't want to give him the satisfaction of seeing me gracefully subside. He dishonored Marian and my mother, and he's raised me to be—to be a *lie*, Marcus. Marian feels the same way."

"I know," Marcus said, with the weariness of a man who had heard at length his sister's feelings on this topic. "I don't mean to make excuses for your father," he said, sounding like he was about to do precisely that. "We both know he's despicable. But when he married this Elsie Terry, he was twenty. It's possible he never thought it was a binding marriage—it took place in a foreign country and in a Catholic church, and neither of them would have been of age in England. It may have been a poor choice, but it's not an inherently evil one."

"Not inherently—" Percy broke off, sputtering.

"My only point is that revenge has never done anyone a bit of good."

Well, of course it wasn't going to do him any good. Percy wasn't fool enough to believe that punishing his father would make him happy. The problem was that letting his father go unpunished would make it impossible for Percy to have any peace. But there was no use explaining that to Marcus. "If it makes you feel better, I fully intend to sell off everything I can in the next month or two."

"Marian is engaged in a similar project," Marcus said.

"I have one more lead," Percy said. "My father's former valet has an inn near Tavistock. His name was Denny."

"Percy," Marcus said gently. "There's no doubt but that your father married this woman. There are people in Boulogne who remember her, and who remember where she came from. And when I visited the village where she was born, there were half a dozen Terrys still living there, including an old woman who says Elsie was her granddaughter. Elsie pays her a visit once a quarter."

"I know that," Percy snapped. "I know, Marcus. The woman's alive, the marriage was valid, and Marian and I are well and truly fucked. What I care about now is Cheveril. Would you please visit Mr. Denny and see if he recalls whether there was a child. I need to know what will happen to Cheveril."

"All right," Marcus said. "I know this all feels impossibly dreadful right now, but there are certain advantages to being a commoner. You won't have to worry about marriage or heirs, and with any luck you could perhaps form a lasting attachment with a person of your own choosing. I know that seems like a small compensation, but—"

Percy laughed bitterly. "Marcus, lasting attachments are the furthest thing from my mind."

Chapter 29

*L*ong after closing, Kit sat in the empty shop, using the broad expanse of the table to spread out maps of the road from London to Oxfordshire and the country surrounding Cheveril Castle. In the margins, he marked information that he still needed. He would have to hire someone to scout out that length of road in advance. In the past, he would have gone himself and committed every farmhouse and hedgerow to memory, but it turned out he could do most of the planning right from his shop.

His work was interrupted by a rap at the door. "Come in," he called, wondering when it happened that people had started to drop in on him at odd hours. His hand went to his knife, more out of habit than out of any actual belief that he was in danger. People who meant harm seldom knocked.

He hoped that it might be Percy at the door. Percy had, after all, left without a word despite the fact that earlier they had more or less made plans to spend the night together. Or at least that was how Kit had interpreted it at the time, but the more he thought about it the more doubtful he became.

But the person who walked in wasn't Percy. It was a woman, wrapped head to toe in a dark, hooded cloak. Only after the door was shut and bolted behind her did she slide the hood off her head.

"Scarlett?" Kit asked, rising to his feet. He could count on one hand the number of times he had ever seen her outside her establishment. "What's the matter?"

"You didn't send word that Flora had arrived safely at her aunt's house."

"It slipped my mind. I apologize. I wouldn't have thought that would merit a clandestine trip across town, though," he said, gesturing at her cloak.

"It's cold," she sniffed. "Nothing clandestine about it. And you're hardly across town." She glanced around the shop, not bothering to conceal her interest, and Kit realized she had never set foot inside the place before.

"Sit," he said. "I'll get you something to drink."

"Tea, please," she asked, sitting primly on the edge of one of the benches that lined the long table. "You took Lord Holland with you in the carriage today."

He decided not to ask her how she already knew that, figuring he wouldn't like the answer. "And?" he asked, not turning away from the kettle.

"I came here to tell you that you're in over your head," she said. "Without Rob to look out for you—"

Kit laughed, and it came out bitter and startled. "You of all people know that I looked out for Rob, not the other way around. Don't tell me that grief has made you forget what kind of man he was." Kit had spent half his life getting Rob out of scrapes, and he'd give up the use of his good leg for the chance to do it again.

Scarlett pressed her lips together in a line of displeasure. "He'd have kept you away from Holland."

"I see." Kit could hardly deny it. Rob would have tied Kit to a chair before letting him get cozy with a lord.

"No, you don't. Tonight, Lord Holland is at a ball."

Kit recalled how abruptly Percy had left that afternoon. "I imagine he goes to a good number of balls."

"No, he doesn't, because he spends his time drinking coffee here and doing what I can only imagine in your back room. Tonight, though, he made an exception, because an old friend of his was to be at the ball—the duchess's brother, Marcus Hayes. Holland's childhood playmate. Tonight, Lord Holland was seen embracing Mr. Hayes and then proceeded to spend an hour privately with him in the gardens."

Kit glanced at the clock. "It's not even ten o'clock. I'd love to know how you already know all this."

"Whatever it is that he's doing with you, he's also doing it with your betters."

"I'll be sure to offer him my felicitations the next time he drops in."

"Betty's worried about you."

Kit sighed and slid a cup of tea in front of Scarlett, shoving the maps to the side to make room. "Betty's always worried about me."

"When I was a girl, I let my head get turned by a man who was handsome, rich, and titled, not to mention charming. When we were together, he made me believe I was the only person in the world who mattered. I left my home and only learned when it was too late how cheaply he held me." She held the teacup in her hands, as if to warm them. "Understand me. I don't regret what came of that. But I will never forgive him for making me believe that I was worth as little as he valued me."

Kit knew enough of Scarlett's history to understand that it

was a common one. But he also knew that the moral of Scarlett's story wasn't that rich men abandon their conquests; it was that when you're treated badly, you start to believe you don't deserve any better.

He could hardly disagree. He could hardly tell Scarlett or even himself that he expected Percy to do otherwise. The truth was that he didn't expect anything different.

"I hope you know," he said, "that I realize how lucky I am to have women like you and Betty looking out for me."

"Spoken like a man about to ignore some good advice," Scarlett said ruefully.

As there was no answer he could possibly make to that, he simply raised his teacup in a silent toast.

Chapter 30

*P*ercy had to concede that he wasn't precisely making the *best* decisions.

His last attempt at prizefighting had ended with injury and mortification. The prospect of more of the same did not deter him so much as serve as enticement. He thought another slice to the arm might shake him out of his dismal mood, or at least give his melancholy something to focus on other than his future.

Besides, he wanted a sword in his hand. And, God help him, he wanted to win that purse. He wanted to know that he could take what he was and make it amount to something.

"My lord," said Collins from the door to Percy's dressing room. "I took the liberty of making some purchases." In his arms he held a mass of black objects of some sort.

Percy watched as his valet placed a pair of black leather boots before him. They were soft, probably kidskin, and laced up the front in the way a woman's boots might. But unlike a woman's boots, they were tall enough to almost reach Percy's knees.

Next to the boots, Collins laid out a pair of black breeches. They, too, were made of soft black leather, far softer and thinner than even the kidskin of the boots.

"I understood that your lordship wished for ease of movement," Collins said in the tones of a man who believed ease of
movement an unworthy goal for the son of a duke. "Nankeen
would be the obvious choice, but I inferred that your lordship
desired some protection in the event of . . . falls." The last word
came out on a frigid whisper.

All the *your lordships* and the pained tones gave Percy to understand that he would be giving Collins several afternoons out
in the near future. "You are a genius and a saint, Collins," he
said, already stripping out of his buckskins. "A credit to your
profession and Englishmen in general."

It took some doing to squeeze into the leather breeches. They
were soft enough to move in. They were also scandalously tight.
Percy was delighted with them.

The boots, too, fit precisely. He laced one as Collins did up the
other, then regarded his reflection in the cheval glass.

Aside from the white of his shirtsleeves, he wore black leather
from the top button of his jerkin to the tips of his toes. His hair
was tied tightly into a queue, as he typically wore it while fencing. On an impulse, he untied the leather cord and let his hair
fall in a curtain around his shoulders, half concealing the false
scar Collins had once again affixed to his cheek.

The black leather made a sharp contrast with his pale skin,
pale hair, and pale linen shirt. His hair would be in his eyes while
he fought, which was annoying, but—he turned quickly on his
heel and watched in the mirror as his hair whipped around him.
Yes, that was good. After all, the purpose of this was to entertain
the crowd. Swordsmanship had to come second to showmanship
today. This would have bothered him not so long ago, but he
found that having thrown out a good number of his principles

and reorganized the remaining ones, it was getting easier and easier to make room for new ideas.

"Oi, if it isn't the Baron," said Brannigan when Percy arrived, joining the other men beside the scaffold. "Didn't think we'd see you again. We thought you were scared off after Meredith sliced you up last time."

"If by sliced up, you mean received a two-inch paper cut, then I'll gladly let all you gentlemen slice me up so long as you give me half the fight Meredith did," Percy said, taking his swords from their cases and checking each blade.

"Meredith," Brannigan called, "I think the Baron paid you a compliment."

"He can go fuck himself, whoever he is," called the man who must have been Meredith.

Percy raised his hand in a salute.

"Oh, Christ, it's you again," said Clancy. "Can you make sure each fight lasts more than two seconds this time?"

This time, Percy didn't enter until the third fight, and he did make it last, even though it went against every instinct he possessed. When he was perfectly poised to knock his opponent to the ground, he instead twirled away and made it look like he had managed a narrow and dashing escape. He heard the crowd gasp. He let his opponent get his blade within inches of Percy's sword arm and then ducked and rolled in the way Kit had shown him. His Florentine fencing master would have wept from the inefficiency of it all, but the crowd fell silent, and that was more important, because at that moment Percy was more worried about rotten vegetables than he was his opponent's swordsmanship. He carried on like that for fifteen minutes before disarming his opponent.

Before the next match, Clancy returned to the scaffold. "Blood," he shouted in Percy's ear, making himself heard over the din of the crowd. "They're going to want blood. No more of this disarming shite."

If he had to, Percy would cut an opponent; he was used to fighting with practice swords that had blunted tips, but he supposed he could scratch his opponent's arm in such a way as to spill a satisfying quantity of blood without causing the man any serious harm. He really, really did not want to do so, however. He had, he supposed, the usual qualms about harming his fellow man. But, more importantly, he did not want to risk a fainting spell in the middle of a sword fight. That was not at all the effect he was aiming for.

Next, he was paired against a man who called himself Friedrich and spoke with a heavy Continental accent. For this match, they were to use sabers, according to some method or whim of Clancy's. The most Percy could say about the saber was that he enjoyed the sound the curved blade made when it sliced through the air. In every other capacity it was inferior to the smallsword and even the clumsy rapier.

The crowd oohed and aahed when Percy's opponent demonstrated the sharpness of his blade by slicing through a piece of canvas. Percy rolled his eyes.

While they fought, Friedrich muttered under his breath in what Percy assumed was German. He was very good, possibly as good as Percy, but Percy could tell he was used to fighting with a lighter weapon, because he quickly began to pant.

To give the man time to catch his breath, and to give the audience their money's worth, Percy began leading his opponent around the scaffold, dancing backward and not attempting any kind of offense. Percy ducked under the other man's arm, tumbled out of reach, and spun with a flourish of his sword.

Eventually, when he was beginning to worry about exhausting himself, he disarmed the man. Instead of simply taking hold of the hilt, he tossed it high in the air. As he watched the weapon turn over, he hoped that from the audience's perspective it looked like the weapon had been thrown when Friedrich let go.

Percy caught the saber by its hilt, held both weapons out to the side, and bowed first to Friedrich, and then to the audience.

Friedrich said something that Percy strongly suspected was German profanity when Percy handed him back his sword.

"No blood," Percy said to Clancy, who was not paying him any attention, because he was busy collecting coins while his assistant took bets.

Next were backswords, then an appallingly clunky broadsword, which Percy had to borrow from another fighter, as he did not possess one of his own. Then came a rather amusing fight against Brannigan with a smallsword in one hand and a dagger in the other. The last fight was once again smallswords, and Percy made sure it lasted a full half hour before he threw the sword in the air and caught it with a flourish.

When Percy was presented with the purse at the end of the afternoon, he figured he needed to buy some goodwill with these fellows if he wanted to fight them again. "I see a tavern on the corner," he said as loudly as he could. "I'll stand you all a pint and a supper as thanks for the most entertainment I've had in months."

His first thought had been to figure out some way to fairly split the purse among the lot of them, but he thought that would come across as too high-handed, and—for reasons he could not quite articulate—he wanted these men to like him. It had, after all, been a long time since he had enjoyed anything that could be called an evening out with friends. All the swordsmen except the German, and including Clancy, who Percy definitely had not invited, joined him at the tavern.

Percy spent half his winnings on ale and beefsteak that night. The rest would go to Collins. In the future, he'd need to save that money. The idea of saving money that he had earned, even such a small sum as this, felt better than clandestinely selling jewels and snuffboxes.

He felt like he had accomplished something. And he realized that this might have been the first time he had ever felt anything of the sort.

Chapter 31

*Y*ou need to come now," Betty said, barging into the shop on her day off.

"You may have noticed that I keep a coffeehouse," Kit said. "I can't just—"

"I'll take over. Do you know the scaffold where they sometimes have prizefights? You need to go there. Now."

"I don't suppose there'd be any use to asking you why," he sighed, already grabbing his walking stick and stepping out from behind the counter.

"Go," she said, all but shoving him out the door.

Kit's leg was in an especially recalcitrant mood, so he was in a sorry state by the time he reached the corner of Covent Garden that Betty had specified. The square was crowded, people standing shoulder to shoulder in front of a timber stage. At first Kit thought he was watching a play or some kind of exhibition, and it took a long moment of confusion to understand that the people who were dancing about the stage were swordsmen. One was large, with cropped hair, and the other was thin, with blond hair that hung to his shoulders.

Despite the size of the crowd, the only sounds were the clatter of blades and the clinking of coins, punctuated by occasional crowd-wide gasps as one or the other of the combatants nearly got his throat cut.

"Move," Kit said, shouldering his way forward through the crowd.

"Hey!" said a man who quite understandably did not enjoy being shoved aside. Kit did not care.

The world was filled with men who had hair that precise shade of gold, surely. There was no reason to think that this was Percy with an enormous fucking weapon being thrust at his idiotic neck.

Kit still wasn't near enough to see their faces, but he could see the way the fighters moved. And he knew the way that blond man thrust and parried, because he did almost the same damn thing with his fist. Kit knew the way that man favored his left arm, knew that senseless little half step he did with his back foot. Kit was going to fucking murder him.

He was close enough to see their profiles now, and that was either Percy or his identical goddamn twin. The fighters circled one another, and Kit gasped aloud like a half-wit when he saw that Percy's cheek was split with a red gash. He had to firmly tell himself not to storm the stage, and then realized that the gash he was seeing was a scar. He had seen Percy in broad daylight only yesterday: the scar was false, Percy was uninjured, and Kit was a prize idiot.

Kit wasn't even sure he breathed for the rest of the fight, or the next one, or the one after that. When Percy was awarded the purse and the crowd finally dispersed, Kit resisted the urge to approach. Instead, he hung back, then followed Percy and apparently all the other swordsmen to a nearby tavern, where Percy spent a fortune feeding and toasting his fellow combatants.

Kit paid for a pint and settled into a shadowy corner where he could watch Percy undetected. From the way Percy hung back, Kit could tell he wasn't quite comfortable, but he didn't think he'd have noticed if he didn't know how Percy acted when he was at his ease—loose limbed and overly talkative. This was how Percy had been that first time or two he sat at the long table at Kit's—a shade too quiet, as if trying to learn the rules that governed his new companions. Kit would have bet anything that the next time Percy broke bread with these swordsmen, he'd be at ease.

Percy, who had been leaning against a wall, approached the table where most of his comrades had gathered. Kit, who had not properly appreciated Percy's attire during the fight, as he was distracted by such matters as the sharpened blades coming within inches of Percy's vital organs, got a good view of the very close-fitting leather breeches that Percy wore.

The leather waistcoat with all its little metal buttons had been bad enough. The breeches were an atrocity. Kit wanted to throw a cloak over the man. Surely, the law was being broken. Where were magistrates when you actually wanted them? He could make out the perfect, indecent curve of Percy's arse, which had been quite distracting in worn buckskins and poncey silk but was heart-stopping in black leather.

As he watched, the redheaded fighter tried to touch Percy's cheek.

"Leave it be, you oaf," Percy said.

"Take it off," the redhead urged. "Show your pretty face."

"No, damn you, it's a disguise. I do not need my people finding out I've been consorting with the likes of you ruffians."

Kit clenched his teeth in jealousy. He did not like watching Percy insult anyone who wasn't him, which was probably a mad thought, but if insults and flirtation weren't synonymous for Percy, then Kit was very much at sea.

"Your people!" the redhead laughed.

"Yes, my people. I did not emerge from the sea, sword in hand."

That was as much as Kit could take. He rose from his seat and sidled around the edge of the room until he was within reach of Percy's table.

He dropped a heavy hand onto Percy's shoulder, then watched in satisfaction as Percy turned his head and realized who he was looking at.

"Out," Kit said.

"No," Percy responded coolly. "Join us, Mr. Webb. We are dining like kings."

"Out," Kit repeated.

Percy looked at him, vastly unimpressed. "Alas, gentlemen," he told his companions, "but I'm being summoned."

"This your people, Baron?" asked one of the men.

"Good heavens, no. God forbid," Percy answered. "I'll settle with the barman," he told the table at large, then got to his feet and turned in the direction of the bar without acknowledging Kit. He continued to ignore Kit while he dropped an eye-watering amount of money on the bar, while he walked out the door into the dusky early evening, and while he continued across the square.

"What in hell did you think you were doing?" Kit growled, barely keeping up.

"Eating and—"

"The swords, Percy. I'm talking about the fact that apparently you like to risk your bloody neck in front of a crowd."

"Yes, well, evidently I do," Percy said, coming to a stop and reeling on Kit. "Do you have a problem with that?"

"Do I— Yes, I damned well do have a problem with that." Kit was almost inarticulate with helpless rage. He kept remembering the sword slicing through the air, inches away from Percy's throat. He had the insane urge to pull back the man's collar and check for wounds. "This is how you got hurt the other day! You let some blackguard—"

"Kindly lower your voice," Percy said, taking hold of Kit's sleeve and pulling him into a lane. Kit was put in mind of the last time they had been in a dark, secluded lane, when Kit had punched Percy. At the time, he had noticed that Percy seemed to know how to duck to avoid a hit, and now he bloody well knew why. He also knew why Percy seemed to know how to fight, even when he had hardly been able to make a proper fist.

"You don't think that your talent with swords might have been useful information for me to have before I taught you to fight?"

"Why, Kit, you think I'm talented," Percy said, regarding Kit through his lashes. "Thanks ever so."

"You know bloody well how good you are, so save your breath. Why did I teach you to fistfight when you can use a knife and sword as well as any man I've ever seen? We could have had this robbery over and done with."

Kit hadn't realized how close they were standing until Percy drew back. "I do apologize for wasting your time, Kit. It had occurred to me that you might have been enjoying yourself, but now I see how silly I've been."

"Don't be like that. Come now."

"Don't be like what, exactly, Kit?" Percy asked, his eyes glittering with anger. "Annoyed that you're being impossible? You never asked me if I knew how to fight with a sword. You may have noticed that every gentleman in this town wears a sword on his belt, but it didn't occur to you that some of us know how to use them? You never asked me," he repeated, "so how was I to know it was relevant? You just threw me in front of Betty and told me to hit her. I've never witnessed a highway robbery. I don't know what they involve in terms of weaponry. That is why I came to you, if you recall. It was your bright idea to teach me to do it, so you can hardly blame me for not being able to read your stupid, stubborn mind."

Kit was stunned by this volley of words. He wanted to defend himself by pointing out that any idiot could have understood that fighting of any variety would come in useful during a robbery, but he remembered how tentative and awkward Percy had been during their first lessons. He had been almost silent, for God's sake. Kit remembered how willingly Percy had let Kit take his hands and make them into fists. He had put himself entirely in Kit's hands, assuming himself to be an absolute novice.

"I apologize," Kit said. "You're right."

"I—I beg your pardon?" Percy looked flustered. Color seemed to be creeping up his cheeks, barely visible in the half dark.

"I made too many assumptions. Do you have any other hidden talents? Knife throwing? Archery? I don't know—juggling, perhaps?"

"Now you're mocking me."

"I'm not," Kit said. "I'm really not. You looked—Christ—amazing up there, you know."

"I'm well aware," Percy sniffed, sounding slightly mollified. "I generally do."

"That's a fact." Kit moved in a little closer.

"I was making new friends and you dragged me away," Percy said, glaring anew at Kit. But there wasn't any real heat in it. Percy wanted something from Kit, and whatever it was, Kit wanted to give it.

"That was wrong of me."

"You're forgiven."

"Is that so?" Kit moved closer still, until they were chest to chest. He put a hand lightly on Percy's waist, feeling like he was trying to coax a stray cat closer.

"And last night I didn't get to go to bed with you. Instead, I had to go to a dance and get lectured by a former lover while getting my bollocks frozen off outside. It was highly unpleasant."

Kit forbore from pointing out that Percy had been the one to leave without a word. Instead, he moved his hand to the small of Percy's back. "You'd have rather been in my bed?"

"Obviously," Percy said, sounding just a tiny bit outraged. Outraged, and like he wanted to be pacified.

Kit bent his head to kiss the soft underside of Percy's jaw. "We can still do that," he said. This was all so excessively . . . tender, Kit supposed. It shouldn't be anything of the sort. He had tried to tell himself that they would just be having fun together. But here in a dark and damp alleyway, they had crossed into something different and dangerous.

Chapter 32

*P*ercy watched Kit frown at the door to the coffeehouse.

"What's the matter?" Percy asked.

"It's not locked. I thought Betty would have locked up and gone home, but I guess she waited for me."

Percy wanted to say that of course Betty waited for Kit. Betty and Kit worried about one another to an extent that was frankly comical. They were both notorious criminals and accomplished fighters, and yet they each acted like the other was as helpless as a kitten.

Kit opened the door and called out. "Betty!"

There wasn't any answer. Percy saw that the candles and lamps were all extinguished and the fire in the hearth was safely banked.

"Maybe she left it open for whoever is staying upstairs this week," Percy suggested. There always seemed to be somebody occupying the garret, and Percy would have bet his new leather breeches that Kit had never once asked for rent.

"No lodgers this week," Kit said, and Percy could just tell that he was about to get very boring about checking to see whether imaginary housebreakers were hidden in every corner, so instead he took hold of Kit's coat and pushed him against the wall.

"Shut up," Percy said, and then kissed him before he could argue.

Kit Webb kissed in a way that was positively unfair. It was an injustice. It was sweet and tentative and totally at odds with the bad grooming and the criminal past. He kissed Percy as if he wasn't sure he was allowed, as if he were worried about being woken from a dream.

Percy preferred to keep his lovers at a safe and cordial distance, and that was precisely how he had planned for things to be with Kit, but all this sweetness was ruining his plans. He was sure that's what was happening as he bit Kit's earlobe and felt the man shudder gently against him. This was Percy's plans being ruined.

"I need to ask you—" Kit started.

"Shut up and keep kissing me," Percy snapped. Or, he tried to snap. It came out as a purr, which was definitely Kit's fault.

"—what in the name of all the saints it is that you're wearing. I have never seen so much leather on one person. It's obscene," he said into the corner of Percy's mouth. He cupped his hands around the swell of Percy's arse, then down lower, where his arse met his thighs.

"You probably ought to take it off," Percy said. "I'll warn you that there's about five miles of lacing and more buttons than I know what to do with."

Kit made a frustrated sound, then ran his hands up Percy's chest, then back down to his arse again, as if by touching he could make the clothes evaporate.

"Before we undress, we ought to get to that bed you promised me," Percy said, sliding a fingernail under his false scar and tearing it off with a wince, then sliding it into a pocket.

Kit led them in the direction of the stairs. One of them must have got distracted halfway there because Percy found himself being kissed again. They crashed against the wall near the bottom step, Kit's weight crushing Percy rather pleasantly. Percy was beginning to doubt whether they could make it to Kit's bedroom, and was beginning to consider whether getting fucked on the stairs was such a bad thing, when Kit changed course and steered them to the back room.

"My leg's too fucked for the stairs" was all he said by way of explanation.

The fact that the back room had nothing approaching a proper mattress, let alone a bed, would ordinarily have been a serious objection, but at the moment Percy could only groan his approval.

"God, I want you," Kit said, his gaze raking hungrily up and down Percy's body. "Can't stop thinking about it."

Percy all but dragged Kit into the back room and kicked the door shut behind them. He was nervy and exhilarated from the prizefight, from his victory, and from the knowledge that Kit had been watching him.

"How do you want me?" Percy asked. His erection was straining painfully against the unforgiving leather of his breeches. He palmed himself in a futile effort at readjustment and heard Kit hiss.

"Take it out," Kit said.

With fingers that felt clumsy and frantic, Percy managed to undo his laces and comply. He had just enough presence of mind to be mortified by his reaction to Kit's hand closing around him—a strangled sob. Until that point, he hadn't realized how much he wanted this, how long he had been craving Kit's touch.

He thrust helplessly into Kit's fist, his face buried in the warm skin of Kit's neck, lips moving over stubbled skin, breathing in the scent of him.

With one hand he began unfastening Kit's buckskins, finally shoving them down. He almost sobbed again when his fingers reached Kit's cock, thick and hot in his hand.

It would be best not to rush. He wanted to take off Kit's clothes item by item and touch every patch of skin that he exposed. He had been thinking of this for so long that he wanted whatever followed to do his imagination justice.

But he also knew he wasn't going to last. This, at best, would just take the edge off. They could go about things more sensibly next time, with more leisure and fewer clothes. Next time could be in half an hour. Right now, he just needed to come, and judging by Kit's erratic breathing and throbbing cock, he was in much the same state. Rutting against Kit's hip, while still stroking up and down his length, Percy grasped Kit's arse with his free hand and pulled him close, hoping he'd get the idea.

Kit thrust back, groaning and swearing. "Wait," he said, and turned around so his back was to Percy, his hands braced on the wall. "Fuck me," he said, his voice raspy and ragged. "Please."

It was the please that did Percy in. He very much had his heart and other parts set on getting fucked this evening, but who was he to deny a politely phrased request, especially one delivered by a gorgeous man with his breeches around his thighs.

"You certain?" Percy asked, thinking of Kit's leg.

"Christ. Please. Can't stop thinking about it," Kit said, sounding desperate. "Oil's in the cupboard by the door."

Percy threw open the cupboard, uncorking the bottle with an

overheated hand. He returned to Kit, crowding him against the wall. He let his cock slide against Kit's arse as he kissed Kit's neck. He was rapidly becoming obsessed with Kit's neck.

"Like this?" Percy asked.

"If you don't stop asking questions and fuck me, I'm never speaking to you again," Kit said, pressing back against Percy.

"All right," Percy laughed. "Calm down." He poured some oil onto his palm and slicked up his fingers. Once again kissing Kit's throat, he slid his fingers along the crease of Kit's arse, lingering over his puckered entrance.

Kit swore and rested his forehead against the wall. "Please," he said, and Percy breached him with the tip of a finger. Lord, the man was tight. Percy couldn't press in any further, let alone add a second finger.

"Let me in," Percy said, and Kit's only response was some garbled profanity. "Right," he added after a minute, "we could stand here like this all night, with my finger barely up your arse, or you could let me fucking *in*, Christopher."

Kit laughed at that, rich and deep and not at all what Percy expected at that moment. "I knew you'd be like this."

"Like what?" Percy asked.

"Impatient. Talkative. A little mean."

"Christ. And you like that?" Percy asked, the words escaping his lips before he could think better of them.

"Something's very wrong with me."

Percy did not know whether to be affronted or not, but then something gave way inside Kit and Percy's finger slid in further. "Yes," he said rubbing circles onto Kit's hip with his free hand. "That's it. More, now."

"I told you," Kit panted. "I've never done this before."

"You've— I beg your pardon?"

"I don't fuck men. Or, I haven't. I told you that."

"Yes, but men often tell me they don't fuck other men, often right before—or after—we've fucked, so you'll excuse me if I take those proclamations with a grain of salt." Percy pressed his chest flush against Kit's back and took Kit's erection in hand. He stroked it slowly, lazily, while carefully moving his finger inside Kit.

Percy tried to remember the last time he had been someone's first in this way, and thought it was probably when he was still at school. In all likelihood, he had been careless and ignorant, and he didn't want to be that way with Kit. He wanted to take care, wanted to make this good, wanted to make it something Kit would feel good about when he remembered it.

He whispered praise and gentle instruction into Kit's neck and only after a while did he realize he was speaking in the way Kit had during their fighting lessons.

"You sure you don't want to get on the floor?" Percy asked when he had another finger inside Kit.

"Can't," Kit breathed. "My leg. Oh *fuck*. Please, Percy, just do it."

Percy slicked himself up and tugged Kit's hips back to make him bend at the waist a little. Then he pressed the head of his cock against Kit's entrance. Kit went tense—of course he did, Percy had been expecting that—but then visibly forced himself to relax.

Percy moved slowly, slower than he had ever done anything in his life. And he kept talking, coaxing and soothing Kit through it. He couldn't help it, even though he knew Kit was going to laugh at him later for not being able to shut his mouth. He told Kit how good he felt, how gorgeous he was, how well he was taking it, how much he wished Kit could see. Kit's palms were flat against the wall, his fingers curled as if looking for something to hold. Percy put his own hands over Kit's, lacing their fingers together.

When Percy was fully seated, Kit rested his cheek against the wall, and Percy could finally reach his lips for another kiss. Percy kept babbling—*Christ, fuck, look at you.* He spoke the words into Kit's lips and ear, into his neck, turned his words into kisses and his kisses back into words.

They were too close and too badly angled for anything more than grinding together, Percy sliding his length over the spot that made Kit's swearing take on a desperate edge. It was all too much for a backroom fuck, for a quick stand up against the wall. It was too much for who they were to one another.

And throughout it all Percy couldn't stop talking, could not stop saying things that were lamentably true and just as ill-advised. He ought to be concentrating on making this better for Kit instead of nattering on about how *beautiful* Kit was, how lovely Kit was being for him. A voice inside Percy's head told him to stop being like this—weak, needy, desperate—but at the same time he saw the way Kit was responding to all of that, and thought that maybe it wasn't so bad.

He extricated one of his hands and brought it to Kit's cock. Kit gasped at the contact, clenching around Percy's length in a way that made Percy almost sob. A few strokes later and Kit was coming, Percy's name a strangled sigh, his body hot and grasping around Percy's. Percy pulled out and came into his own fist, his climax so hard it nearly knocked him off his feet. He collapsed against Kit and could have stayed there if he hadn't remembered Kit's complaints about his leg.

"How's your leg?"

"How's my *leg*? You've just had your cock up my arse and you're asking about my *leg*?"

"It was meant to be more of a general inquiry as to your state of well-being, but if you wish to give me an itemized list of your body parts and their various conditions, please don't let me stop you," Percy offered graciously.

Kit's shoulders started shaking, and Percy realized the bastard was laughing.

"Oh, who even cares about your leg. Or your arse, for that matter. You can all go straight to hell," Percy sniffed. But he stepped away only long enough to take a blanket from the cupboard, throw it to the floor, and urge Kit down.

"What—"

"Oh, shut it," Percy said, tucking himself away. He ducked into the shop to fill a pitcher with still-warm water from the kettle and to grab a few cloths. He wet one and brought it to Kit, who he found propped up on an elbow.

"This is for whichever of your body parts you feel most requires it," Percy said, primly holding out the cloth. "Or you can use it to polish furniture, for all I care. Please don't feel constrained to—"

Kit pulled on the edge of Percy's boots in a way that caused Percy to trip. Percy caught himself in time to land on the blanket beside Kit.

"Ugh, I don't know why I like you," Percy said, and then immediately regretted it. And then immediately after that, he allowed himself to briefly wonder why it was a bad thing to admit. In addition to the past half hour—which admittedly could be explained by a host of other things besides anything so tender as *liking*—there had been weeks of laughter and conversation. Admitting it shouldn't even be significant.

Happily, he was spared further reflection on this boring and fruitless topic by Kit's mouth sliding over his own. It was different from their earlier kisses, slower and less urgent. Lazy, even. One of Kit's hands sifted through Percy's hair and Percy arched into the touch. Right when Percy was starting to wonder if this might be the time to take off the rest of the clothing that they both still, unaccountably, wore, Kit went still.

At first, Percy didn't realize what had happened. He thought, perhaps, that Kit had hurt his leg. Then Kit climbed to his feet, shoving Percy behind him. He took out the knife he kept on his belt and snarled, "Show yourself," at a figure that had emerged on the threshold of the door that Percy had left open.

Percy was calculating how long it would take for him to reach the case of weapons he had stupidly abandoned near the front door.

"Yes, well, I plan to, Kit," said the stranger. "Keep your hair on, will you."

A funny thing happened to Kit's face, then. He went so pale that Percy thought that maybe he really had been injured. And he dropped his knife hand to his side at the same moment that his jaw went slack.

"Rob?" Kit breathed.

Chapter 33

Isn't this an interesting sight to come home to," Rob murmured, glancing between Kit and Percy. "I want to know *all* about this."

"He's not important," Kit said. "What I want to know is where the bloody fuck you've been and why you let me think you were dead for a year?"

"I missed you, too," Rob said, stepping into the back room and letting his gaze travel around the place. "Home sweet home."

"I asked where the fuck you've been," Kit repeated.

"It's a long story, darling, and I think it's best saved for when we're alone. Speaking of which, I'm dreadfully sorry to have interrupted you. It seems you've learned all manner of interesting things while I've been away."

"It's not what it looks like," Kit said.

"It looks like you've been shagging a lordling."

Kit knew that Rob was trying to distract him, but he also couldn't stand the idea of Rob coming back and thinking that Kit had abandoned all his principles and gone to bed with the enemy. "Shut up about that. Where were you?"

"I'll take myself off," Percy said, casting an acid glance at Kit.

"Enchanted to make your acquaintance," he said to Rob, executing a graceful bow. "And you can fuck yourself," he said to Kit. He shouldered past Kit, stopping only long enough to grab his coat and his bag. "It's been illuminating, gentlemen." The door slammed on his way out.

Kit knew he should go after Percy. He had said something wrong, something that would no doubt occur to him much later and for which he'd feel appropriately contrite, but at the moment all he could think of was Rob. And he was, truth be told, slightly annoyed with Percy for having been there to distract him.

"I reckon you bungled that," Rob said, shaking his head ruefully.

"That is *not* what we're talking about. For Christ's sake, Rob, it's been an entire year."

Rob sighed as if this were all terribly boring. He sauntered over to the hearth and grabbed a fire iron, then used it to prod the fire back to life. "Do you know, I had forgotten you had a wood fire here? I've thought of this place a thousand times over the past year and completely forgot about your baseless prejudice against coal."

"It ruins the beans," Kit said automatically, as he had every other time they had had this argument over the years, and then looked away so he wouldn't see whether Rob was smirking.

Rob peered inside the kettle, presumably to check that there was enough water for two cups of tea, then hung it on the hook over the fire. "I was injured on that last job."

"You were shot in the chest. I saw you fall." There had been so much blood. The last thing Kit had seen before losing consciousness was all the blood. After Kit escaped from jail, Janet and Tom explained that they had fled the scene as soon as shots were fired, and that when they went back, there was no sign of Rob's body. They had all assumed their friend was in a pauper's grave.

"It went through my shoulder. A remarkably clean shot, and it doesn't bother me in the least anymore. I see you weren't as lucky," he said, frowning at Kit's walking stick. "I had to lie low for a few days, though, and when I returned to London, there was a message waiting for me from my mother. It took me several months to, ah, deal with that."

"Your mother knew?"

"No, God no." For the first time, Rob looked distressed. "I was furious with her. Trust me when I say it was better for me not to be in the same country as her. I didn't plan on faking my death and vanishing for a year, Kit." His jaw set. "Believe me when I say I had to leave. I hope you know me well enough to trust that I wouldn't have done it unless I was left with no other choice."

Kit wanted to believe that, he truly did. "Exactly what did this letter say?"

"I wish I could tell you." Rob sounded sincere, damn him. "There are some things I don't want to saddle you with, my friend."

Kit ran a frustrated hand through his hair and sat in one of the chairs by the fire. "You're going to need to say something, all right? I thought you were *dead*." Kit had grieved this horse's arse. "Betty *cried*."

"Well, that's horrifying. I dare say the plants beneath her feet withered and died. Tears of pure vitriol. So who's this fellow with the yellow hair, and how long has that been going on? I have to say, I'm offended that you never tried to have one off with me. You know perfectly well that my tastes are expansive. I'm wounded, I tell you, wounded."

"Are you coming back from the dead to complain that I'm fucking men who aren't you?" asked Kit in disbelief. "Are you serious, now?"

"Well, yes. It does need to be addressed."

"No, it bloody well does not. I can go to bed with who I please, without having to explain myself to you."

"You seldom go to bed with anybody. Is that because you don't care for women?"

"No," Kit said, striving for patience. "I seldom go to bed with people because I seldom meet anyone I really want to go to bed with. The fact that he's a man isn't what matters." Too late, Kit realized he had said too much.

Rob let out a low whistle. "You're . . . fond of him, then?"

It was on the tip of his tongue to deny it, but based on the look on Rob's face, that would be pointless. And Kit had spoken dismissively of Percy once tonight and didn't want to do it again. "Yes, not that it's any of your business. And that's all I wish to say on the matter. Now, if all you're going to tell me is that your mother left you a mysterious message that required all your friends *and your mother* to think you were dead, then I suppose I'll just take myself off to see your mother."

"I wouldn't do that, old friend. She might not be feeling particularly hospitable. You're taking the news much better than she did."

Kit took a sip of the tea that Rob had placed beside him. As always, Rob had added too much sugar. Kit winced.

"If it makes you feel better, I didn't mean for you to think I was dead. Not at first, at least. It was just that I thought you were dead. The broadsheets got that wrong, if you recall."

"Bugger." The broadsheets Kit had been shown while in prison had been a confused jumble of hearsay. A few days after Kit's arrest, another robbery had occurred in roughly the same part of the country and which ended in the highwayman being shot dead. Details of the two incidents got jumbled, and as always, nobody seemed able to keep highwaymen's identities straight, so the papers had reported that Gladhand Jack had died. At the time, Kit assumed that Rob was dead and decided that Gladhand Jack would die with him.

"It wasn't until much later," Rob said, "that I realized you were alive."

"Where did you go?" Kit asked. "You can tell me that much, surely."

"France," Rob said, wrinkling his nose. "If I never set foot on a fishing boat for the rest of my life, it'll still be too soon."

"Did you finish whatever you set about to do?"

"No, I have not," Rob said, staring at the fire. "But I'm afraid I'll need to."

There was a grim determination in his tone that took Kit back to the first months they had spent on the road after their lives went to shit and neither of them could even see straight for the anger and sorrow. It made the hairs on the backs of Kit's arms stand on end.

Rob let out an abrupt laugh. "You've really fucked things up with your gentleman, though. My God, it reminds me of when Jenny threw all your linens into the garden. What did you do that time?"

"I let the dog into the house, and he ate an entire ham," Kit said, smiling despite himself. "I still don't know whether Jenny was more upset about the lost ham or the sick dog."

Rob laughed again, and the firelight shone onto his face.

There were lines that hadn't been there a year before, and it looked like it had been a long while since he had a decent night's sleep or a full meal. He looked rawboned and weary.

"Your old rooms on the third floor are empty," Kit said. "I boxed your things up and put them in the attic, but I'll help you get them down tomorrow."

"Are you still letting every vagrant and vagabond in greater London have a bed for the asking?"

"Only vagrants and vagabonds I like and trust," Kit said, smiling into his tea.

"Does your gent count in that lot?"

"Do I like and trust him? I like him," Kit said. "Can't trust him."

"Good."

"He came to me a month ago and asked me to do a job for him," Kit said. "I couldn't, because of this bastard"—he patted his leg—"but I've been showing him how to do it himself."

"A gentleman?" Rob asked in apparent disbelief. "Shagging him is one thing, but—"

"What *did* you think I'd do while you were off playing dead? Did you think I'd be happy to spend all day pouring out coffee? Or did you think I'd carry on like before, just without you?"

"I tried not to think about it," Rob said. "Why are we having this conversation sober?" He took out a flask of what Kit knew would be gin and poured some into his tea. Kit covered his own cup with his hand. "Really?" Rob asked, but corked the flask and returned it to his coat. "Sober, bent, friendly with toffs. Anything else I ought to know about how you've been spending the past year?"

"Don't forget crippled," Kit added lightly, and then felt bad when Rob looked stricken.

"Is it that bad?"

Kit realized Rob hadn't seen him walk more than a few steps. "Yes," he said. "It's that bad." He realized that the words hadn't come out bitterly, though. A month ago, he couldn't think about his injury without feeling as if he had lost a part of himself. But now he was starting to feel like he was still Kit Webb, just with a leg that didn't work.

"What in hell is that spider doing?" Rob said, getting to his feet and striding to the stairs. "Have you gone blind as well?" He reached up, as if to sweep away the cobwebs.

"Don't you dare," Kit said, getting to his feet. "Just duck your head under it as you go upstairs." Rob turned and stared at him. "It's just living its life, all right?"

Rob continued to look at him like he was speaking in tongues but held his hands up in surrender, and then poured them both new cups of tea.

Chapter 34

*K*it woke with his entire body in outright revolt. Yesterday's traipsing around town had done his leg no good, and he must have leaned badly on his walking stick, because his shoulder and back were in a pitiful state. He spent a full minute staring at a crack in the ceiling, dreading the prospect of hauling himself out of bed, before he remembered that Rob was back.

And then he could add a sick stomach to his list of complaints. Rob was up to something, which was pretty much his permanent condition, but this time it didn't involve Kit. Kit could only think of a handful of reasons why Rob wouldn't spill a secret to Kit, and he didn't like any of them.

He grumbled and swore the entire time he washed and dressed. By the time he got to the top of the stairs, he was wondering how bad it would be to just . . . slide down, maybe. It surely couldn't hurt more than walking down would, and would provide a bit of novelty to his day.

"There you are!" Rob called from the bottom of the stairs. Kit could smell burnt coffee and something else equally burnt—toast or oatcakes. Rob could burn anything he put his mind to. During the months they spent living rough, Rob had managed to burn soup; apparently a year of being presumed dead had done nothing to improve his cookery skills. "Had a bit of trouble with breakfast," he admitted. "I think I'll just go out and get us a loaf of bread. Why are you just standing there?"

"I'm trying to convince my leg that it really wants to do this."

"Do you need a hand?" Rob asked a little too brightly.

"No," Kit said, schooling his face to not show pain as he took that first step down. "Just go away and stop staring at me."

"Touchy," Rob said, but he left.

"You're going to give Betty the fright of her life when she comes in," Kit said when he finally made it downstairs.

"Oh, I saw her yesterday when she let me in here. About two minutes after she kicked me in the bollocks and punched me in the gut. Really, you're taking this better than anybody else."

"I can't believe you told Betty before you told me."

"I came here to tell you *and* Betty. I just happened to see her an hour earlier than I saw you, because you were busy getting fondled by gentlemen. Who is he, by the way?"

At the mention of Percy, Kit remembered what they had done together. He had worried that it would be strange and different with a man. And, obviously, the physical act was different, which his body was still reminding him of. But at the end of the day it was getting off with someone he fancied—fancied a great deal. When he remembered Percy's words in his ear, alternately soothing and chiding, he could almost feel the other man's body pressed against his back.

"Kit?" Rob asked, jolting Kit back to the present. "Does he have a name?"

"Percy," Kit said. He didn't feel any pressing need to explain who Percy was—or, rather, who his father was. Rob was already going to think that Kit was out of his mind for getting friendly with an aristocrat, and it would be infinitely worse if he knew that Percy's father was the Duke of Clare.

"Whoever he is, he did not look pleased with you when he left last night. People don't much care for being referred to as unimportant."

Kit winced, remembering his own words. But if Percy had become upset by being called unimportant, that was everything but an admission that he wanted to be important to Kit. And that thought made Kit's heart leap with hope. He wanted to find Percy right that minute and apologize, but it would have to wait until his leg settled down.

Throughout the morning, even though it was a Sunday and the shop was closed, people stopped by as word spread that Rob had returned. By the evening there was a festive mood at the coffeehouse, with people Kit hadn't seen in over a year coming in to visit Rob. Every time the door opened, Kit turned, hoping that it would be Percy, even though he knew how unlikely that was. Kit was surrounded by nearly everyone he knew, but the person he most wanted to see was across town, in a fine house, an entire world away from Kit.

Even Janet stopped by, a swaddled baby in her arms. He had known she was expecting, but seeing proof of it was still somehow startling. She looked well, though—tired, but plumper than he had ever seen her.

"I don't suppose you'd be interested in a job," Kit said, taking the baby from her and cradling him against his chest. The child was an insubstantial weight, still at the stage where it seemed like a stiff wind might carry him away. He settled his hand more firmly at the baby's back.

She gave him a dour look. "Do I look like I'll be climbing into trees any time soon? And I'd like to know how to shoot an arrow with these in the way," she said, gesturing at her chest. "I told you to talk to Hattie from the fair."

Kit hummed his agreement and turned his nose into the baby's head, breathing in the smell of milk and fresh linens and whatever else made babies smell the way they did. "What's his name?"

"Sam. Not that we've got around to christening him yet."

Hannah hadn't been christened, either. Kit couldn't make himself do it alone, not with Jenny in prison. And then, after everything, it was the least of his concerns. "That's a good name," he made himself say. "Go on and let me look after him for a bit. If he needs you, I reckon you'll hear him holler."

Janet, who maybe knew something about Kit's past, or maybe just saw something in his face, or maybe just was grateful to have a few minutes without the baby, leaned over and kissed Kit's cheek before vanishing into the throng.

Somebody produced a bottle of gin, and somebody else arrived with a stack of pies. Baby Sam still sleeping on his shoulder, Kit carefully lowered himself into a chair. The child startled slightly at the movement, and Kit patted his back, whispering hushing noises into his ear.

Betty came over with a tankard of ale. "You all right?" she asked.

"Not quite over the shock," he admitted. "You?"

"He's lucky I haven't broken his nose. Has he told you where he was all this time, other than that it was a secret?"

Kit shook his head.

"I'll tell you, I don't like it."

Kit stayed silent for a while, thinking only of the slow breathing of the child in his arms. "Neither do I," he finally said. He wanted to say more, but didn't know how to express how glad he was to have Rob back, but how profoundly uneasy he felt about it. It crossed his mind that what he really wanted was to speak to Percy; Percy, he felt certain, would understand what it was like when a thread of distrust worked its way through love. Kit imagined what it would be like to be able to unburden himself to Percy, and even for Percy to be able to do the same to Kit. It felt out of reach, miles away from their tentative alliance, miles away from what they had done together the previous night.

But he wanted it, and he thought Percy did, too. He didn't know if they'd manage it, but Kit intended to try.

Chapter 35

It was beginning to occur to Percy that highway robbery was only going to be the beginning of his life of crime, because he was also going to need to dip his toes into the world of kidnapping. He wouldn't put it past the duke to attempt to keep Marian from Eliza. Spiriting her away was not the problem—even as loud and inclined to wriggle as she was, she could be concealed under a cloak and then—well, Percy hadn't the faintest idea what one did with children, even if one acquired them by more traditional means than kidnapping.

"You're admirably portable," he told her. "We at least have that working in our favor." She responded, as per custom, by making a noise that sounded like "fffff" and squeezing his finger in her fat little fist.

"Yes, quite," he agreed.

Percy had sent the nursery maid back to bed and could hear her soft snores through the closed door. He could simply walk out of the house with the baby in his arms and be halfway across town before anyone even noticed the child was missing. He would probably even have time to stop in his rooms and fill his pockets with a handful of valuables.

They could live off that for some time, if he could figure out how people lived in an ordinary sort of way. He could ask Kit how one went about hiring rooms and acquiring food and milk. He was extremely cross with Kit at the moment but didn't doubt that the man would have no problem being an accessory to kidnapping—not under these circumstances, at least. How very humbling, needing to ask for lessons in how to live like a normal person.

Eliza made a rude noise, and Percy raised his eyebrows. "Yes, terribly common, I quite agree," he said, feeling ashamed at the prospect of plunging his sister into obscurity. Because at the very least, even the illegitimate daughter of the Duke of Clare and Lady Marian Hayes ought to live like a lady, not as an anonymous orphan in a shabby set of rooms in some backwater where they would never be discovered.

After returning the baby to her cradle, he began assembling a collection of items for Collins to sell. Three brooches, his least favorite snuffbox, and an ornamental sword that was so badly balanced, it annoyed Percy even to look at it. He didn't know what kind of price he'd get for those items, and couldn't even recall what he had paid for any of them in the first place, but he had the sense that they wouldn't go terribly far in keeping him in the manner to which he had been accustomed. He added a sapphire ring, a set of jeweled dueling pistols, and a small golden looking glass.

It all fit in a small satchel with room to spare, and his apartments were still filled with trinkets and baubles. How much of it did he really need? He had reconciled himself to the loss of his least favorite snuffbox, but what about the other five? He didn't even like snuff. And how many rings did a man need? He had a dreadful certainty that the answer was zero.

"My lord?" asked Collins when he found Percy kneeling before a small mountain of glittering objects.

"Do you happen to know what it costs to hire a decent set of rooms?"

"My lord?" Collins repeated, this time with a note of alarm.

"I will soon find myself in reduced circumstances," Percy said carefully. "I've put aside some items that I believe I can do without. Do you happen to know how one goes about selling things?"

If Collins thought this an ignorant question, he didn't let it show. "Yes, my lord. Am I correct in assuming that my lord and his father—"

"You can speak freely, Collins. And you might as well sit down."

"Is the duke cutting you off?"

"Not yet," Percy said, because that much was true. "But I thought it would be best to be prepared."

"Very wise."

"It's a secret, Collins."

"Of course, my lord."

"You ought to know that—" Percy swallowed. This was harder than he had anticipated. "You might not wish to remain in my service. Some unpleasant truths are about to emerge. I'd keep you on, but for your own comfort, you may wish to begin looking for another post."

"I believe the customary course of action is to go to the Continent, my lord."

"I beg your pardon?"

Collins's cheeks went dark with embarrassment. "If one fears prosecution for the sort of activity that might be described as—"

"Ah," Percy said. "Quite." If Collins thought Percy was about to be prosecuted for sodomy, that was all to the good.

"We can be on the packet to Calais before nightfall, my lord."

Percy gaped. "If my ship is to sink, there's no reason for you to be on it. I can find you a place with a respectable gentleman, Collins. People have been trying to poach you off me for years."

"No, thank you, my lord."

"Collins—"

"If you wish to dispense with my services—"

"No, no, nothing like that," Percy said hastily.

"If I may make a suggestion, perhaps my lord would be cheered by dressing in something other than dirty riding clothes? Those breeches would be enough to put anyone in a melancholic frame of mind."

Percy glanced down at himself and saw that he was, indeed, still wearing his riding clothes from that morning. "Good thinking, Collins," he agreed, and let himself be dressed in one of his more stylish ensembles—plum with lilac embroidery, purchased in Paris at significant expense. Admiring himself in the cheval glass, he had an alarming thought. "I suppose I'll have to sell some of my clothes."

"Some of it, my lord. But whatever fate awaits you, you'll need to meet it wearing something other than rags and sackcloth."

This advice was both sound and soothing. When Collins left, Percy considered what to do with himself for the rest of the day. It had been some time since he visited Kit's wearing anything respectable. He could stop by now and give Kit a small thrill by allowing the man to surreptitiously ogle his ankles. But Kit had behaved abominably yesterday, and Percy was not in a frame of mind to reward the man.

If Percy allowed himself to see through the cloud of anger and humiliation that blanketed the memory, he could perhaps understand that Kit had been startled. Startled might even be too mild a word for whatever one felt when confronted with someone returning from the dead. It was, arguably, ungenerous of Percy to put too much stock into what Kit had said at that moment.

Ordinarily, if a lover treated Percy with less than perfect civility, he would walk away and never look back. He usually carried on his affairs with the same sangfroid with which he did almost everything else. He had been taught to keep people at arm's length, and just to be on the safe side he typically kept them even further.

That rule applied not only to lovers but to everyone. Marian was the only real exception, and he always suspected that she had gotten in on a technicality due to the fact that they had known one another before he learned how to get the better of his emotions. *Fond is another word for weak*, his mother had always said.

He had believed her. He still did. His mother had taught him how to survive despite the weakness that was at the core of who he was. She had taught him how to shield himself in a carapace of pride and power.

Right now, he wanted to go crawling to Kit and demand reassurance that Kit hadn't meant what he'd told his friend. He wanted to admit to Kit how very much he liked him and say it again and again until Kit said it back. What was worse, he wanted to tell Kit all about his problems—from his father's bigamy to the contents of the book to the fate of his sister and

Marian—not because he thought Kit could do anything about it, but because he wanted a friend to tell him that everything was going to be all right.

It was pathetic. It was the pitiful need for reassurance and affection that he thought he had long since subdued.

That night, when he heard tapping at his window, he was not surprised.

"I got your message," Marian said, climbing into the room and dropping a bag onto the floor, causing its contents to clatter. "What's wrong?"

He poured them each a glass of brandy and sat in one of the chairs before the fire, gesturing for Marian to take the other one. "What if we called the robbery off?" he asked.

She took a long drink of brandy and tapped her fingers on the arm of the chair. "I was wondering when you'd suggest something like that."

He was almost dizzy with relief. Surely, the pair of them were mad; this entire highway-robbery scheme was nothing more than a folie à deux. "So you agree," he said.

"Of course not, Percy," she snapped. "Not in the slightest. Your father has done something unforgivable to both of us and I don't know if I can live out the rest of my life if I know that he hasn't been punished for it."

"People do it all the time," Percy said, thinking of Kit. "Live their lives, knowing that someone who wronged them is alive and well."

"But we have a chance to take something back from him." She leaned forward, her eyes bright. "We have a chance to make things—not fair, not equal, but just a little less unfair. I know it's small and petty, and I know I'm being spiteful, but spite is all I have right now."

He nodded, remembering his conversation with Kit. "It's honor."

"I feel far from honorable right now, Percy."

"The feeling that you and I have of something being taken away from us? That's our honor. The need we have to make the duke pay isn't any different from calling a man out in a duel. It's not small and petty. I was raised on stories of the honor of the Talbots and the honor of the Percys, and all those stories come down to people taking unaccountable risks to stand up for what and who they value."

Percy could gather up his brooches and his rings and sell every last yard of silk in his wardrobe and eke out a plain existence. Marian could live with Marcus, or perhaps even stay on at one of the duke's lesser properties. They could both be sufficiently content despite the niggling sense of incompletion that came when they remembered that the duke still had his name, his fortune, his coronet.

But Talbots didn't let their honor be sullied, and neither did Percys.

Percy realized he had had it all wrong when he told Kit that honor is just spite dressed up; spite was honor when it was the only weapon you had against someone more powerful.

"You're right," Percy said slowly. "I just had cold feet." He extended his hand, and Marian grasped it for a long moment before she got to her feet and threw open the window. "The entire house is fast asleep," he said. "You could simply walk to your apartments like a sensible person."

"And so I could," she replied, looking over her shoulder, one foot already on the windowsill, "if I didn't have business taking me elsewhere this evening."

"Evening," he repeated, scandalized. "It's past two in the morning."

"By the way," she said, gesturing at the sack she had left on the floor, "fence those for me, will you?"

Before he could protest, she was already gone.

Chapter 36

*I*t took another day for Kit's leg to get into a state that was amenable to being walked on for more than a few yards, and even then, he had to hire a hack to take him to the park.

He knew that Percy went riding early most mornings and found him easily enough. The park was still mostly empty, except for shadowy figures returning from whatever mischief they had been up to in the dark. The ground was blanketed in a mist that drifted across the grass. Most people would take this as a sign that greater caution was needed, but Percy was reckless with his own safety, and so Kit followed the sound of hoofbeats until he caught sight of Percy racing along the path, disappearing into the fog and then reappearing as if by magic.

Percy rode like he did everything else—he was graceful enough to make risking his neck look easy. He was fast and lithe, and it was a pleasure to watch him. Even in his loose riding clothes, even with his hair tied back and tucked under his hat, the long lines of his body were visible.

Kit already knew Percy was beautiful—had known it the first time Percy walked into his shop, and every further encounter had only served as redundant proof. But the pleasure Kit took in watching him wasn't simply because Percy was beautiful, or even because he was talented. It was because Percy was *Percy*. He enjoyed looking at Percy for the same reason he had been frightened out of his wits to see Percy sword fighting: he just liked the man.

Kit told himself that he liked a lot of people, even though he knew that wasn't true. He told himself that it was nothing unusual to like a person, even if, on paper, every single thing about them was antithetical to one's staunchly held beliefs about what a person ought to be.

He told himself that liking didn't mean one held any tenderer feelings, and neither, for that matter, did kissing.

He told himself all of this and didn't believe a word of it. He clutched the parcel he held in his free hand, and when the fog cleared, he stepped closer to the path of Percy's horse.

"Please watch your step," called Percy, breathless and pulling up on his reins. "I'm afraid I don't have the patience for bloodshed this morning." Then he must have recognized Kit, because his face closed off entirely.

"I came to beg your forgiveness," Kit said immediately.

"For what?" Percy asked after hesitating for only the space of a single breath.

"For saying you were nobody. For saying you didn't matter."

"Are you apologizing for hurting my feelings with an unpleasant truth, or for lying?" Percy asked.

"For hurting your feelings with a lie," Kit said.

That must have been satisfactory, because Percy dismounted and came to stand face-to-face with Kit. "Why did you do it?"

"I didn't want Rob to know that I was—that I'm fond of a person like you."

"And what kind of person am I, exactly?"

"A bloody rich one."

Percy let out a startled, slightly bitter laugh. "And that's what you thought when you saw that your friend, who you had believed dead for the past year, was alive and well? You thought—better not let him think I'm overly friendly with this man I'm rolling around with on the floor."

Kit didn't know how to explain that Percy seemed to occupy the foremost portion of his brain, nor did he know exactly when that had happened. "Yes" was all he said. And then, because Percy's eyes were searching his face, looking for something that Kit couldn't hope to hide, "I don't know how not to think about you. I don't know how to stop, and I don't want to." He swallowed. He had felt like this once before, and the result had been him and Jenny standing before a priest as soon as the banns were called. He knew what it was, and he knew he wasn't foolish enough to say so out loud. "I brought you something." He held out a parcel wrapped in brown paper.

Something gratified flickered across Percy's face. Kit smiled, because of course Percy was the sort of person to be delighted by presents. "What is it?"

"Nothing much." Kit placed the parcel into Percy's outstretched hand, then watched his face as he opened it.

"It's cake," Percy said, not as if he had expected a golden snuffbox or something, but as if there was nothing in the world better than cake. He broke it into two pieces, giving one to Kit and popping the other into his mouth. "Oh, it's very good."

"I thought you might like it." In fact, Kit, arriving at the bakery as soon as they unlocked their doors, had picked out the cake that seemed the most unnecessarily complicated. The baker's sleepy daughter had informed Kit that this cake had orange peel, rosewater, and a number of spices. It cost twice as much as the other similarly sized cakes. Kit knew at once that it would be Percy's favorite.

"Where did you get it?"

"A bakery."

"Which bakery?" Percy asked, impatient.

"That's my secret. You'll just have to let me get you another cake sometime soon."

"If you haven't figured out by now that I'll let you buy me as many cakes as you please, as often as you want, you're stupider than you look." That, from Percy, was as good as a declaration, and Kit drew in a breath.

"Me too," he said.

Percy turned away and smoothed his horse's mane. "If my mother knew I was acting like this, she'd roll over in her grave," he said, avoiding Kit's eye.

"What about this situation would bother your mum? Is it that I'm a man or that we're about to rob your father? No shortage of causes for worry."

Percy snorted out a very ungentlemanlike laugh, and Kit bumped their shoulders together. And then, because the fog was thick and Percy's face was bleak, Kit tucked a loose strand of hair behind Percy's ear. Percy shuddered, as if the contact were too much for him, but he didn't step away.

"One of her earliest lessons was never to act like one needed the approval, company, or affection of any earthly being," Percy said.

Kit hadn't been expecting that. "Everybody needs those things," he said.

"Yes, but one isn't supposed to let on. That's what's dangerous. And she was right, you know."

With anyone else, Kit might have argued that not only was it not dangerous, but it was the only way to live. But he could see that Percy believed it as a basic tenet of his existence. "Aye, but you like danger."

Percy laughed. "No, I do not. You are badly misinformed."

"What would you call sword fighting, then? And don't tell me you're too talented to get injured, because I've dressed your wounds."

"Wound, singular," Percy corrected him.

"And what would you call carrying on with men if not dangerous?"

"It's hardly my fault that the laws are what they are. You can't expect me to be celibate."

"And associating with hardened criminals?"

"What hardened criminals do I— Oh, I suppose you're referring to yourself."

"Yes," Kit said, laughing. "Had you forgotten?"

"Hardened criminal sounds like someone who goes around frightening old ladies, when really you're just a darling."

"I've frightened scores of old ladies," Kit protested.

"No, you didn't. You charmed them. I've heard the ballad, you remember."

Kit frowned. "Maybe they were charmed after the fact, but I think a lot of those stories are from people who were only relieved that they got away with their lives. I promise they were frightened when their carriages stopped. I saw their faces. That's something I don't miss."

Percy looked carefully at him. "It's a pity you can't arrange for the carriages of villains to be empty of any innocents. Well, my father won't have anyone in the carriage with him other than his henchmen, and I'm hardly going to wring my hands about frightening *them*."

"As I said, you really don't seem to have any problems with danger." Kit took the remnants of cake from Percy's hand, broke off a piece, and held it up to Percy's lips. "I'd even say you seek it out. So you ought to be perfectly fine letting on that you need me."

Percy stared at him, and for a minute Kit thought he'd protest. But he leaned forward and ate the cake from Kit's fingers.

Chapter 37

The next morning at breakfast, the duke announced his plan to visit Cheveril Castle in two days' time.

"Indeed," Percy said, managing a bored air as he cut his ham into ever smaller pieces. "Will Marian be joining you?"

"*The duchess*," his father said severely, "must call on her mantua maker, and therefore must remain in town."

Throughout this, Marian remained very still, and Percy inferred that it had not been easy for her to negotiate her unsupervised stay in London. If everything went as planned, Marian would only need to endure two more days of silent cold meals and the ever-watchful eye of the duke. Two more days. Percy hadn't known it was possible to feel terror and relief at the same time.

Percy excused himself from the table and went directly to Kit's. When he arrived, Kit was at his usual station by the hearth, but he looked up when he heard the door. He didn't quite smile, but an expression of pleased surprise crossed his face, followed by a slow and careful appraisal of Percy's fine attire.

Sitting on a stool nearby was Rob, and he was staring at Percy in a way that left no room for Percy to hope that he had not been recognized as the man Kit had been with several nights ago. Feeling that it would be more awkward to feign ignorance of the man's presence, and also possessed by the lamentable urge to be on his best behavior around Kit's friends, he bowed his head at the man.

Rob did not return the nod. Instead, he looked shrewdly, but not quite unkindly, at Percy, then flicked his gaze to Kit, and then back again. Percy wasn't sure if it was his imagination or if he detected a somewhat mad glint in the fellow's eye. One had to be a bit mad, he supposed, to let one's friends think one was dead for an entire year. But no matter; Kit cared for the man. Kit also seemed to care for Percy, which not only gave him and Rob something in common, but proved that Kit was a terrible judge of character.

Rob was somewhere between Kit's and Percy's ages, which was to say about twenty-five, with hair that could only be described as carroty and a build even leaner than Percy's. Even sitting, he seemed strung tight with a dangerous tension, like a whip pulled back and about to strike. He looked familiar in a way that Percy could not quite put his finger on, but before he could think further on this, Rob spoke.

"I can't decide whether I'm more surprised by his being rich or his being a man," Rob said, his eyes still on Percy but his words plainly directed at Kit. It was an impertinence, to talk about him as if he weren't there, and Percy was shocked to find that he didn't care. Perhaps it was that with so much else to worry about, the petty trappings of rank and courtesy did not even merit a second thought. Perhaps it was that he was willing to be generous with Kit's friends. Neither explanation pleased him.

"I need to speak to you. In private," Percy said, remembering the purpose of his errand and trying to ignore the flames of fear and anxiousness that licked at the edges of his mind.

Kit gestured at the door to the back room, and then, apparently thinking better of it, made toward the stairs. The office, Percy supposed, was a much more suitable place for a meeting with Lord Holland.

When the door shut behind them, Percy cleared his throat. "This will probably be too short notice to arrange the robbery, but my father will be traveling to Cheveril in two days."

Kit frowned. "Two days is plenty of time. You already know your part. The main difficulty was always going to be knowing your father's route beforehand, and then separating him from his outriders and the other carriages in his party. Now we have the first part settled, and with Rob around, the second part will be child's play."

"You've told him?" Percy didn't know why he felt betrayed. Of course Kit would have told Rob who Percy was and what Percy planned. Of course Kit's loyalty would be to Rob, not to Percy. Percy knew this, knew better than to assume otherwise. Never in his life would Percy have valued a mere lover—not even that, just someone who had fucked him in a seedy back room—over one of his inner circle. He was being childish and naive to expect Kit to behave differently.

"No," Kit said, his gaze horribly soft, as if he knew something of Percy's thoughts. He reached out as if to touch Percy's shoulder reassuringly, God help them both, but then pulled back. "Not yet, I mean. He doesn't know your father is our mark, but he'll have to know in order to do the job."

"All right," Percy said. "You mentioned that you already engaged the other people who I require?" They had discussed a sharpshooter and another man to actually hold the carriage up alongside Percy.

"A girl named Hattie Jenkins will be our sharpshooter. As for the other man, I've decided that I'll do it myself."

"But you can't," Percy said immediately, then regretted it when Kit clenched his jaw. "We both know you wouldn't be able to get away fast enough, if it came to that."

"It won't come to that."

"You can't know that."

"You don't get to make choices for me," Kit said, his voice low and dangerous for reasons that Percy did not understand. "I'm not in your pay or your service."

"Of course you aren't! This was supposed to be *my* job," Percy protested. "When I tried to hire you, you wouldn't do it! That was the point of our entire arrangement."

Kit looked like he wanted to argue, but instead he just shook his head. "I don't need to explain myself to you. Let's just say that I want to satisfy myself that the job is done right."

"About that," Percy cut in. "You've never told me what makes you so eager to see my father's downfall."

"That makes two of us."

Well, of course Percy hadn't. He could hardly go around blabbing about his own illegitimacy. And yet—in a few short days, he and Marian would see that it became common knowledge. The only risk in telling Kit now was that Percy had not yet told another soul about his predicament and did not wish to start. He wanted to take his secret—the one that exposed every facet of his existence as a fiction—and bury it under layers of tissue paper, the way Collins had packed all Percy's most fragile treasures before taking them off to be sold.

But Kit was looking at him, something hard in his eyes that hadn't been there a few minutes earlier. Percy shouldn't give a fig what was or wasn't in Kit's eyes, or in anyone else's eyes, for that matter.

Every day is market day for secrets, his mother had always said. Secrets could be traded for favors, for countenance, for trust. Secrets could be kept for the same price.

Sometimes one shared a secret so it wouldn't be a secret anymore. Sometimes one shared a secret to take away a bit of its power. Maybe that was what Percy would be doing if he told Kit about his father.

But secrets could also be shared to show that one trusted the recipient. *Here, hold this, I know you won't break it*, his mother had said when handing him a delicate glass bauble. And Percy had remained so still that he had forgotten to breathe.

"My father's marriage to my mother was invalid," Percy said, "because he was already married at the time. Someone who knows about this is blackmailing Marian. You see what this means," Percy said, aware he was rambling and unable to stop, because that would mean looking at Kit's face. "I'm illegitimate and so is Marian's daughter. I'm not particularly concerned about myself, beyond the loss of my name, my station, and my fortune, but I can't forgive my father for doing this to Marian. That's why I need the book—we're going to ransom it until my father pays enough for Marian and the baby and me to live on."

Kit remained utterly still, leaning against the door as he had since entering the room. "Beyond your name, station, and fortune," he echoed. "Mere trifles."

"Don't pretend you care about dukedoms and estates."

"I don't," Kit said promptly. "I do care that you've lost things that matter to you."

"Things you hate."

"Yes."

"I don't want you to pity me."

"I don't. I couldn't." Kit managed to deliver these last words without any trace of affection, which Percy didn't think he could see without feeling sick, but with a sneer. Percy didn't know what that sneer meant, but it put him on familiar ground.

"A friend," Percy said carefully, "suggested that I ought to regard my father's first marriage as a youthful peccadillo. And that my quest for revenge is ungenerous of me."

"The world is filled with people who quietly choose to forget the marriages they made when they were young and didn't know any better. Sometimes that's the only way people have a chance at happiness. But your father isn't some traveling tinker. He had a responsibility."

"To the estate," Percy said, nodding.

"Fuck the estate," Kit said with venom. "No, he had a responsibility to you. He let you believe a lie—a lie about who you are and what your place is. He let you prepare your whole life for a purpose you don't have."

"What else could he have done?"

"Other than tell the truth? Well, instead of letting you believe that your worth hinges on your place in a hierarchy that men like him made up centuries ago—a hierarchy that is deranged and infantile and does a great deal of harm, I'll point out—he could have rebuked all of it. He could have given away his wealth, renounced his title, and lived like the rest of us. He could have lived the sort of life that you're now meant to live."

"I don't think one can renounce a title," Percy said, because that was the only part of Kit's speech he could engage with. The rest was not only radical but felt somehow blasphemous, possibly treasonous.

"He should have done it anyway."

There were moments when the world appeared to remake itself. It had already happened to Percy once this year, when he had learned of his father's betrayal. And now it was happening again—everything tearing apart at the seams, only to be sewn up in a different shape altogether. The world he now saw was Kit's, a world where one could refuse to accept the existing order of things, a world where old truths could be jettisoned and new ones put into place.

Percy felt oddly vulnerable, newly hatched in a world where he didn't know his way. He leaned instinctively toward Kit, not realizing he was doing it until Kit reached out and pulled him close. Percy shut his eyes and rested his forehead against Kit's.

"Sorry," Percy said after a few moments, unsure what he was apologizing for but aware that he was taking up Kit's time.

"Shut up," Kit said, and kissed him.

Chapter 38

Stay," Kit said, speaking the words against Percy's mouth. He had spent weeks committing to memory every detail of Percy's various appalling ensembles and now wanted to remove every stitch of this one. The gold braid alone could—and should—be snipped off and sold for enough to put bread in the mouths of all Saint Giles's urchins for an entire week, and those buttons could pay the rent on a decent set of rooms for a year. But he also wanted to trace the line of that gold braid with his heated fingers, then undo each button with his teeth.

He decided not to inquire too closely into either of these urges.

"I only have an hour," Percy said, pulling away but leaving his hands on Kit's hips. "I need to accompany Marian on her visits."

"She's important to you," Kit said looping his arms around Percy's neck. "Did you hope to marry her?" It was probably a tactless question, considering who she was married to—or not married to—presently, but Kit wanted to know, for reasons he had firmly decided were not jealousy.

Percy furrowed his brow. "I thought it might come to that,

although of course I always hoped Marian would make a match with someone who could be a proper husband for her."

"Do you not ever fancy women?" Kit asked, weighing his words carefully.

"Oh, no. Never even bothered trying to fool myself on that score. I take it you're, er, more broad-minded in your preferences."

"Mmm." Kit was momentarily distracted when Percy began kissing his neck. "But not broad-minded enough to let you leave that wig on while you're kissing my neck that way."

Percy complied without taking his lips from Kit's neck, tossing the wig onto Kit's desk. Kit undid Percy's plait and then ran his fingers through the silky strands with something like relief.

"How much else do you want me to take off?" Percy asked.

"If we only have an hour, not much. It probably takes a full hour to button you into that getup."

"You're not wrong." With that, Percy took a handkerchief from the recesses of his coat and spread it on the ground before dropping to his knees. Kit promptly decided he was very enthusiastic about Percy remaining dressed for this encounter, from the heart-shaped birthmark to the sword at his hip.

Kit reached behind him to slide the bolt shut on the door.

"I've been wanting to do this," Percy said conversationally as he unlaced Kit's buckskins.

"Ngh," Kit said articulately, his palms flat against the door behind him. And then, recovering himself, "Be my guest." He searched for something else to say, but then Percy's hand was drawing Kit's erection out and holding it lightly in a loose fist, and Kit's thoughts deserted him again.

"I didn't get a chance to get a good look at you the other night,"

Percy said, moving his hand so slowly and languidly that Kit wanted to cry. "It was dark, we were rather hurried. But now," he said, his voice trailing off as he swiped his tongue over the head of Kit's cock.

Kit was fully hard now, hard and wet and wanting. "Next time we do this with our clothes off." Surely it wasn't presumptuous to talk about a next time; they both clearly enjoyed this. Maybe the problem was that Kit was thinking of a string of next times stretching out into the future.

Percy's only answer was to suck lightly on the tip of Kit's erection. Kit groaned and let his head fall back against the door. Percy was doing something with his tongue that made Kit want to cry out, want to thrust forward, but Percy's hands were firm on his hips, keeping him in place.

"Next time," Kit repeated, hoping Percy couldn't hear the hopeful pleading in his voice.

Percy drew him deeper then, and Kit watched his length disappear into Percy's mouth, lovely and obscene and fascinating. Something of that must have shown on his face because Percy gave him a look that somehow managed to be a smirk despite the fact that his mouth was full of Kit's prick.

Kit didn't even want to blink, lest he miss a second of this. He wanted to memorize the way Percy's hair fell over his face, the way the silk thread in his coat caught the light, the way that absurd birthmark was now a mere inch from where his lips stretched around Kit's erection. Somehow, he looked angelic, with his golden hair and the halo-like glow that came from his clothes, and the fact that he was currently sucking Kit's cock did nothing to detract from that. Kit took one of his hands off the wall and gingerly brushed a few stands of hair off Percy's face so as to get a better view.

"Whatever you're doing," Kit managed to rasp, and then stopped when he felt the head of his cock nudge the back of Percy's throat. At that point, all he could do was swear. "Stop," he finally said, pulling at Percy's hair to signal his urgency, while gripping the base of his erection with the other hand.

Percy pulled off with an obscene noise and sent Kit a bewildered look. "Everything all right?" he asked, his voice sounding hoarse and wrecked in a way that made Kit shudder.

"Yes," Kit said emphatically. "I just want it to last. You're so good. I've never felt anything like your mouth. Never had it done like that."

Percy narrowed his eyes. "How? Competently?"

Kit gave a desperate laugh and ran a thumb over Percy's cheekbone.

"Will you permit me to resume?" Percy asked with an exaggerated air of forced patience.

Kit murmured his assent and then groaned when Percy swallowed him again.

"Because," Percy said when he pulled off again, in the same slightly snide tone he had used a moment before, "let me tell you, this isn't even particularly skillful. I wouldn't even consider my talents above middling in this arena." And then he resumed sucking and licking and doing miraculous things with his tongue.

Kit was—there was no other word for it—overcome. He expected his good leg to give out any minute now. Not only was Percy's mouth hot and wet and wonderful, but it was mocking and impatient and a little mean. It wasn't that Kit liked Percy being mean—well, no, he definitely did like it, which was something he would think about some other time—but it was who Percy was. The person giving Kit this pleasure was the same man

who held a sword like an extension of his arm and told him secrets like they were blood oaths. It made Kit feel unspeakably
fond.

"I adore you," Kit said, and the worst part of it was that he
had paused a full second before speaking to weigh his words as
well as his lust-addled mind was able, so he couldn't even blame
his frankness on the sort of whim that struck a man right before
coming. "I adore you," he repeated for good measure.

Percy glanced up at him, openly skeptical and maybe a little
pitying, but his only answer was to take one of Kit's hands and
bring it to the back of his head, and to remove his own hands
from Kit's hips.

Kit opened his mouth to ask whether Percy was sure, but Percy
must have anticipated this because he was preemptively glaring
up at Kit. Kit tilted his hips forward, his palm cradling the back
of Percy's head. Percy put up one knee and braced a hand on the
door behind Kit. Kit heard himself make an unhinged, desperate
sound.

After that it was just pleasure and sensation, tempered by the
hope that he wasn't hurting Percy and the vague sense that Percy
would be very cross indeed if Kit expressed this concern aloud.
Kit gasped out a warning and came with his eyes squeezed shut
and his hands fisted in Percy's hair.

Percy kept at it, slowing his mouth, moving almost tenderly,
until Kit could take no more and attempted to haul Percy up.
That, unfortunately, was when his leg finally gave out, and he
would have landed in a heap if Percy hadn't neatly caught him
with one arm.

"You're strong," Kit said as he lowered himself into the nearest chair. His words came out regrettably soft and sweet, when truly Kit had meant it as no more than an observation.

"You're delirious," Percy scoffed, and Kit grabbed him by the hem of his coat and pulled him down for a kiss. He had the satisfaction of realizing that Percy was, momentarily, startled. Percy so seldom let himself be seen as anything other than controlled and composed.

"Your turn," Kit said, fumbling with the inscrutably complicated opening of Percy's breeches. Beneath the silky fabric, he felt the hard ridge of the other man's erection. "How the hell do you get this thing out?" he grumbled.

Percy sighed and got his breeches open with what appeared to be one deft flick of his wrist, then stood before Kit, his erection in his hand. Kit, at eye level with Percy's groin, had never been this close to another man's cock before, and rather wished the room weren't so dimly lit. He hooked a finger into Percy's waistband, thinking to draw the man closer and return the favor.

"I think not," Percy said tartly. "If you think that what I did was so marvelous, I shudder to imagine what mediocrities you plan to visit upon my cock."

Kit grinned. "Coward."

Percy narrowed his eyes. "Fine, then. Have it your way."

Before Kit could decide which one of them had just goaded the other into this, he firmly tugged Percy's breeches lower and cupped his hands around the swell of the other man's arse, pulling him closer.

It was almost certainly true that whatever he did was mediocre at best, but Kit grasped the fundamentals. He got the first inch of Percy's cock into his mouth, using one hand to stroke the base.

Whatever he was doing, it couldn't have been too awful, because it wasn't long before Percy's breaths were coming fast and his fingers were tangled in Kit's hair.

When Percy came, Kit swallowed because he couldn't figure out any other way not to ruin Percy's clothes, and he was so appalled with his priorities that he nearly choked himself laughing.

"So pleased you found that amusing," Percy said, fastening his breeches. "One strives to entertain."

"I do adore you," Kit said, gazing up at him with an expression that caused Percy to become intensely interested in the buttons of his coat.

"You really shouldn't," Percy said.

"You can't stop me, you know," Kit said. "I'll care about you as much as I please."

Percy pressed his lips together and left the room without another word.

Chapter 39

*D*ownstairs, Percy found Betty behind the counter.

"I have a favor to ask you," Percy said. "It relates to your other line of employment."

She narrowed her eyes. "Kit ought to know better than to talk about that."

"Give Kit some credit. Give *me* some credit, for that matter. I've been here most days for a month. I have noticed things."

She sniffed. "Hand it over and I'll give it a look later on."

He passed her the bag in which he had stowed all the teaspoons and other knickknacks that Marian had evidently taken to pinching. Percy decided that Marian turning thief was not even on the list of the ten most troubling things he was contending with at the moment, and therefore he was not going to worry about it at all.

"You know," Betty said, glancing in the bag, "you're plainly up to no good, and I don't usually hold that against a man, but if you hurt Kit, I'll come after you. You hear me?"

"I never doubted it for a minute," Percy said. "Speaking of which, Kit seems to think he's coming with me on the, ah, errand

I'm running. Do you think you could persuade him to stay in London?"

"I don't think I could keep him away from you unless I locked him up. Even then, he'd find a way. And I think you know that."

"Surely, he knows it's a bad idea, what with his leg."

"Kit does a lot of things that are bad ideas," Betty said, pointedly flicking her eyes over Percy.

"Seriously, Betty, he listens to you."

"That's right. He does. And so should you. When the pair of you are done with this job, let him be. He deserves better. There's more to him than you know, and he's had enough misery in his life without you adding to it."

"I see," Percy said, because while he didn't care for being ordered about, he also couldn't disagree with anything that Betty said.

Betty looked like she was about to say something, but then something over Percy's shoulder caught her eye. "Well, I'll be fucked," she said.

Percy turned and saw a woman enter the shop. She wore a cloak of black velvet and had unpowdered red hair. At first, he thought he was looking at Flora Jennings, so strong was the resemblance, but then realized this woman was several years older, at least forty.

"And who would that be?" Percy asked. "Does Kit have a policy of only allowing women into the shop if they have red hair?"

"That's Scarlett," Betty said. And then, when Percy snorted in disbelief, she added, "Obviously it's not her real name, but she's Mistress Scarlett, you know?"

"Ah."

"And she's also—"

Betty was interrupted by the entrance of Rob from some-where else in the building. He strode over to Scarlett and em-braced her, all but lifting her off the ground. "Mother, darling," he said.

"She's Rob's *mother*?" Percy asked, astonished. "Which means that Flora is his sister?"

Betty gave him an appraising look. "I'm not sure about that. It could just be an uncanny likeness."

Percy regarded the pair and tried to recall Flora's face. Rob and Scarlett didn't resemble one another terribly, apart from the red hair and a suggestion of sharpness about the jaw and cheek-bones. Flora, in fact, looked more like Scarlett than Rob did. Rob looked more like— Percy tilted his head and searched his memory, but couldn't quite arrive at the resemblance.

Through the general din and clatter of the shop, Percy heard a heavy, uneven tread on the stairs and automatically turned his head in time to see Kit duck underneath the spider web. Percy had watched that blasted thing grow to shocking proportions in the past few weeks, and he would have taken it upon himself to dispose of it if not for the fact that Kit seemed to like it there. This time part of the web caught in Kit's hair—which, given the state of Kit's hair, was hardly surprising—and Kit carefully dis-entangled it. Then he murmured something that looked awfully like "beg pardon" to the spider.

Percy stared, some combination of emotions he preferred not to identify roiling in his heart. Then he crossed the room. "You're an industrious little monster," he told the spider. The spider did something ghastly with one of her neatly wrapped trophies. Percy decided not to think about that, either. "You wove a pretty web, but you are not in the least bit practically minded. One relates.

This is a terrible place for your home, however lovely I'm certain it is." He reached his hand up toward the creature.

"What are you doing?" Kit asked, sounding irate.

"She's going to wind up lost in your hair, and that's no life for an honest spider. I'm going to move her someplace where nobody will bother her and she can eat all the flies and midges she pleases. All right?" When Kit didn't object, Percy let the spider crawl onto his hand, somehow managing not to faint or shriek while doing so. "All right, madam, away you go," he said, carrying it over to the bookcases. "You'll make your home on the very top shelf, over where the proprietor sees fit to keep Mr. Hume. Nobody is in the least likely to disturb you there."

That accomplished, he dusted his hands off on his breeches and found Kit looking at him oddly, but escaped into the street before he had to figure out why.

Chapter 40

 hat's this?" Rob asked when Kit and Betty were sorting through the contents of the parcel Percy had left with them. The shop was closed, and they worked by the light of an oil lamp, separating out the items that could be sold immediately from those that would need to have monograms or other marks polished off.

Kit didn't answer right away, because it was more than obvious they were receiving stolen goods. The objects on the table were a motley assortment of silverware, handkerchiefs, earbobs, and buttons. Kit hadn't been surprised that Percy wanted to raise some quick money—in his circumstances, selling off a couple of shirt studs was honestly something he ought to have done quite a while ago. What surprised him was the sheer assortment of silverware on the table: Kit had counted spoons with at least eight distinct monograms. This could mean that Percy had been busily pilfering from every dinner table he visited, but given the earbobs, Kit rather thought he had help from the mysterious Marian.

"What did your mother want?" Betty asked Rob.

"To scold me, which is all anybody wants from me these days."

"Poor you. Imagine, people being upset with you after the stunt you pulled."

"I keep telling all of you that it was unavoidable. Consider how much it hurts my feelings not to be believed." Bending over the table, Rob picked up a spoon and held it up to the light. "Monogrammed," he said disapprovingly. Then he looked at a silver hairbrush. "And so is this. This is the Duke of Clare's coat of arms. Do you want to tell me what you're doing with the Duke of Clare's hairbrush?"

"More likely the duchess's, I should think," Kit said, his mouth dry. He had known he'd need to come clean to Rob at some point but had put it off time and again. "You know the job I've mentioned? The Duke of Clare is the mark."

Whatever Kit had expected from Rob, it wasn't total silence. It wasn't Rob putting a shoulder on Kit's arm and taking the seat beside him. Kit kept his attention on an ornate silver soup spoon. He didn't want to look at Rob, and he certainly didn't want to look at Betty.

"I would have told you before the job," Kit said. "It's only that the situation is a bit complicated."

"You're going to hold up the Duke of Clare's carriage. Yes, I'd damned well say it's complicated, especially since you're fucking his son."

Kit dropped the spoon to the table with a clatter. "I—what? You recognized him? You knew?" Kit's mind reeled. Rob and Betty were looking at one another, and Kit glanced between them. "What am I missing?"

"I told him not to involve himself in this mess," Betty told Rob. "But do you think he listened?"

Rob buried his head in his hands. When he looked up a moment later, he seemed to have come to some kind of decision. "You're in love with the Duke of Clare's son."

"I didn't say—" Kit began, but Rob cut him off.

"And together you're going to hold up his father. And why, exactly, is the duke's pretty son so eager to steal from his papa?"

"There's an item he wants. I believe it belonged to his mother. He says we can have everything else in the carriage."

"You idiot. He means to kill his father and let you hang for it."

"I don't think so."

"You would if you were thinking straight. He's used some combination of lust and knowledge of what the duke did to completely addle your senses. This scheme ought to be obvious even to a baby."

"When he first came here, he didn't know I had any particular reason to hate his father," Kit said, the excuse sounding feeble to his own ears.

"Where did he get your name, Kit?" Rob demanded. "Is there anyone who knows you're Gladhand Jack who doesn't know that the Duke of Clare had your wife transported? Because I can't think of any. He knows who you are, and he's setting you up."

"If Percy wanted to kill his father, I don't think he'd choose such a roundabout way," Kit said. "And I don't think he could—" He broke off. He had been about to say that he didn't think Percy could feign affection for him, but Percy could probably feign anything he pleased. And yet, Kit didn't think Percy was doing so.

When Kit told Percy that he adored him, he had been speaking the truth. And Percy's only response had been that Kit shouldn't. But that hadn't sounded like a warning so much as the protest of a person who didn't believe he deserved to be loved. It could all be an act, and Kit's refusal to believe so might just be because his prick—or, even worse, his heart—was not reliably rational.

He couldn't have said exactly when it happened, or why, but Kit found that he had come to trust Percy, had come to have faith in the man. He knew there was more to Percy's scheme than Percy had confessed: he had seen the way Percy measured out his words when speaking of his father's bigamy, weighing each one to make sure it wasn't too much. There was a good deal the man had left untold, but Kit felt certain it wasn't anything that would harm him.

"My mother told me someone was asking about you," Rob said. "I'd bet it was your lordling."

"Your mother was as surprised as I was to discover that I was doing a job for the Duke of Clare's son. She tried to persuade me not to," Kit said.

"If you think my mother isn't an accomplished actress, you've gone even softer in the head than I had thought, and believe me, I already think your judgment is frighteningly impaired," Rob said. "Have Tom do the job. Stay away from it."

"I need to be there."

"Oh, of course. You need to see Clare punished."

"No," Kit said immediately. "I do want Clare punished, and I'll be glad to see it happen with my own eyes. Of course I will." He felt his face heat as he spoke, knowing how much he was revealing. "But I need to be there to make sure Percy's all right."

Rob raked his hands through his hair and groaned. Betty swore and got up from the table.

Thinking he'd just as well give his friends time to complain about him behind his back, Kit reached for his walking stick and hauled himself up the stairs and into his bedroom. He sat on the edge of the bed, his heart racing and his stomach churning.

Even through the closed door, he could hear Betty and Rob talking. About him, no doubt.

Kit absently patted his hip in search of a flask that hadn't been there for a year. Instead, he stretched out an arm for the jug of water that sat on the washstand and swallowed a mouthful.

It was a long while before he heard footsteps on the stairs. It was Rob, of course.

"Mind if I come in?" Rob asked, cracking the door open. He had a cup in his hand.

Kit gestured for him to enter, and Rob sat on the bed beside him and handed him the cup of tea. "Betty made it, so it's all right."

"Thanks," Kit said.

"So," Rob said. "What do you need me to do to help you with this job?"

Kit didn't ask whether Rob was agreeing to help as an olive branch to Kit or as a way to ensure Kit didn't meet any trouble. "Only the usual things. Make sure something happens at the coaching inn to delay any other carriages in the duke's party—a loose axle or a horse needing to be reshod. Check the carriage for any pistols stowed under the cushions. The drunker you can get the coachmen and any outriders, the better. If they have any weapons, see if you can pinch them. After the duke's carriage leaves the inn, ride ahead to where Percy and I are waiting."

"Percy is he now?"

"I'm hardly going to call him Lord Holland."

"I suppose not," Rob sighed.

"I know you and Betty think I'm being foolish, but I've

planned this job as well as I planned any other job. Better, even, because it's amazing how much more clearly you can think when you aren't foxed half the time. I've spent time in the duke's stables and know that his horses are skittish and his servants are a close-mouthed group. He'll travel with his own horses, even though that slows his pace, because he doesn't trust them to strangers."

"I only want you to be safe, and the more emotional a job is, the less likely it is to go off without a hitch. You lose your instinct to back off."

Kit had the distinct impression that Rob was talking about himself. "Are you certain you don't want to tell me what's been bothering you?" Kit asked.

"Nothing's bothering me," Rob answered.

"I'm not going to pry, but we both know that you haven't been yourself since you got back. And that's fine. Obviously, whatever kept you away was serious enough to—well, serious enough to keep you away. But if you want to talk to someone, you know I won't spill your secrets." Kit swallowed, suddenly overwhelmed by the sense that he was losing the best friend he had ever had. "I never have, you know."

"I do. I do know. But I can't. Trust me when I say that it would complicate your life more than you can even imagine."

"Even so, Rob. When haven't we been willing to complicate our lives for one another? That's how friendship works." At least, Kit had thought so.

Chapter 41

The weather, Percy decided, was suspiciously fine. It was the sort of crisp and clear late autumn day that made summer seem a distant and slightly vulgar memory and the coming winter seem almost implausible. Hardly fifty miles outside London, the fog and smoke were nowhere to be seen in the Oxfordshire countryside.

Truly, Percy could not have chosen more pleasant weather for a highway robbery.

Before leaving, Kit had shown Percy a map, pointing with one callused index finger at a place between Tetsworth and an area simply marked "pasture."

"See that bend in the road? There'll be a copse of trees right there," Kit had said, a glint of excitement in his eyes. "It's not so different from the place I showed you in Hampstead. Be there at dusk."

They traveled separately, Kit and the sharpshooter together in a stagecoach, Percy on horseback, and Rob by his own means.

Early in the morning, Percy dressed in his finest riding costume and told Collins not to wait up for him, hoping the valet would interpret this to mean Percy planned a spree of debauchery. Then he rode to an inn, bought a round of drinks for the patrons, loudly announced his plan to buy a hunting dog from a man in Kent whose dog had recently given birth to a litter of puppies. That accomplished, he got back on the road in the direction of Oxfordshire, changed into nondescript clothes and removed his wig, and arrived at the designated copse of trees well before dusk and with a horse who had a distinct air of being hard done by.

He had brought with him a loaf of bread and a flask of ale but was too nervous to do more than break off crumbs of crust and roll them between his fingers. He checked the position of the sun in the sky. It was not quite dusk, but it was close, and still there was no sign of Kit.

There was some shameful part of him that hoped Kit and the girl did not turn up. Then Percy wouldn't have to go through with this.

There was an even more shameful part of him that desperately needed Kit to come, because otherwise Percy would know himself to be abandoned.

Right when he was about to give up deciding which hope was more shameful, he heard soft footsteps and turned to find Kit approaching him. With him was a slight figure in breeches and which Percy would not have guessed to be a girl if Kit hadn't informed him beforehand.

Percy was certain he had schooled his face into something suitably bland but still Kit greeted him with a long look and a warm hand on his shoulder. Then Kit reached into the satchel that was slung over his shoulder and pulled out Percy's black prizefighting leathers, which Percy had given him the previous day. "Change," Kit said.

Percy, spurred more by the vestiges of some old and defunct sense of propriety than by any actual principles, opened his mouth to object on the grounds that a girl was mere yards away. But then he went behind a tree and did as he was told. He plaited his hair and tucked it into one of Kit's decrepit tricorns, then took the false scar, which was still intact after he had peeled it off the last time, and stuck it to his face.

When he emerged, Kit looked him up and down. "Good," he said. Then he took a flask from the satchel and handed it to Percy. "Drink."

"Are we only speaking in monosyllables today?" Percy asked, and only when he had spoken did he realize that those were the first words to have left his mouth since Kit arrived. He opened the flask and sniffed it, dismayed to discover that it contained gin. It was filled to the very top, so he guessed that Kit must not care much for gin, either. He took a sip, and then took another one. When he made to hand it back to Kit, the man shook his head.

"You keep it."

"Is my terror that obvious?" Percy asked, pitching his voice low enough that the girl, who was sitting on the ground examining the fletching of her arrows, would not hear.

"No," Kit said, looking him in the eye. "You always hide it well. Do you remember what I told you about the trick to a good holdup?"

"Not caring whether you live or die," Percy said immediately, because how could he forget that?

"I lied."

Percy looked at Kit closely. Kit wasn't as bad a liar as Percy had once supposed. He was just out of practice and hadn't quite got control of his tells. Now, for instance, his eyes were opened a bit too wide, as if he were actively trying not to look shifty. And his hands were fisted at his sides, as if he were trying not to fidget.

Percy decided not to call him on this lie. There would be no point to quarreling over it right now. And besides, this was Kit's way of telling Percy to be careful, which was just another way of Kit saying that he cared.

Instead of answering, he leaned in and kissed Kit on the cheek.

Every time a coach passed, Percy thought he might be sick, even though he knew it wouldn't be his father's coach. The plan was for Rob to ride ahead and warn Kit and Percy when the duke had left his last inn.

But the sun set, and still there was no sign of Rob. Hattie climbed a tree and got into position.

"Oi, Kit," she said after a while. "I can see a coach and six coming up the road. There's a picture painted on the door."

"Bugger," Kit said. "Something must have held Rob up."

"Do you want to go to the inn and see if he's all right?" Percy asked.

"No, I want you to go into the road and hold that carriage up."

"We don't even know if that's my father," Percy protested.

"It's a coach and six on the right road at the right time." He spoke with a calm that Percy would have thought impossible in the circumstances. "You have one minute to decide. It's your choice."

In the silence, Percy could hear the hoofbeats in the distance, indistinguishable from the beating of his heart.

"All right," he said, and from his pocket he pulled the kerchief that he meant to use as a mask. "All right," he repeated.

Kit took the kerchief from him and deftly tied it around the back of his head, then did the same for himself. He handed Percy a pistol and patted him on the shoulder, then Percy walked into the road.

Percy waited, feeling exposed and alone in the middle of the dusty road. As the carriage bore down on him, he saw that he recognized the horses and the coachman. Even though they had gone over this countless times, he was amazed that the carriage actually stopped.

"Your money or your life," Percy called out, deepening his voice so it wouldn't be recognized, and trying very hard not to pay attention to the fact that one of the outriders—a man he recognized as one of his father's enormous guards—had drawn a pistol. "But I'd rather have the money."

On that signal, Kit cleared his throat and held up his pistol, letting the moonlight glint menacingly off the steel, and Hattie fired an arrow directly over the heads of the horses.

He heard rustling from within the carriage and sauntered over as if he weren't terrified.

But when he opened the carriage door, what he saw didn't make sense. Because it wasn't his father holding out a coin purse. It was Marian.

"Take this and leave," she said haughtily, her face angled toward him so he could see her plainly in the moonlight, while his father remained half-concealed by shadows.

"I'm a highwayman, not a crossing sweep," he answered. "I choose what I take and when I leave. Empty your pockets, sir," he said to his father.

For a moment he thought his father wouldn't comply, but then, with a sigh, his father pulled off one of his rings and handed it to Marian. Then he reached inside his coat pocket.

He could see the outline of the book through his father's coat. And then his father shifted, and he could see a corner of the book visible above the edge of the pocket. He could reach out and take it. And so he did. As his hand darted out, he met his father's eyes.

The last thing he remembered was the sound of the pistol being fired.

Chapter 42

$\mathcal{L}$ ater, Kit went over the events of that night again and again, trying to figure out when exactly he ought to have known that something was wrong.

Rob's absence ought to have tipped him off, of course, but he had been able to explain that away.

The way Percy's hands shook might have been a clue.

But then everything had gone as planned. Percy spoke his lines, the carriage stopped. The outriders drew their weapons, but none aimed with anything like intent. It was all perfectly typical.

But there had been a woman in the carriage, and that hadn't been right at all. The duchess was supposed to be in town, and Percy hadn't mentioned that his father might travel with a mistress.

Before he could make sense of the woman's presence, a pistol shot rang out, one of the horses startled, and as the coachman tried to get the animals settled, there came the sound of another shot. Then Percy emerged from the carriage, covered in blood.

Kit started for him, but then one of the armed outriders dismounted, aiming a pistol directly at Percy's head. From where he stood, Kit could see Percy's eyes, wide and dark.

"Go to the duke!" the outrider shouted to the coachman.

"Stay exactly where you are," Kit called out. He drew his own weapon. From above, an arrow flew past, missing the outrider's arm by inches.

Then the woman's voice sounded, loud and clear above the shouting outriders and whinnying horses. "Get back on your horse, you oaf. You're of no use to the duke lingering about here. We must get the duke to safety. Drive, Higgins! Fast!" The carriage took off down the road in a cloud of dust and accompanied by the sound of braying horses.

"Where were you hit?" Kit demanded. Percy was walking, at least, so it couldn't be too bad, but even in the moonlight Kit could see that he was pale. "Hattie!" he called.

"I don't think I was hit," Percy said, his voice thin. "I can't be sure."

He was in shock, Kit realized. "The lantern, Hattie!"

"I got the book," Percy said.

"Bugger the book," Kit snarled. "And bugger all these buttons." His hands felt all thumbs as he tried to open the blood-soaked waistcoat.

"And I got Marian's coin purse," Percy said, with a slightly hysterical laugh.

"And what in hell was she doing there?"

"Kit, I don't know."

Hattie had arrived with the lantern by then. "Kit, we have to move him."

"He's injured."

"Getting hanged won't make him any better. We need to get out of here."

The girl was right. "Run. Take this." He took the coin purse from Percy's hand and thrust it at Hattie in exchange for the lantern. "Run. I'll take care of him. When you get to London, tell Betty exactly what happened. Do you know how to get back to town?"

She nodded and ran off.

"Kit," Percy said, looking down at himself and at the blood-soaked clothes that were now illuminated by the lantern. "Damn," he whispered, and fainted.

"I've got you," Kit said, even though he didn't have Percy so much as he broke Percy's fall. "Wake up," he said, shaking Percy's shoulders. "Damn you, this is not the time. I'll bring you—Christ and all the buggering saints, I don't know where to bring you or how I'm meant to get you there." He held the lantern up, while patting Percy down with his other hand, trying to find where the blood was coming from.

Finally, he found a tear in the fabric, a hole in the leather breeches the size of his thumb. Percy hissed when Kit touched it, which at least meant he was coming to. Even with the light from the lantern, Kit couldn't tell how bad a wound he was dealing with, and he didn't dare waste another minute in this spot when they could be found at any moment. He tore the kerchief from his own neck and tied it around Percy's thigh, hoping it would at least slow the bleeding. He tied the knot, counted to ten. And when he touched the spot over the wound, his fingers came away dry.

"Percy, please, I'm begging you to wake up." He took the flask from Percy's pocket and splashed some gin onto the man's face. "Come on now." Percy's eyelids began to flutter, and Kit let out a shaky breath.

"My father," Percy said.

"Later. Now, see if you can get to your feet." Kit stood and held out a hand, bracing his own weight on his walking stick.

When Percy reached out, his hand was cold, but he stood with little effort. "As I said, I don't think I'm injured."

"The blood that's all over you argues otherwise."

"I don't believe that's my blood," Percy said. "And the less we talk about blood right now, the better."

Kit realized for the first time that Percy didn't have the pistol in his hand. "Where is the weapon?"

"I believe it's in the carriage."

"If you can mount your horse, you need to do it."

It took Percy a few false tries, and in the end Kit had to all but shove him into the saddle. Kit still couldn't tell whether it was blood loss or shock that was affecting Percy. All he knew was that they needed to get far away from this place, and they needed to do it now, but between them they only had one horse and two working legs.

And this was why Kit should have hired someone else for this job. Kit should have stayed in London, because in his condition he was worse than useless to Percy. Well, he could take himself to task later; now he needed to get Percy to safety. If he remembered this part of Oxfordshire at all correctly, a short walk through the woods would bring him to Jenny's gran. Kit's leg was in a sorry state, and he'd pay for this tomorrow, but he still had some strength left.

"Get on behind me," Percy said.

"Your horse can't hold us both," Kit said. Christ, the horse looked like he needed food and water, too. "Come on."

Percy didn't even ask where they were going, which could not be a good sign. He let Kit guide him through the woods, quiet and almost docile. Every few minutes—every few seconds, if he were honest with himself, Kit brushed his hands over Percy's wounded leg and checked his fingers for blood. It didn't take long for them to come away bright red.

The moon was high in the sky when they came to the part of the woods he knew. Past an old well, across a shallow stream, and there was the cottage, firelight flickering in the windows and smoke coming from the chimney.

Jenny's grandmother might not even live there anymore. It wasn't as if Kit had kept in touch. Well, even if strangers answered the door, it was better than sleeping rough or raising suspicions at an inn where news of the robbery may have already spread. This was their best bet.

When he raised his arms to help Percy down from the saddle, Percy scoffed and tried to dismount on his own, and would have fallen if not for Kit's arm around his middle.

"We're stopping at this cottage," Kit said into Percy's ear. "You're Edward Percy. You're no relation of the duke. You're a friend of mine from London."

When Kit knocked, the door was answered by a woman with a long white plait. It took Kit too long to realize it was Jenny's grandmother.

"Granny Dot," Kit began, then corrected himself. "Mistress—"

"Christopher. I should have known that if I ever were to lay eyes on you again, it would be on a moonlit night in the company of a blood-soaked stranger. Dennis!" A lad of about seven or eight appeared behind the old woman's skirts, his mouth open in a yawn. "Set up a pallet bed in the barn and light the brazier." Then, to Kit, "That's John's youngest."

"And how is John?" John had been Jenny's oldest brother.

"Dead," Dorothy said curtly. "They're all dead, except you, me, and Dennis."

Kit realized Percy was looking between him and Dorothy. "This is Mr. Percy. He fell off his horse and injured himself. We need a place to sleep for a night or two, some supper, and some hay for the horse, if you can spare it."

"You'd be welcome to stay longer than that, but I imagine you have your own reasons for not lingering. I imagine you always have," Dorothy said, not unkindly.

The lad came back then and showed them to the barn, which was little more than a shack that Kit thought might at one time have housed a milk cow. Kit could hardly look at the boy for how much he resembled Jenny, for how much he seemed like a ghost of what Hannah might have looked like.

"Sit," Kit ordered Percy once the boy had left them to go tend to the horse. "And strip. I need to check you for wounds."

"Are you mad? It's freezing in here."

The barn was drafty and smelled of damp old straw, but it wasn't the worst place Kit had ever spent the night, and once the brazier was lit it would be fine.

Kit unsheathed the dagger at his hip. "Strip or I'm cutting those breeches off you."

Percy raised his eyebrows. "In another context that would have been a very fun game indeed."

Kit supposed it was a good sign if Percy was talking like that. It was not a good sign, however, that Percy couldn't seem to un-lace his boots. Kit, ignoring his leg's screaming protests, managed to kneel on the ground before Percy and get his boots off. He untied the bloody kerchief. "Lift your hips up," he said, and tugged Percy's breeches off. Percy gasped when the leather peeled off the wound, but he kept still and didn't complain.

"Drink," Kit said, handing Percy the flask of gin. Percy complied, and then before capping it, Kit poured a generous slosh over the wound.

Percy flinched and swore. "You could have warned me."

The blood cleaned away, Kit could make out the contours of the wound. It was about two inches long on the outside of Percy's thigh, as if Percy had been trying to step out of the path of the pistol ball and had nearly managed it. Kit let out a breath he hadn't realized he was holding. From the satchel, he removed a clean kerchief and tied it around the wound.

And then he bent and rested his forehead on Percy's knee and let the relief and exhaustion wash over him.

"Shh," Percy said, his fingers tangling in Kit's hair. "It's all right."

Kit opened his mouth to protest that of course it was all right and Percy could just shut up about it, but when he tried, all that came out was a sob, and he realized his cheeks were wet with tears.

So he let Percy pet his head, and it occurred to him that Percy wasn't as awkward at soothing as Kit might have guessed. He said things like "hush, hush," and "there, now, I have you," as if they came naturally to him.

"What have I done to you," Kit said.

"What have *you* done to *me*?" Percy scoffed, his hand stilling in Kit's hair. "You have it all backward, you great lummox. Now let's go to sleep before you say anything even stupider."

And Kit was so relieved to hear that edge of comfortable

rudeness in Percy's voice, more reassured by it than he could have been by any gentle words.

The night was cold, so Kit told himself that it was only practical for them to lie pressed up against one another. Kit fell asleep with his head buried in the fine hair at the base of Percy's neck, one arm thrown around Percy's middle. And if he was dimly aware that Percy was still wide-awake, he didn't let that stop sleep from overtaking him.

Chapter 43

*P*ercy had never slept on the ground in his life. He had also never been shot. Nor had he spent an entire night in another man's arms. It was an evening of firsts, all of which combined to put him into a state quite unfit for sleep. He shut his eyes and might have managed to doze off once or twice, but he kept being startled by the sounds of owls hooting and leaves rustling, or by the solid presence of Kit behind him.

Or by the throbbing ache in his thigh.

Christ, he knew it was only a graze. He had known as soon as it happened—before it happened, even, because he had thrown himself against the side of the carriage to avoid being hit directly. He knew it was hardly any worse than the gash he got in his arm during the prizefight, but its existence was an unwanted reminder of the predicament he was in.

All their efforts had come to naught, even though Percy now had the book. The central problem remained: a blackmailer was about to expose the duke as a bigamist. If the duke was dead, they could not hope to extract funds from him, and as his illegitimate son and false wife, they could not inherit anything from the estate. If he lived, they certainly couldn't plan on extorting any funds from him because—Christ—because Marian had shot him. Percy could hardly believe it. If the duke lived, they'd be lucky to escape the gallows. He supposed he'd have to run away.

Percy didn't know where this left him. He didn't know what his next step needed to be, or what his future might look like. The less he thought about what Marian had done and why, the better. By all rights, he ought to be miserable. And yet he felt strangely—not peaceful, exactly, nor resigned, but somewhere in between.

Kit began to stir well before dawn. Percy, taking this as a sign that it was time to give up any hope of sleep, tried to sit up, only to feel Kit's arm tighten around him. Kit grumbled something along the lines of "Not yet," and "Stay," and Percy was sorely tempted. But he also knew what would come next, and sure enough, he felt Kit go still, heard a sharply drawn breath. And there, that was Kit realizing where he was, who he was with, and what had brought them there.

"I'm so sorry," Percy said, because he hadn't said it the day before.

"So am I." Kit's voice was sleep rough, and the words were more growl than actual speech. He still hadn't loosened his hold on Percy, though, so Percy turned in his arms.

"How is your leg?"

"How is *my* leg?"

"It didn't escape my attention how badly you were limping by the end of the night."

"It's pretty fucking terrible," Kit said after a moment. "But nothing I haven't been through before. It'll be fine to walk on."

Percy decided to postpone that argument. He got to his feet, gritting his teeth through the pain in his thigh. The pistol ball had torn through about an inch of muscle. The scar would be unsightly and he was afraid nothing could be done to salvage those leather breeches, but the shot had missed both bone and artery; as long as he escaped fever, he would recover. Carefully, he stepped into his riding breeches, thankful for once that they were loosely tailored.

The barn door creaked open, and the little boy stuck his head in. He carried a jug and a basket. "Gran thought you might be hungry. We haven't any tea or sugar," he added, shifting from foot to foot.

Percy looked between Kit and the boy. Last night, even through his fog of pain and confusion, he noticed the way Kit looked at the child as if he were seeing a ghost. Kit had said little about his past, but from what Percy had been able to piece together, it was filled with ghosts.

"Thank you," Percy said, taking the jug and basket from the boy.

"Your horse doesn't like me very much," said the boy.

"Balius doesn't like anyone very much. Including me," said Percy. "But he's strong and fast and he puts up with me. Did he try to hurt you?"

The child gave Percy a withering look. "I know how to take care of horses."

"Ah. Silly me. Thank you for taking care of him for me, then."

"Dennis comes from a long line of horse thieves," Kit said after the child left. "So he really does know how to look after horses."

"Do I need to worry about my horse being stolen out from under my nose?"

"I don't think those two are still in the business," Kit said dryly.

Percy uncovered the basket, revealing a pile of oatcakes. He couldn't have eaten if he tried, so he handed the basket to Kit. Instead, Percy sniffed the contents of the jug. It was beer, probably home brewed, and really not something Percy would have chosen, but he took a long drink anyway. It was bitter and strong, and Percy suspected that given his empty stomach, it wouldn't be long before he felt the effects. He passed the jug to Kit, but Kit waved it away.

"Dorothy's beer is too much for me," Kit said, and Percy realized that apart from a few sips of ale, he had never seen Kit drink anything but tea and coffee.

"Well, I intend to get fully soused, thank you. You'll have to tie me to the horse."

Kit snorted. He was being very patient in not asking Percy too many questions about what had happened during the robbery, and Percy couldn't tell if Kit didn't want to know or if he guessed that Percy didn't know how to talk about it.

"Marian was there," Percy said when the jug of beer was half-empty and his thoughts had begun to take on a gauzy texture. "She was supposed to be in London."

Kit paused in shaking the hay out of a blanket. "I gathered."

"I think—" But Percy didn't know what to think, or rather he didn't want to know, so he took another drink.

"If there's any chance she's going to identify you as the man who shot the duke, then we need to lie low for a while," Kit said.

This was putting it very generously, Percy realized. Kit had refrained from speculating about whether Marian had set Percy up, even though he surely had to suspect as much. Hell, Percy had let the idea cross his mind as he lay awake, trying to make sense of what he had seen.

Percy's instinct was to protect Marian. His instinct was to lie through his teeth if it meant shielding Marian.

But there was something else tugging at him, some sense of—duty, maybe, to Kit. He had brought Kit into this predicament, and he owed Kit at least the bare bones of information.

"My father tried to shoot me. Rather, he did shoot me," Percy said, gesturing at his leg.

Kit nodded slowly. Presumably, he had guessed as much.

"But he recognized me. Before he shot, I mean. I shouldn't be surprised. There was no love lost between us, and I knew he valued that book over everything else. I shouldn't be surprised," he repeated. "I really shouldn't be."

Kit was looking at him very closely now, and for a minute Percy worried that Kit planned to comfort him, as if "I'm sorry your father tried to murder you after you pulled a pistol on him" were a reasonable sort of sentiment, but instead he stayed sensibly across the barn.

"What about the second shot?" Kit asked.

Percy passed a hand over his jaw, cringing at the unfamiliar sensation of stubble. "Marian took the pistol from my hand and shot my father." She had shot the man in the chest at close range, then all but shoved Percy out of the carriage and ordered the coachman to drive on. Those were the facts Percy was certain of, and now Kit had them as well.

"Do you think she planned to kill him all along?" Kit asked after a minute. This, Percy supposed, was a polite way of asking whether Marian had set Percy up.

"I don't know," Percy said honestly. "If she just wanted to kill him, she could have done it a dozen different ways. There was no reason to bring me into it." He didn't bother saying that Marian would have let him in on any plan she was concocting, because it wasn't true. He had known for weeks that she was up to something, sneaking in and out of the house in the middle of the night, dressed as she was.

"There was a moment," Percy went on, "after my father shot me, when Marian looked stunned. I think she saw that my father recognized me. I could be wrong, but I think she realized that if my father could kill one child, then her own daughter would never be safe." Percy swallowed. This might be nothing more than a fairy story that he had invented to make himself feel better about being betrayed by not only his father but his closest friend.

"She may also have realized that *you'd* never be safe," Kit said.

And that was the kindest thing Kit could possibly have said. It settled something within Percy's chest. "When do you want to leave?" he asked.

"I think you and your horse—and me, really—could do with another day of rest. I'd like to know your leg has stopped bleeding before I put you back on a horse."

"All right," Percy said, and for a moment let himself enjoy the novel sensation of being looked after.

When Kit stepped out to talk to the old woman, Percy rooted through his satchel until he found the book. Other than the cover now being splattered with blood, it was exactly as he remembered. He ran a finger over the faded gold leaf on the cover, the worn leather of the binding.

When he opened it, he saw that it was indeed a Bible, as his cousin had insisted, and Percy hadn't believed. It was a Bible, with a list of names, dates, and locations written in his mother's tight, spidery handwriting. When he flipped through the pages, he saw what appeared to be random words underscored, and with a dizzy sense of realization, he understood that he was looking at either an encrypted message or the key to a code.

Chapter 44

Dorothy looked at Kit as if she half expected him to disappear. When Kit took her kettle outside to fill at the pump, she seemed surprised that he came back, as if maybe she expected him to run off and take the kettle with him.

"I'll send Dennis to the village to see if there's any news," she said. "I reckon that whatever brought you here might be the sort of news that travels. He knows better than to talk about any strangers who might be sleeping in the barn."

"Thank you," he said sincerely. "I don't suppose the——" His voice caught, and he broke off. "Is anyone living at my old cottage?"

She gave him a look that was equal parts soft and reproachful. "It fell down years ago, Kit."

He swallowed. "Of course it did." He went outside then, desperate for fresh air. He found Percy hauling buckets of cold water from the pump to fill an old tin washtub that he had set up in the barn.

"Are you going to heat that water?" Kit asked.

Percy's cheeks turned pink. "I didn't want to bother anyone."

"Well, you freezing to death would be more of a bother. Dennis!" Kit fished a halfpenny from his coin purse and gave it to the boy in exchange for his trouble, and then leaned against the barn wall.

Percy came to lean beside him. "Do you know," he said in a confiding tone, his forehead wrinkled, "I saw that child walk past earlier with a brace of pheasants. I think these people are poachers."

Kit laughed. "That they are. And so was I. And so was my wife. So were a lot of people who lived on your father's land, if we wanted to make ends meet." After the words left his mouth, he held his breath, not knowing how Percy would react.

"I wondered why you hated my father. If you were one of his tenants, that would certainly explain it," Percy said, not without bitterness. He didn't ask about Jenny, but he took Kit's hand and squeezed it, as if he knew the story there wasn't a happy one.

Once the bath was full, Kit closed the barn door to shut out the worst of the drafts. He watched in some amusement as Percy drew a bar of pure white soap from his satchel, followed by a sponge and a sheet of linen.

"What else do you have in there?" Kit asked. "A feather bed?"

"I assure you that if I had a feather bed, I would have brought it out last night. Not that I'm complaining about your friend's hospitality," he quickly added.

Kit didn't pretend not to watch as Percy stripped. First, he wanted to be sure Percy wasn't hiding any wounds—there was only so much he had been able to see by the lamplight the previous night. And second, well, he wanted to.

Percy pulled his shirt over his head and cast his eyes around, obviously looking for somewhere to put it, before finally shoving it into his satchel, unfolded. Presumably, he was used to always having a servant at hand to deal with things like clothes that needed washing. Kit wondered what Percy's plans for the future were. If the duke were dead, what did that mean for Percy's extortion scheme? Would Percy know how to live without fine soap and hot baths? And then Kit felt stupid for even wondering—of course Percy would figure it out. He had gone from being the pampered scion of a noble family to consorting with criminals and prizefighters. Kit knew a bone-deep longing to be around long enough to watch Percy find his feet again.

Percy pulled off his boots and buckskins and stepped into the bath.

Kit had known that Percy was strong, but it was something else to see the lean muscle that lay under his fair skin. And he had known Percy was beautiful, but it was something else to see the span of his shoulders and the curve of his arse.

Percy looked over his shoulder at Kit before lowering himself into the bath. "If you're staying, you should come over here."

Not needing to be told twice, Kit dragged a stool beside the tub and sat. "There something you want?" Kit was decidedly not in the mood himself, but there were stranger things than getting aroused by narrow escapes from danger.

Percy swallowed and shook his head, not meeting Kit's eyes. "No, I just had too much of that beer and I'm maudlin. I figure having you nearby will stop me from crying into the bath as I wash my father's blood from my hands, almost literally."

"Sometimes you need to cry into the bath."

"Somehow I doubt you ever do that," Percy said, soaping up his arms. The cut Kit had dressed over a week ago was now an almost invisible pink line, soon hidden by soapsuds.

"You'd be surprised. Well, not into the bath. For me it was crying into my gin, but same principle."

Percy slid lower in the tub, wetting his hair and working some suds through it. "Collins will be outraged that I used bath soap in my hair. He probably won't speak to me for days and will leave bottles of hair tonic around my apartments in retaliation. Assuming, that is, that I'm not forced to flee for my life. A life of anonymous exile probably doesn't involve much in the way of hair tonic."

Kit could have reassured him that the duke was almost certainly dead, but that wasn't what Percy needed to hear. "You'll get by," he said instead. "You're clever and you're strong."

Percy gave him as incredulous a look as a man could deliver with bubbles all over his head. "I'm the opposite of strong. It's all a facade. It's acting."

Kit's heart twisted with some unspeakable, unwanted fondness. Percy was somehow still young or naive enough to think that there was any difference between being strong and acting strong. And again, Kit found himself wanting to be there when Percy figured it out, when he learned what he was worth.

As Percy struggled to wash his back, Kit wordlessly took the sponge from his hand and took over.

"My father used to let me win at chess," Percy said as Kit ran the sponge over the nape of his neck. "I thought it was because he didn't want me to feel bad about losing, but then I realized it was because that made the match faster."

Kit didn't understand at first why Percy was telling him that, why that fact mattered now, more than any other detail he could have called up about his father. But he realized that Percy was sharing with him one moment of stark disappointment, when a gesture he had thought to be one of love was revealed to be one of indifference. He had been shot by his father, who had been indifferent to him. And now he was trying to figure out how—or whether—to grieve a man who simply hadn't cared.

Kit dipped the sponge into the warm water and washed the shell of Percy's ear. He couldn't imagine anyone being indifferent to this man. Hating him, maybe. Loving him, certainly. But indifference just seemed impossible.

Percy rinsed his hair and stood. Kit watched the water sluice off a body that was unmarred but for yesterday's wound and felt a surge of relief that nothing worse had befallen the man. He shook out the sheet of linen and held it out for Percy to step into, then wrapped him in both the sheet and his arms and held him there, just for a moment.

The water was still warm, and Kit figured he ought to take advantage of it, so he shucked his clothes and stepped into the tub. He felt Percy's gaze on him, and didn't need to check to know that he would have been looking at Kit's scar. It was a spiderweb of ropy red marks that spread from the side of his thigh to above his hip. His instinct was to hide himself in the water, but he made himself turn to face Percy.

"It looks worse than it feels."

"I'm certain you're lying."

"Yeah, well. No use complaining." He sat, conscious of how it hurt even to bend at the hip to fold himself into the tub.

Still wrapped only in the sheet, Percy sat on the stool that Kit had occupied. "Have you ever thought about not walking so much?"

Kit snorted. "Every day. Betty only wants to tie me to the

chair most afternoons." He lathered up, using the soap Percy had brought. It smelled like flowers. "Christ, what did this cost? No, never let me know. Look, before I got hurt, I was always either on my feet or on my horse. I'm still figuring out how to be still, how to—how to be me, I suppose, but with a leg that doesn't work. I'm not there yet."

Percy's eyes were fixed on him, clear and wide and filled with an expression that Kit didn't dare give a name to. "You're good at figuring things out. We both are."

Kit nodded, and evidently Percy decided he had had enough of earnestness, because he spent the rest of Kit's bath alternately insulting his hair and ogling him.

"That was something I wanted to do better," Percy said after they were both clean and dressed and eating hard cheese and apples. "Taking care of the tenants, I mean. When I inherited, I wanted to be more reasonable about rents and maybe build a school." His cheeks colored. "I know that's all a moot point, now. I can talk all day about the fine things I planned to do, but none of it will ever come to anything. And I'll never know if I'd have been a better landlord than my father."

"No such thing as a good landlord," Kit said, his mouth full of crisp apple.

"I— What?"

Kit swallowed. "There are horrible ones, like your father. And there are ones who manage to refrain from doing actual evil. But I've never heard of a good one."

Percy opened his mouth, then snapped it shut. He was turning over Kit's words instead of immediately protesting, which was more than Kit would have expected.

"Come on," Kit said, when they had finished eating. "Can you walk five minutes?" Kit wasn't sure if *he* could walk five minutes, but he was going to try anyway.

He led Percy along a still-familiar path through the woods, much more overgrown now than it had been ten years earlier, when either he or Jenny or one of the others walked it every day. Now, he supposed, Dennis and Dorothy still walked this route to get to the village, or it would have been completely absorbed by the forest.

He was glad Dorothy warned him that the house had fallen down, because its absence was so disorienting that Kit at first thought he had taken a wrong turn. A couple of saplings were already growing where the floor had once been. Most of the stones had been taken away to repair walls or build new homes.

"This was where I lived when I first got married," Kit said. "We were eighteen," he added, as if that were an explanation. "And then—things went wrong." He wasn't going to recite the series of events. He was going to give himself that kindness, at least here, in front of the rubble that had been his hope. "The pub was gone and my parents were dead. It all happened so fast. And then Jenny had a baby." He swallowed, trying to collect himself, conscious of all Percy's attention on him. "It was a bad winter. She shot a deer. Her lot were all horse thieves, sheep thieves, poachers, coin clippers. I think an uncle was a counterfeiter." He wasn't going to get into how he had asked her not to, begged her not to. That wasn't the point, and he didn't want to make himself out to be overly bothered by breaking the law, when the ten years since had thoroughly put the lie to that notion. "She was caught and your father sentenced her to be transported. She died on the ship." He tried not to remember when she had been taken away from him and Hannah; he tried not to imagine her last weeks on that ship. But standing here, it was hard to keep those thoughts at bay. He gripped the end of his walking stick until his fingers cramped.

"And the baby?" Percy asked in a voice that was hardly louder than the sound of the breeze moving dead leaves around the forest floor.

Kit gestured at the base of the ancient oak tree that still stood at the east side of what had been his home. "I thought the tree was as good a grave marker as any, but I was half out of my mind and possibly not making the best choices. Rob dug the hole," he added, although he didn't know why that seemed like an important detail.

"What was the baby's name?"

"Hannah. She was six months old. I did my best after Jenny was gone, but—" He couldn't go on unless he wanted to start blubbering, and he didn't think he could stand to start shedding tears about this again. Not after so much time. Not with the bloody Duke of Clare's son beside him.

But when he dared to look at Percy, he saw that the man was doing a terrible job himself of fighting back tears. Something about Percy's secondhand grief dragged Kit out of the past, and he was seeing his own grief through the space of ten years' time, removed enough that he could feel sorry for the person he had been while remembering who he was now.

"I would have thought you'd be a prettier crier than that," Kit observed, hoping it would cut the tension, and failing miserably due to the catch in his voice. "Percy, love, you don't want to be that man. You don't want to be the man handing down sentences, ruining lives. Your life isn't what you expected it to be, but—" He didn't know how to finish that. He didn't know how to say that he was glad to know that Percy would never have the sort of power that could ruin lives on a whim.

Percy nodded. "I'm so sorry. And thank you for telling me."

They walked back to Dorothy's cottage in silence.

Chapter 45

"I need to see Marian," Percy said that night when he couldn't hold it in anymore.

"You don't know if you're wanted for your father's murder," Kit pointed out. They were lying on the barn floor, tucked under a single blanket, staring at the roof beams as if they were particularly interesting.

"You can wait here. Or go back to London. Or do whatever you please. I'm going to Cheveril Castle and talking to Marian."

"You realize she might have said *I* shot the duke, don't you? She might not have been setting you up, but me." Kit groaned and rubbed a hand over his jaw. In the darkness, Percy could hear the rasp of a callused thumb over stubble. "Rob tried to convince me that you were setting me up, that you had found out about my history with your father and were trying to take advantage of me. I told him that was impossible. But Marian may have done precisely that. Where did she get my name?"

"I'm not certain. She was rather cagey on that point." Percy didn't want to concede that Marian had been setting anybody up, but he also didn't want to waste his breath arguing that point.

He turned his head so he could see Kit's profile. "I'm glad you knew I wouldn't do that."

Kit didn't turn his head. "So am I."

"In any event, I don't think you need to worry about being set up for the robbery or the shooting. The coachman and outriders saw a slim, fair man with a scar who walked without a limp."

"I was on the side of the road."

"You faded into the shadows. The only part of you that was visible was your pistol. Besides, if you're worried about being mixed up in this, it's all the more reason for you to get back to London and act like nothing happened."

"It's all the more reason for me to stay with you," Kit said. "If she has any scruples about setting you up, then being with you is the best alibi I could hope for. And if she doesn't, then I'm fucked anyway."

Percy glared at Kit's profile. "Well, I'm going to Cheveril Castle. It's only a few miles from here." He could tell that Kit was cross with him, but when Percy turned onto his side to go to sleep, Kit threw an arm over him and pressed his lips to the top of Percy's head. And that was something Percy had never even contemplated—the possibility that someone could be cross with him but also fond of him. Come to think, Percy was more than a little annoyed with Kit—why would the blasted man not go back to London like any reasonable person would—but he didn't think he had ever been so fond of anyone in his entire life as he was of Kit at that moment. He took hold of the hand that rested against his belly and lifted it to his mouth, pressing a kiss onto the knuckles.

"Kit," Percy whispered when a few minutes had passed. The nighttime sounds of the forest seemed increasingly loud, and the space around them impossibly dark and empty. Percy felt small and lost, and like Kit was the only solid and safe thing in the world. "Are you awake?"

"Yes," Kit said, gravelly and low.

Percy knew that it was pitiful to seek out reassurance, but he had never needed it more. "How are you able to look at me after telling me the role my father played in your life?" His voice was more querulous than he would have liked. "Don't you see him every time you look at me?"

"Yes," Kit said simply. "Of course I do."

But he didn't take his arm away, and the fact that he was here despite everything that could have stood between them was more reassuring than any words he could have uttered.

"But I also see you," Kit went on.

Percy fell asleep feeling safer than he had in weeks.

In the morning Percy watched as Kit hugged Dorothy, the old woman looking small and frail beside him. Then Kit knelt and said something to the boy.

Percy mounted Balius, who was still visibly indignant about having traveled nearly fifty miles to sleep in a shed. Kit, with the aid of a tree stump, mounted a bay mare that Dorothy claimed to have borrowed from a neighbor. Percy stowed all his belongings in the horse's saddle bags, except for the little green book, which he kept close at hand in his pocket, and which seemed to grow heavier as Percy began to suspect its purpose.

By midday, they were within sight of Cheveril Castle, the turrets and then the gatehouse coming gradually into view.

It was only a building, Percy told himself. Stone and shingle, plaster and mortar. He knew that it was only the work of his mind that had built it into something more—a legacy, an identity. But still, looking at the silhouette of his home against the gray autumn sky, seeing it for the first time in years and possibly the last time in his life, he had to grit his teeth to hold back a sob.

"I'm going to ride up," Percy said. "Do you want to wait here?"

Kit leveled a dry look at him and rode ahead toward the gate.

When the gatekeeper told Percy that the duke and duchess were not in residence, Percy nearly asked the man to repeat himself, he was so stunned. He managed to ask where the duke and duchess might be, and the gatekeeper explained that the staff expected the duke and duchess two days ago, and could only assume they had changed their plans.

Percy knew he ought to turn around and return immediately to London to see if the duke lived, to confer with Marian, to plan out their next step.

But he was this close to Cheveril, and he might never get to see it again—not, at least, as its heir. He rode through the gates. If Kit was surprised, he didn't let on, just kept riding along at Percy's side.

The drive from the gatehouse to the entrance had been designed to afford a visitor the best view, the facade that had been built during the time of Percy's grandfather. On the approach, one passed through acres of parkland and gardens, then drove between matched fountains that had been imported from Italy.

This was how Cheveril appeared in Percy's dreams—a dozen turrets, an uncountable number of windows, white stairs that were always swept clean of debris. This was how the house looked when he was coming home.

It was also art. It was the work of dozens of architects and God only knew how many craftsmen, gardeners, servants, and laborers. The amount of gold that had gone into the building of

Cheveril Castle was nothing compared to the number of lives that had been devoted to making it what any right-thinking person had to concede was the finest example of sixteenth-century architecture in England, and possibly anywhere, as far as Percy cared.

"It was built two hundred years ago," Percy said, "on the site of what had been Cheveril Priory. One used to approach the house from the south side, but my grandfather commissioned a facade that improved the roofline of the east side, and the result is what you see." He had no idea why he was bothering with a history lesson, and one about rooflines no less, except that he wanted an excuse to linger here for another moment. He didn't want to rush through the last time he'd come home.

"If you look to your left, you can see the Italian gardens," Percy said, cursing himself for sounding exactly like a housekeeper giving a tour to holidaymakers. "My father put them in about a dozen years ago." The view from the front of Cheveril Castle was now intricate garden beds, behind which lay a broad swathe of uninterrupted parkland.

"It was the spring of '39," Kit said.

"Yes, that's right," Percy said, puzzled that Kit would know this. "It was my second year away at school."

"Did you ever wonder how the castle got its name?" Kit asked.

"It was named after the priory that used to stand here," Percy said.

"And how do you think the priory got its name?"

"Oh—there used to be a village, didn't there?" He only vaguely remembered it as a place he was occasionally allowed to visit with his nurse, his cooperation secured with a boiled sweet. At some point, the village hadn't been there anymore, but he had been too occupied with school to ask what had become of it, and in any event conversation with his parents did not extend to the duke's improvements to the property.

"Yes," Kit said flatly, then rode ahead of Percy.

They probably ought to ride around to the stable block, but Percy wanted to walk up the broad white steps one last time. There was the usual awkwardness that attended arriving home unexpected, but Percy took advantage of the general confusion to avoid explaining Kit's presence. "Really, I was hoping to see my father and the duchess, but if they aren't here, then I'll only stay long enough to rest the horses," Percy said airily. "No, no, don't trouble yourself about supper."

Eventually he and Kit were in the great hall, alone except for the small army of servants that no doubt were just out of sight.

"This is the great hall," Percy said redundantly, because it was fairly obvious where they were, with its enormous hearth and its minstrel gallery. "And this is the Grand Staircase," he said. "We lack a certain creativity when it comes to naming things, I'm afraid. You'll never guess what color the Blue Library is." He spun on his heel and saw Kit standing in the middle of the hall, not looking at the ornately carved ceiling or the impressively large, if tragically ugly, oil painting of a battle scene that hung above the hearth, but rather at Percy himself, and with an inscrutable expression on his face.

"Can you climb stairs?" Percy asked. "Frankly, I'm not certain I can, and there's a solid chance a footman will have to carry me down, but would you like to give it a try?"

Kit shrugged. Percy's wound pulled a bit with each step, and he regretted this idea by the first landing.

At the top, he led Kit toward the portrait gallery. "That's my grandmother," he said, gesturing at the portrait of a raven-haired lady who had an affronted-looking pug on her lap. And then, indicating a gentleman with an enormous black wig who was sitting in what was obviously the great hall downstairs, "That's the ninth marquess, shortly before he was beheaded. He had several pet monkeys. Too many monkeys, if we're honest. And this is my mother." He hadn't planned to stop, hadn't planned to stare, but this was the first time he had seen his mother's face since he left England. And while this portrait was a poor likeness, it was close enough to take his breath away. It had been painted shortly after her wedding, so when she was about twenty. The portraitist had contrived to give her a dreamy air, which was far from the sharp-eyed, quick-witted woman he had loved.

"You look like her," Kit said. They were the first words he had spoken since entering the house.

"Thank you," Percy said, even though it wasn't exactly a compliment, given how daft his mother looked in that portrait. But he knew Kit meant that Percy looked like his mother, *too*. He let himself stare shamelessly at the portrait for another minute. "It's a pity it's so large, or I'd smuggle it out in my coat." Most people didn't even have the option of stealing portraits of their dead mothers, so leaving this behind wouldn't really be a loss, he reasoned. Eventually his memory of his mother's face would fade. It was fine. He would cope, just like everybody else.

"And these are my apartments," he said, pushing open a heavy oak door. The rooms had been dusted and aired recently, and smelled fresh and clean despite having been unoccupied for over two years. "The Talbot family tradition of obvious naming continues unbroken, as these chambers have been known as Lord Holland's Rooms since my first ancestor used the courtesy title."

Kit stood in the doorway, his jaw set and his expression dark. Again, he looked at Percy, rather than at the objectively impressive collection of Dresden figurines that sat on the chimneypiece, or at the honest-to-God Caravaggio that hung beside the door to the inner chambers. Nor did he seem interested in the thick carpets or silk draperies.

Percy passed through the antechamber into the sitting room, then through that into the bedchamber. He knew Kit followed only from the muffled sound of his walking stick thumping against the carpeted floor. Percy lifted a hand to touch the pale blue silk bed hangings. A few motes of dust scattered, catching the light in a way that almost sparkled.

Then the dust settled, and he knew he must have been staring into space for minutes. He felt his cheeks heat, and he turned to Kit, who was leaning in the doorway. "I'm sorry." His voice was thick, and if he didn't know better, he'd think he was about to cry. "The clock above the mantelpiece is—"

"I don't give a fuck about the clock."

"Of course you don't, you barbarian."

Kit's mouth twitched. "What do you need?" Percy must have looked as confused and lost as he felt, because Kit clarified. "What do you need to do here? We can't stay. I'm sorry, Percy, but we have to go to London. What do you need to do before we leave?"

What he really wanted was to shrink the entirety of Cheveril to the size of one of the Dresden figurines and put it in his pocket to keep it safe. What he really wanted was to burn it down so nobody else could have it, or maybe because he hated caring so much about brick and stone.

He glanced at the bed, then at Kit. "Will you—would you

fuck me?" His voice was small, doubtful, the opposite of seductive. "The mattress is very comfortable," he added, because he was thoroughly committed to being a moron.

"Is that what you need?"

Percy nodded. Kit crossed the room, still not touching him, still looking at him too closely.

"All right, then," Kit said, and kissed him.

Chapter 46

Make it so this is what I remember," Percy said as they fumbled with one another's clothes.

"You may be overestimating my abilities," Kit said. He wished he could, though. He wished all it would take was a thorough fucking to obliterate Cheveril Castle and all it stood for from Percy's mind. From who Percy was.

Percy had cast off the last of his clothes and stood naked in front of blue bed curtains that Kit strongly suspected had been picked to flatter its occupant. The idea simultaneously struck him as sinfully extravagant and an admirable use of funds.

Kit tugged off his boots. "Get on the bed."

Percy arranged himself on a coverlet of the same sky-blue silk. "Oh, there's oil in the pocket of my coat."

"Optimistic, were you?" Kit shucked his jacket and his shirt, letting them drop to the floor.

"Shut up and do your job," Percy said, spreading his legs and taking himself in hand.

Laughing—and wasn't that a marvel, to be laughing in this place, with this man—Kit got the oil and tossed it to Percy. "You know I haven't done this, right?"

"Why haven't you, Kit?"

Kit sat on the edge of the bed and palmed one of Percy's bent knees. "It never seemed worth the risk."

Percy stared at him, propping himself up on one elbow. "Let me understand. You, while routinely committing highway robbery and other capital crimes with such wild abandon you're almost a household name, balked at a little buggery?"

"Well, it sounds silly when you put it that way."

"I think we need to acknowledge that your priorities may be overdue for some realignment."

Kit grinned, but he knew Percy was right. Maybe Kit hadn't thought his own pleasure should matter. Maybe Kit had only thought it was all right to risk his neck when it was for somebody else's benefit—or somebody else's punishment. But when he touched Percy, the idea that he was risking his neck made him as furious as it did when he thought about places like Cheveril existing while regular people went hungry. Any law against this was the sort of rule Kit wanted to break on principle alone. Whatever they had between them, for all its confusion, was good, and it was theirs, and they should take it. Fuck anything that said otherwise.

Percy licked his lips and pulled Kit down beside him. "You think that being with me is worth the risk?"

Kit heard the uncertainty in the other man's voice, and it broke his heart. "You're worth any price I could pay," he said, and then kissed him. Usually Percy kissed like it was a fight, like he planned to kiss until he was the last man left standing. But now he was pliant, his mouth soft beneath Kit's. Kit took the leather cord from Percy's hair and undid his plait, letting the golden strands spill over the pillow.

Percy poured some oil onto his fingers and stroked himself, then trailed his fingers lower, over his bollocks and then along the crease of his arse. Kit sat up, watching intently as two of Percy's fingers disappeared inside himself. He put a hand on the inside of Percy's knee, nudging his legs further apart so Kit could watch better. Percy obligingly tilted his hips up, and Kit heard himself make a punched-out-sounding noise.

When he looked up, he saw that Percy's eyes were on him, watching Kit watching him. Kit felt his face heat, and saw an answering flush on Percy's neck and down his pale chest. "Look at you," he breathed, and had the satisfaction of watching Percy redden to the tips of his ears.

Kit bent down and kissed him. Then he skimmed a hand down Percy's chest, circling a nipple, palming his erection, before coming to rest on his wrist. He kissed Percy some more, rutting his hardening cock into Percy's hip, feeling his desperation mount.

"Please, Kit," Percy breathed.

Kit got to his knees between Percy's legs and just looked at him for a moment, pale limbs against the expanse of blue silk, bright hair fanned out on the pillow. And the expression on his face was so candid and open that Kit had to look away.

He lined himself up and paused, just letting himself enjoy this feeling of almost breaching Percy, prolonging that moment when need overwhelmed every other sensation. Then he pushed in a little and swore at the grasping heat, watching himself sink in inch by inch.

Percy started to boss him around, because of course he did. "Wait, yes, keep going, right there, do that again." Kit complied and buried his face in Percy's shoulder, half laughing and half overcome with the pleasure of it, the joy of it being Percy he was doing this with. He slowed his thrusts and kissed Percy, lazy and slow.

Kit took one of Percy's legs—the uninjured one—and put it over his shoulder. "This all right?" he asked, turning his head to kiss Percy's ankle.

"No," Percy said, his words belied by the fact that they were spoken while he arched up into Kit's touch. "You're doing this all wrong."

Kit stilled. "Oh?"

"You were supposed to make it dirty. I wanted to—God, yes, do that again—desecrate this place. And instead, you're being lovely."

Kit looked down at him. "If it makes you feel any better, the bedcovers are going to be ruined."

Percy snorted. "See, this is what I mean. I'm not supposed to be laughing. You're so bad at this, it's quite a—" He broke off when Kit tilted his hips up at a different angle, his words trailing off into a guttural moan. "Quite a disappointment."

Kit carried on disappointing him until Percy reached down and stroked himself until he came, whispering Kit's name, digging his fingernails into Kit's shoulders, and Kit tumbled over the edge after him.

After, they lay side by side, catching their breath.

"If you think," Kit said, getting out of bed, "that anything we do together could desecrate a single fucking thing, you're an idiot." He stepped into his buckskins. "And I don't think you want to desecrate this place, or your memories of it. You love it. It's your home, for all I'd like to see it rot. But you aren't going to use me and make out that what we're doing, what we are to one another, is something vile." He dug through his satchel until he came up with a cloth to hand Percy, then turned his back while Percy got dressed.

"I meant," Percy said, coming up behind him, "that this isn't something I could have if I were who I thought I was. The Duke of Clare can't have his—lover, I suppose—in his chambers." He put a tentative hand on Kit's shoulder. "As an equal. I wanted to do something he couldn't. And I meant what I said about you being lovely. You always are."

Kit turned. Percy's hair was loose around his shoulders, tangled from Kit's hands. His lips were kiss swollen, his shirt was wrinkled, his neck was red and rough from Kit's stubble.

"Percy, I know." He tucked a strand of hair behind Percy's ear. "I know that. Let's get going."

Percy left with many thanks to the servants and a liberal distribution of silver coins, then mounted his horse with a good deal of muttering about how he never learned to plan his days around a good buggering.

"Can we make it to London by nightfall on these horses?" Percy asked.

"You can," Kit said, glancing at the sky, and then looking at the horses. "I'll take the stagecoach from Tetsworth and arrange for this mare to be brought back to her owner."

"I can wait for you," Percy offered, and he was a good enough liar that Kit thought he might actually mean it.

"You really can't. You need to get back to town as soon as you may, and your horse, however much of a fuss he might make about it, will get you there faster than the stagecoach."

Percy stroked his horse's mane. "Balius's pedigree is too refined and his sensibilities too delicate to live in this common sort of way," Percy remarked, seemingly for the benefit of the horse. "He was raised in the lap of equine luxury and has been quite at sixes and sevens without a steady supply of apples and other treats. I know, my darling," he told the horse. "I feel quite the same way."

As they proceeded down the drive, Kit gestured across the broad expanse of parkland. "Remember that village I told you about? Cheveril? Do you know what happened to it?" When Percy shook his head, Kit went on. "Your father razed it to the ground to provide a better view from the castle."

"I remember it," Percy said, his eyes fixed on the empty stretch of grass where Cheveril had once stood. "I'm ashamed to say I never thought about what became of the people who lived there."

"My father's inn was pulled down. He tried to make a go of it two villages over, but that village already had a tavern. He and my mother caught sick and were dead by spring of '41."

"1741," Percy said slowly. Kit could almost see him doing the sums. "It was the same year your daughter died. You lost them all at once, didn't you?"

"It was a bad winter," Kit said. He hadn't known until years later that the winter of 1740–41 had been bad for the entire country and even beyond rather than a private torment visited on him alone. "Needless to say, your father didn't lift a finger to help."

"And instead, he had a girl transported for poaching," Percy said. "A mother."

"Rob and I couldn't spend another minute in this part of the country, and, well, neither of us had much interest in making an honest living at that point."

"No, I imagine not." Percy swallowed. "I knew my father was a bad landlord, but I didn't realize how bad."

Kit shook his head and turned his gaze to the empty expanse where Cheveril used to stand. "Maybe you didn't realize about

Cheveril, and maybe you didn't realize about my family. But you know that your family's fortune was built on the losses of others. You know that your father has property in the West Indies. You can't possibly think that anything built with that money is good. Surely, you know the cost of all this." He gestured around them, encompassing the castle, the garden, the grounds. "You shouldn't need to hear about the destruction of a village a stone's throw from your home, the story of a man you've gone to bed with, a baby whose grave you saw. I don't care about your staircase and your gardens. They're beautiful, but they aren't worth the price, and I don't want to know anyone who thinks they are."

He hadn't looked at Percy while he was speaking. Partly because he didn't want to see any sign of skepticism, partly because he needed to deliver that speech with as few concessions to Percy's feelings as possible and was afraid that the sight of his face would make him soften the blow.

"Now let's go," Kit said, and led the way through the gate.

Chapter 47

By the time Percy approached Clare House, it was nearly midnight. Leaving a furious Balius with the grooms, he saw no sign that they regarded him as a wanted man. So that, at least, was a good sign. They did, however, whisper among themselves, too softly for Percy to overhear. News of his arrival must have spread quickly, because Collins met him at the door.

"My lord," Collins said, looking as frazzled and unkempt as Percy had ever seen him. "I expected you yesterday morning."

"Too much brandy," Percy said, and regretted it immediately. He lowered his voice. "I'm sorry to have given you cause to worry."

"Your father, my lord. I'm afraid he was injured on the road to Cheveril. Her Grace said that he was shot while defending her from a footpad. But, I'm afraid . . ." Collins faltered.

Percy's heart was beating so hard, he worried Collins could see it through his waistcoat. "Out with it, Collins."

"He's alive but unlikely to remain that way for long."

"I see. Where is Marian?"

"Her Grace disappeared soon after bringing the duke home."

"Disappeared?" Percy repeated.

"In the confusion of His Grace being carried in and the physician being called for, she simply . . . disappeared. She didn't ask for the carriage or have a footman call her a hackney. I can only imagine that she went on foot, although she must have changed her clothes at some point, because she was"—Collins cleared his throat—"quite covered in blood upon her arrival."

Percy shuddered. He could not think why Marian would have left or where she would have gone. Nothing about their plan could be furthered by her absence—indeed, the reality was quite the opposite.

"Her encounter with the footpads no doubt did in her nerves," he added firmly. "What have the coachman and outriders said about this attack?" Percy tried not to look like he was holding his breath.

"They've all said the same thing. The duke's carriage was held up outside Tetsworth. Two pistol shots were heard, and then Her Grace called out for the coach to drive on because the duke was injured."

That much was good. Percy allowed himself to feel something like relief, because at least nobody had connected him or Kit with the holdup. There was another matter he needed to discuss with his valet, though. He steered Collins into an empty parlor and shut the door behind them. "Do you remember hearing that when I was an infant, my father moved his mistress into the north wing of Cheveril Castle?"

"I'm afraid it was discussed for some years, my lord."

"Did anyone ever mention what she looked like?"

Collins furrowed his brow. "Red hair, rather buxom."

Percy's heart thumped, because that fit the description of Elsie Terry. "Why did she leave?"

Collins shocked Percy by barking out a laugh. "The duke brought her there to irritate your mother, but your mother spiked his guns by befriending the girl at once. They were fast friends at the end of a twelvemonth, and when the duke caught on, he made her go. To hear the older servants speak of it, by the time your mother was done with her, she was as much a partisan of the duchess as you or I."

"Well, how the devil did it never come up between them that Elsie Terry had married my father?"

"She did *what*?" Collins gasped.

"Goodness, have I finally succeeded in shocking you? Yes, a good year and a half before the duke purported to marry my mother, and she—or somebody who knows her well enough to be in on the secret—is blackmailing Marian and me."

"But she apparently doted on your mother," Collins said.

"Well, she did wait until my mother was dead. And she is, lawfully, the Duchess of Clare."

"Oh dear," Collins said, blanching.

"I really ought to have broken it to you more carefully. Here," he said, directing Collins to a chair. "Sit down and I'll send for some brandy." He clapped Collins on the shoulder and pulled the cord to summon a servant. "I ought to see my father," he said, and departed.

The only light in the duke's chambers came from a branch of candles at the bedside. The physician left after bowing to Percy and telling him a number of things that all amounted to the duke's imminent death.

Percy stood at the head of the bed. "I don't know if you can hear me," he said, taking the book from his pocket. "But I suspect that you've left me with enough to destroy the Talbot name for generations. Well, to be fair, you destroyed it with a clandestine marriage and a lifetime of bigamy, but let's not get mired in details." Percy opened the Bible to the list of names on its flyleaf, then flipped through the pages of apparently random circlings and underscores. "What I have here is a list of Jacobite supporters. I suspect that the rest of the book contains the particulars—amounts of money, promises made, and so forth. That's all entirely in keeping with my mother's priorities, and I suppose the only question is whether the evidence in this book involves past treason or a future plot. But what can you have been up to? I doubt you've become a Jacobite. I can only imagine that you were using this book either to blackmail the people listed on the first page or to otherwise bend them to your will."

Percy didn't know if it was his imagination, but he thought his father's eyes flickered. "The question is, what shall I do with it? I suppose I could carry on blackmailing people and then use that money to pay my own blackmailer, and we'd have an entirely blackmail-based economy. I must confess that doesn't appeal to me in the least. Alternatively, I could give this book to His Majesty and see what the Crown's gratitude will do for me. If I also hand over the key to this code—and, Father, I know where it is—I bet I could get a title of my very own. Not a dukedom, but something that my descendants could build up into a suitably impressive legacy."

The duke's mouth opened and closed, and Percy thought he was trying to talk. Percy found he didn't care. He didn't care about what might be his father's dying words. On his list of things that mattered to him, this ranked far below Marian's whereabouts and the question of what to do with the book. Possibly lower than whether Balius needed to be reshod.

"Or I could throw the book into the river. I could live my own life, not one either of my parents wished for me. You shot me," Percy said. "And I was hardly even surprised. I robbed you at gunpoint and never had a single qualm about extorting funds from you. I don't want to be that person." As he spoke the words, he realized that he didn't want to be the person his mother had shaped him into or the person his father wished he were. He didn't want any part of their expectations.

Percy's eyes prickled and he cursed himself. But he wasn't grieving his father's imminent death so much as he was sad about not having anything to grieve.

The next morning, he woke to the news that the duke had died.

Chapter 48

*K*it returned to a coffeehouse that remained relentlessly normal, frustratingly unchanged. The seats were filled with the usual patrons, who demanded their usual drinks and had the usual conversations. The weather continued to slink from a damp and foggy autumn toward a dismally cold winter. His leg was as uncooperative as ever. Betty was her typical self, even if she directed glances toward Kit that seemed to go right through him.

Throughout the day, every time a man in a wig and a fine coat walked in the door, Kit's heart gave an extra beat, even though he knew Percy would be busy doing whatever men did when their friends shot their fathers after holdups gone wrong. Kit frankly couldn't imagine what that entailed, but he wished Percy would come by and tell him. He wanted to know that Percy would ever come back and would continue to come back. It seemed a small thing to ask for, an almost pitifully modest bit of reassurance.

They had parted on less-than-ideal terms at the gates of Cheveril Castle. Throughout the interminable stagecoach journey back to London, Kit wished his parting words to Percy had been about how much he thought what they had between them was

worth keeping rather than a rant about the evils of the landown-
ing classes.

But the truth was that what they had between them wasn't
worth keeping if Percy didn't understand that the things he
valued—the things whose loss he felt as a calamity—were terrible and dangerous, both to Kit and to everyone who lived under
the thumb of people like Percy's father. If Percy didn't understand that, then maybe he shouldn't come back.

When Kit looked around his shop, it felt empty and dull without Percy. He tried to remind himself that Percy had never belonged there, just as he had never belonged anywhere near Kit.
Kit had known that all along, even if he had lost sight of that fact
somewhere along the way.

He tried not to think about how very badly he had lost sight
of that fact. He tried even harder not to think about how Percy
seemed to have done so as well.

He tried not to think about the two nights they had spent on
the dirt floor of a barn, nor about the hour they had spent on silk
bedcovers in that godforsaken palace.

More often than he liked, he thought back to that afternoon
at Cheveril Castle, and wondered if maybe all along Percy just
wanted him as a bit of rough, a criminal for hire. He pictured
Percy among all his luxuries, spread out cool and clean on that
blue silk, like something Kit had never wanted to want. Kit was
coarse and rough, and it was too easy to believe that Percy truly
had wanted Kit to sully the place.

He couldn't quite make himself believe that, though. Whenever he tried, he instead remembered something domestic and
mundane—Percy absently tearing his cake into two pieces and
giving half to Kit, Percy's lips brushing a kiss onto his knuckles—

and he knew how Percy felt. He couldn't even convince himself that he was deluded or foolish—he knew how Percy felt with a bone-deep certainty, with a surety that was something like faith.

That didn't mean he'd come back, though. The world was filled with people who felt all kinds of things and couldn't manage to shape those feelings into something that would last. But Kit knew he wanted that, and knew he was prepared to do whatever it took to make it happen.

Perhaps spending time with Percy had knocked something loose inside him, as if maybe being with Percy had made Kit take stock of what exactly he needed to be content. Weeks ago, Betty had teased him about pining away for a life of crime, but what he had really missed was the sense of setting things right. In a world that was teeming with unfairness, Kit wanted to be a hand on the scale of justice, or maybe he wanted to tear the scales down.

And, ideally, he would do all that with Percy, if not at his side then at least near at hand.

"The lads at table five started a betting pool for when Rob will come back and how bad his excuse for buggering off will be this time," Betty said while they were closing up.

Kit snorted. Neither hide nor hair had been seen of Rob in the days since the robbery. All Kit could think was that maybe Rob had taken a liking to disappearing without a trace. Perhaps this was going to be a regular occurrence—vanishing for a year and then returning without warning. "I probably ought to go see his mother," Kit said, feeling very resigned about it. "Maybe he told her this time."

After walking Betty home that night, he took his time on the trip home. There was no hurry, and he had made up his mind to go easy on his leg. But when he approached the darkened coffeehouse, he saw a figure leaning against the door, obscured by shadows.

Kit gripped his walking stick a little more firmly but didn't break stride. The figure was lean and dressed in nondescript clothes; he bent his head in a way that would shield his face from view, even though the street was dark. A pale strand of hair escaped from beneath the brim of his hat, catching the moonlight.

"Loitering," Kit chided when he reached the shop.

"I prefer to think of it as skulking," Percy countered. "Maybe even lurking."

"You'll have to work on your technique." Kit opened the door and held it for Percy to enter before him. Percy immediately sat in his usual seat at the long table. "I wondered if I'd ever see you here again," Kit admitted.

"It's hardly been a day since I saw you," Percy said, not bothering to conceal how amused he was, damn him.

"More like a day and a half," Kit grumbled. And then Percy smirked at him and, really, Kit could not stand for that, so he hauled Percy up by the collar and kissed him hard.

"It's almost all I've been thinking of," Percy said, his words little more than a breath against Kit's cheek. "Well, in between bouts of scheming and coming up with plans to bankrupt and defraud the estate of the next Duke of Clare."

Kit's heart gave a wild thump as he processed the ramifications of that statement. He pulled away just enough to look Percy in the eye. "You've been busy."

"Rather." From his shoulder, Percy removed the strap of what Kit could now see was the case in which he carried his swords. "I have something for you. It's not much, but as you certainly didn't profit in any way from our job—"

"I don't need to be paid for that," Kit said.

"No, no, I know that. I shouldn't have phrased it that way. It's actually something I got for myself while I was abroad, but I've never used such a thing and don't plan to. In any event, I thought you might like it." He held out a walking stick.

Kit took it. It was a little heavier than the stick he presently used, and made of a wood that felt silky smooth and warm to the touch. The handle was carved in a way that made it feel molded to fit his palm. He could tell at a glance that it was a fine piece of craftsmanship and likely cost a pretty penny, but it wasn't ostentatious. It wasn't something he'd feel silly using. Frankly, he was surprised Percy would have chosen something so understated for himself. "Thank you," he said. "It's a very nice—"

"Yes, yes," Percy said impatiently. "It's all that and more. But you haven't seen what it can do." He reached out and did something to the handle so that the body of the stick fell away, revealing a long, thin blade. "It's a swordstick. Since you always have your walking stick as well as various weaponry, I thought it might be convenient."

"I don't know how to use a sword," Kit said.

"Well, you're very fortunate to know someone who does and who would very much enjoy the chance to teach you." Percy fiddled with the hilt of the swordstick, his fingers brushing against Kit's. "If you like."

"You ought to be worse than this," Percy called out half an hour later. They had stripped down to their shirtsleeves, and the only light in the back room came from two lanterns that Kit hung from hooks. Silhouettes of limbs and swords danced across the walls. "Fix your grip and stop making your wrist do all the work."

"I don't see how I could possibly be worse," Kit panted. In order to make things more equal, Percy used a blunt practice sword in his left hand and was clearly only using a quarter of his skill to parry Kit's attacks. Kit, meanwhile, was making a shambles of the thing.

"No, no, I've seen dozens of novices make asses of themselves," Percy said. "You, at least, know how to fight. Yes, see, just like that," he added as Kit blocked one of his thrusts. "You're using the strength from the core of your body rather than making your arms do all the work. And you aren't afraid of hurting me."

"I'm terrified of hurting you," Kit objected.

"However will you manage when I'm prizefighting?"

"Badly, I expect."

"Well, I suppose we have a few weeks left before we need to worry about that. I'll be quite sufficiently busy ruining the estate and so forth. Speaking of which, I ought to warn you. For the next fortnight, you're going to hear people refer to me by my father's title. No, don't lower your blade, Kit, for heaven's sake. The blackmailer said he'd give us until January first, and I intend to use all that time to—well, you'll see. No sense in being tedious about administrative details with you. What matters is that on the thirty-first of December I'll make the information about my father's marriage public. I swear upon everything holy, Christopher, if you don't stop waving that thing about like a May Day streamer, I'll take it away from you and bestow it upon someone more deserving. Do not tempt me."

"Why bother?" Kit asked. "With your father dead and the estate in your hands, you could afford to pay off the blackmailer as long as you pleased."

"Paying off blackmailers does not appeal to me," Percy said

primly. "I've known that from the start. But it turns out that being the Duke of Clare does not appeal to me, either."

"Is that so," Kit said.

"There are choices a commoner can make," Percy said, looking Kit hard in the eye.

"That's a fact." The gift of the swordstick made sense now. Not only was a sharp blade Percy's idea of a lover's gift, but it was a gift that put them on an equal footing. Kit had always enjoyed the democratizing effect of a weapon in his hand, although that was usually in quite another context.

"Oh, you approve, do you?" Percy's effort at sardonic archness instead landed somewhere near giddily thrilled. He let his guard down on his right side, just the slightest bit. If Kit hadn't spent a month sparring with him, then he might not have noticed, but it was enough for Kit to advance on him.

"That's right, I do," Kit said, pressing forward. "And you're glad about it."

"Lamentably accurate," Percy sighed, and took a step back, then another. Kit pressed forward again, then dropped his sword, deciding that he didn't much care for the idea of a sharpened blade too close to Percy. It landed on the floor with a clatter.

"Now I'm going to have to sharpen it," complained Percy as his back met the wall.

Kit took hold of the wrist of Percy's sword hand and turned it, pressing the blunt edge of the practice sword against Percy's neck. "You just wanted me to shove you up against the wall," he growled. "You shouldn't let me win."

"Can't blame a man for trying," said Percy, sounding abominably pleased with himself. He was short of breath, and Kit knew it wasn't from exertion.

"I wonder what I'll do with you," Kit said, casting Percy's sword to the floor and crowding against Percy. Only when their chests were pressed against one another did Kit bring a hand up to Percy's jaw, angling his mouth for a kiss. He took his time about it, sliding a leg in between Percy's, then tucking a hair behind Percy's ear, before finally closing the gap and kissing him. Percy was soft and pliant, the way he rarely was. He opened his mouth against Kit's as if he had been waiting for that kiss all day or even longer.

Kit couldn't have said how long they stayed like that, sharing kisses that were long and slow and only a little heated. "When do you have to go?" Kit finally asked.

"I don't, actually," Percy said, sounding the slightest bit shy about it. "I told my valet not to wait up."

"Stay," Kit said.

Chapter 49

*P*ercy couldn't help but feel a little smug about finally seeing Kit's bedroom after spending hours downstairs nearly every day for a month and even seeing the office a few times. He could tell from Kit's awkwardness that he rarely, if ever, let anyone enter it. He nervously pointed out things like the ewer and the window, as if Percy were unfamiliar with ewers and windows. Finally, Percy had taken pity on him and hauled him down to the bed, slowly stripping him of his clothes and showing him how glad he was to be there.

"So," Kit said later on, his hand carding through Percy's hair. "What are your big plans for defrauding the estate?" Kit's bed was barely wide enough for two people, but it didn't matter because they were all tangled together, Percy's head on Kit's arm, Percy's knee over Kit's leg, a warm quilt tucked around them both.

"You'll see," Percy said. He didn't want to tell Kit yet, because he didn't want to sound like he was asking for credit for good intentions. Only if he were successful with his schemes did he want Kit to know.

"What does Marian think about it?"

"I wish I knew," Percy said. "I haven't seen her since the robbery. Neither has her brother. I'm rather worried." In truth, he was more than a little worried. Under ordinary circumstances, he'd have already started a full-blown search, but these were far from ordinary circumstances, and there was a good chance she had reasons of her own for lying low. He didn't very much like to think about what those reasons might be.

"I haven't heard from Rob, either," Kit said, his hand stilling in Percy's hair.

That did very little to settle Percy's mind, and from the way Kit's body had gone tense beside him, he thought Kit might be harboring similar suspicions. He propped himself up on his elbow and looked down at Kit. "You said that you grew up together in Oxfordshire. Is that where Rob's mother is from?"

"Scarlett? No. She got in trouble, then sent Rob out to be fostered in the country. I don't think she ever laid eyes on him until we came to London ten years ago, and by then he was grown."

"Who was his father?"

Kit raised his eyebrows. "A customer, I imagine."

"But wouldn't it take a good deal of money to send a child out to be fostered for such a long period of time?"

"I think Rob's parents—the ones who raised him—thought of themselves as having adopted him."

"You don't happen to know Scarlett's real name, do you?"

"Percy, what's this about?" Kit asked.

He didn't know how to tell Kit this and only hoped he didn't botch it up too badly. "I might be wrong—Christ, I hope I'm wrong—but I think your friend Scarlett is my father's legal wife. Her daughter has a Bible that's identical to my mother's. God knows I wasn't paying attention when she showed it to me, but I'd wager that it's even bound in the same green leather." Percy

forced himself to stop and braced himself for Kit's inevitable protest that Percy was jumping to conclusions, that he had no proof,
et cetera.

But Kit remained silent, his hand tracing an absent circle on
the side of Percy's knee. "That fits," he finally said.

"It does?" Percy asked. "Fits with what?"

"Well, I've wondered how Scarlett knew Rob's foster parents.
It's not the sort of thing you can ask, though, and they didn't
volunteer. But it makes sense. It also fits in with Rob's disappear-
ance. He was furious with his mother and told me I wouldn't
want to know the truth. I had the impression that his mother had
given him bad news. He mentioned that it took him months to
decide what to do about it."

"Evidently, what he decided to do was blackmail Marian and
me." Percy had gone over this in his head a dozen times. At first he
thought that Scarlett was blackmailing him herself but couldn't
figure out why she'd do that while also deliberately showing him
the Bible. Now he was fairly certain that she and Flora had been
subtly trying to sell him the book, which might contain the key
to the code his mother had used in her own book. Or perhaps it
was the other way around, and Scarlett wanted his Bible—from
what Percy understood, she was a woman who would know precisely how to make use of a book of secrets.

"Scarlett was born Elsie Terry," Kit said.

"And what year was Rob born?" Percy asked faintly.

"He just turned twenty-five, so 1726."

"Well, that's him, then." Percy thought he ought to feel something, anything at this confirmation of his worst fears: Cheveril
would go not only to a commoner but to a very, well, *common*
commoner.

"You really could pay him off, you know," Kit said after a long while. "He might be an arsehole about it and keep coming back for more money, but he doesn't want to be a duke."

Percy looked down at Kit and felt a rush of intense affection. Kit hadn't needed to tell him that, hadn't needed to make it easy for Percy to slide back into a life Kit hated. It was tempting, truth be told. He could return to the world he had come from as if the past few months had never happened. Surely, Percy could do more good as a wealthy and titled man than he could as a disgraced commoner. He could be a principled duke, one with the highest ideals. He could make good on all his plans and then some.

Or he could do something different. He could be his own man, and do right in his own way. "I find that I don't want that anymore," Percy said. It wasn't entirely true, and from the look Kit shot him, he knew it, too. "What I mean is that I've made my choice."

"Why?"

Percy looked away and fiddled with the hem of the bedsheet. "Do I really have to spell it out for you?"

"If it's because of"—Kit gestured between their bodies, as if reluctant to say what they were to one another—"then you'll only wind up resenting me."

"It's not," Percy said. "The fact is that you've ruined me for a life of leisure, Kit Webb. How can I go back to all that when the most principled man I know thinks it's evil."

Kit stared at him. "You've gone daft."

"I love you."

"Like I said."

Percy kissed him, because there was no use arguing with a man so stubborn.

"You all right?" Kit asked after a while.

"Entirely," Percy said, and it was mostly true. "How about you? You seem remarkably unbothered by everything I've told you, I have to say."

"I am bothered, though. Poor Rob."

"Poor Rob?" Percy sputtered, pinching Kit's shoulder. "He blackmailed me!"

"Of course he did." Kit captured Percy's hand and held it. "He doesn't want to be a duke. But here he is, presented with a chance to make aristocrats miserable while also lining his pockets. Of course he blackmailed you. I'd be shocked to hear he did anything else."

"Do you know, that's almost exactly what he said in one of his letters to Marian."

Now, that made Kit sit up. "*One* of his letters? How many letters did he send? And what kind of blackmailer talks about his motives?"

"Not a particularly good one. He wasn't going to get a farthing off us. And there was a period of time when Marian wasn't exactly opposed to murdering him. Blackmail isn't good for one's health."

Kit sighed. "I don't want you to think that I like the idea of him blackmailing you, or anyone else." His hand tightened on Percy's knee. "But especially you."

"I do know that," Percy reassured him.

"You don't think Marian might have killed him after all, do you? I really don't like that they're both missing."

"Neither do I." Percy didn't care for the implications in the slightest. "But I don't think she'd have killed him. We have no way of knowing whether he told anyone else. She's too clever to seriously consider something so shortsighted, however much revenge might please her." Percy dearly wished he could have made a better defense of his friend. "And besides, it was my father she was most angry with, not the blackmailer."

Kit looked at him, and Percy knew they were both thinking of what Marian had, in the end, done to Percy's father. She had, if nothing else, proven that she was willing to kill. "I'll put it about that I'm looking for him," Kit said. "I don't know what good it'll do, but I'll try." With that, he sank back down onto the pillows, bringing Percy along with him. "Our friends are going to give me a heart attack."

Percy felt almost giddy at that *our*, that implication that they shared things now. "I imagine this is how Betty feels all the time." He stretched out, feeling Kit's body long and warm beside him. "Do you mind if I start a fire?"

"Are you cold?"

"I want to burn that book." He had confirmed its location in his pocket no fewer than a dozen times that day, each instance putting him uncomfortably in mind of his father performing that same gesture. And he had slept with it under his pillow the previous night, as if someone might slip in through the window and steal it. Considering the amount of traffic his bedchamber windows had seen over the past month, and considering the steps his father had taken to secure the book, Percy couldn't feel that he had been entirely unreasonable in his fears.

"There's a tinderbox on the chimneypiece. But we might as well use the hearth downstairs. I could do with some supper."

As Percy stepped into his breeches, he reflected that of course Kit could speak of burning evidence of what might amount to treason and eating supper in the same breath and in the same calm tone. They both were simply things that needed to be done. He had been like that from the start; in the world as Kit saw it, getting supper and committing felonies and attempting to dismantle ancestral power were all equally probable events. That struck Percy as about right.

And so they sat before the fire in the coffeehouse, eating bread and cheese. Percy turned the book over in his hands. One last time, he looked at his mother's handwriting. What he was about to do would have disappointed both his parents, and quite possibly Marian, but he felt in his bones that it was right for him, and right in a broader sense. The book was a weapon. If Percy were to wield a weapon, he wanted it to be one he fully controlled, not a book that sat in his pocket like an undetonated bomb, threatening to injure people who had done nothing to warrant harm.

He had spent a lifetime thinking about his role in the Talbot legacy, always with the tacit assumption that his role would be to accrue and consolidate power as his forebears had done. But for too much power to be in one family's hands was a blight on the landscape. Getting rid of this book was a damned good start to making sure that the Talbots' place in history wasn't entirely bad.

With Kit's hand on his shoulder, he cast the book into the fire, and stayed until it was reduced to ashes.

Chapter 50

*T*wo peculiar things happened in the next couple of days.

The first was that the broadsides began bringing news of the new Duke of Clare's latest doings. He altered his tenants' leases and converted several properties to freeholds. Deeds of manumission were sent off to Barbados. Priceless artworks and a dozen horses were sent to auction. Funds were set aside for the building of schools and poorhouses, along with an endowment to keep them going for a generation. Public opinion was divided as to whether Percy had done these things to spite his dead father or because he had gone quite mad.

The second peculiar thing was that Kit returned from walking Betty home to find a note on his pillow.

"Stop fretting. I'm not dead. Tell your gent that Lady M isn't dead, either, as she doesn't seem disposed to do so herself. And for God's sake, call off the hunt. Much love, R," the note read, in Rob's handwriting.

When Kit showed it to Percy that night, he studied it for a long minute. "I can't be certain, but I think it's the same handwriting as the blackmail letters. The way the ink blots at the tail of the R and M is distinctive. I might wish for a reassurance slightly more enthusiastic than 'not dead' but it was kind for your friend to put my mind at ease." He said *kind* as if it were a complicated foreign word, as if his tongue and lips didn't want to shape themselves around it, and Kit knew that Percy was trying to tell Kit that he intended to be civil to Rob and about Rob.

"I saw that you're selling some horses," Kit said.

Percy wrinkled his nose. "How do the papers learn these things so quickly? Yes, I'm selling everything that isn't nailed down. Including Balius, who I can only hope will be as mean and ill-tempered to his new owner as he was to me. Good riddance, and all that."

Kit had seen Percy croon to and cosset that stallion and didn't for a minute believe that Percy was taking his loss well. He had little lines around his eyes hinting that whatever divesting half the Clare estate entailed, it was not easy on him. "Let's go for a walk," he suggested. "I'll stand you a pint."

As they were getting into their cloaks, Betty came over and touched Percy's shoulder. "Please come back and put him out of his misery," she said. "Do it for me? You should see how he's been pining. It's scaring away the customers."

"Christ on a cross, Betty, go away," Kit said, his cheeks heating.

"Since when do you even like me?" Percy asked.

"Who said I did?" Betty answered, blowing him a kiss.

It was cold, the first night of the year that made it impossible to pretend that winter wasn't waiting around the corner. Their breaths clouded the air in front of them, mingling with the smoke and fog that drifted through the streets. It was, objectively, a foul night, but Kit had a sense of hopeful exhilaration that he hadn't experienced since that fresh green springtime he courted Jenny. He had been little more than a boy then, and hadn't known how rare and precious that sort of feeling was. Now he was jaded enough to know that most people never knew what it was like to take a walk side by side with the person they liked best in the world.

"Mind if we stop in here?" Kit asked when they passed the stable where he kept Bridget. It was a little warmer inside, thanks to a brazier the pair of stable boys were using to warm their hands. The boys looked up, recognized Kit, and wordlessly waved him in.

"Her name is Bridget," Kit said when they reached the right stall. "I can't ride her as fast as she likes, but she puts up with me anyway. You're welcome to make use of her as much as you like."

"Thank you. That's—"

"She's my horse, mind. I'm not making a present of her."

"I didn't think you were," Percy laughed.

"You hear me, Bridget," Kit said, holding out his hand for her to nuzzle, "you're still mine. You can be as rude as you please to Percy, and he'll only think it's a sign of good breeding." Percy leaned against him a little, shoulder to shoulder, just enough so Kit could feel his warmth and a comforting bit of pressure.

At the tavern, they tucked themselves into a dark, snug corner. Kit waited until Percy was finishing his second pint, his limbs just starting to get a bit loose and the careworn lines easing from his face.

"So, what happens on January first?" Kit asked. His own pint was only a quarter empty, and he held the tankard between his palms, the pewter warming to his touch.

"I lay out the evidence of my illegitimacy before my solicitor and hope he can figure out how to make it so that I'm not the Duke of Clare. I haven't any idea what that entails, but the important thing is that I've made a number of decisions that I don't think can be easily undone."

"I don't think Rob would want to."

"Fair. But let's say the courts decide he isn't my father's legitimate son, and instead the title and estate go to some horrible Tory cousin. I've tried to set it up so that nothing I did could be easily reversed. You would not believe how cross my solicitors and agents are right now. So much hand-wringing. So many lamentations."

"Fuck 'em," Kit said.

"Fuck them indeed," Percy agreed, and lifted his pint in a toast.

"But that isn't what I wanted to know. What happens to you on January first? You don't plan to stay at Clare House, do you?"

"God no. I, well." Percy traced a finger around the rim of his cup. "I did have something to ask you, and I hope you won't take it the wrong way. And mind you, there are other options, naturally."

"Out with it, Percy." Kit was braced to hear that Percy had decided to go abroad or to live as a recluse in the country, both of which were probably very reasonable choices.

"Would you mind if I hired the house next door?" Percy asked. "You probably think that given my circumstances, I ought to content myself with a set of rooms, but Collins insists that any sister of mine must be raised as a lady, which evidently means in a proper house, and I'm afraid I've put myself in a position where I owe Collins so many favors that I simply must do as he says."

Kit blinked. "You want to move in next door?"

"As I said, there are other suitable houses, if you think it would be, ah, too much of a good thing to have me next door. It's a decent house with large rooms and plenty of light." Percy added quickly, "And I can get it on a long lease. This neighborhood has many advantages, as I'm certain you know; for example, proximity to the prizefights as well as, not to put too fine a point on it, you. But as I said, I can hire a different house with all the above qualities, except that last one, which of course wouldn't be an advantage at all if you'd prefer me elsewhere—"

"I wouldn't prefer that," Kit said. "Not even a little." He hadn't quite realized it, but he had been waiting for something like this—a sign that Percy was choosing him, choosing them. Love, while a fine thing, might be little more than an accident. It was what came next that mattered.

"Really?" Percy looked as if he felt as unsure of what to do with this abundance of hope as Kit was himself. "Well, of course you wouldn't. Who wouldn't want me as a neighbor? Apart from, you know, quite a number of people, as it turns out, if you've been reading the papers."

Kit slid his hand across the table so his thumb brushed once against the inside of Percy's wrist.

"Yes, well, it had to be done," Percy said, even though Kit hadn't spoken.

Percy looked just as much like the old Duke of Clare as he had the day they'd met, and Kit didn't think he'd ever fail to note the resemblance or forget the family connection. But now the likeness was proof that Kit himself had changed; it was proof that Kit had relearned how to hope.

Chapter 51

$\mathcal{W}$hen they got back to the coffeehouse, it was dark and empty. Percy had already slept two nights in a row in Kit's bed, and he was debating whether it would be indiscreet to attempt a third, when he was distracted by the sight of a parcel leaning against the wall. It was large and flat and wrapped in brown paper.

"That wasn't here when we left," Percy said, eyeing it warily.

"It certainly was not," Kit confirmed, walking over to examine it. "There's nothing written on it. No direction or name."

"Might as well open it," Percy suggested.

Percy couldn't have said exactly when he realized what he was looking at. Was it after Kit tore off the first strip of paper and he caught a glimpse of blue paint? Or was it after the second strip was removed and Percy could make out the roofline of Cheveril? In either case, he tore off the remaining paper with his own hands and stared at the life-size portrait of Marian and himself posed before the eastern facade of Cheveril Castle.

The portraitist had caught Percy in half profile, either turning his head toward Marian or away from her, and looking like he was about to laugh. Marian held the baby—who thankfully looked like a human infant rather than a small goblin—close to her chest, and wore an expression that hovered between serene and calculating. As for Cheveril, Percy could only speculate as to who had directed the portraitist to paint in the house in place of the duke.

"There's a scrap of paper gummed to the back," Kit said.

Percy moved to the back of the canvas and knelt to read the note. "'Kiss Eliza for me,'" he read aloud. "What does that mean?" he asked in rising panic. "What can that possibly mean? Does it mean she isn't coming back?"

Kit took hold of Percy's shoulders. "It likely means she needs time."

"Right. Right. That makes sense."

"Who chose the artist?"

Percy raised his eyebrows. He hadn't taken Kit as someone who was interested in art or artists. "I did. I visited Signore Bramante's studio in Venice and liked his work."

"Why? I mean, the likeness is good, and it's not a bad-looking painting, but there've got to be dozens of artists who can do the same, and who wouldn't need to be shipped in from Venice."

Percy cast his mind back to what felt like a lifetime ago but was only earlier that year. "His subjects seemed to like one another." There were other reasons, ones having to do with light and composition and a certain misplaced optimism about getting into Bramante's bed. But the truth was that when he'd learned that his father had married Marian, of all people, he had hoped it was a love match. And so he had hired Bramante, as if spending a silly amount of money on a portrait might make it so.

That answer seemed to satisfy Kit, as little as it pleased Percy, though. He nodded. "You look like family. You and Marian and the child."

Percy, who had more or less kept his cool for the past abominable week, for the past wretched couple of months, felt tears prickle his eyes. "Oh, damn you, Kit Webb. I ought to go," he said, even as Kit pulled him close. "I have more trouble to make for the solicitors. And you might not be aware of this, but it might raise eyebrows if I broke down and started to sob on your shoulder. Commoners must be discreet." He knew he was being absurd; the shop was empty, they were safe and alone. But he couldn't even remember the last time he had cried. It felt rather nice, though, in a self-indulgent and histrionic way, to let himself go a little, and to know that Kit was fond of him just the same.

"There are other things commoners can do, though," Kit said, pulling back and looking Percy in the eye, and Percy knew he was referring to what Percy had said at Cheveril, about how Percy could be with Kit in a way the Duke of Clare never could.

Percy flushed. "I hope so," he said.

He had begun to imagine what his life could look like now, and how it might be a life he could share. He imagined two houses close enough that traffic through the alley behind them might not attract notice, whatever the hour. He imagined shared meals, shared time, coffee cups migrating from one building to the other.

He had thought of his changes in circumstance in terms of loss, but what he had gained was precious. "I find that I have nobody to oblige but myself," Percy said. "Nobody to please but myself. But I want to please you. Of all the choices that I never thought I'd get to make, that's the one I want the most, Kit. If you'll have me."

"I love you, too," Kit said, and pulled him close.

Epilogue

One month later

*O*ne morning in the middle of January, when it was early enough that the winter sun hadn't quite risen and Kit had only just lit the fire, a knock sounded at the door.

"Some of us can't tell time," announced Percy as he entered the shop, looking sleep rumpled and holding a furious baby.

"So I see." Kit ushered them in toward the hearth. "Are you going to burp that child or not?"

"I beg your pardon. Talbots do not belch."

"Give her over," Kit laughed, holding out his arms. "There now," Kit said, firmly patting the child's back.

"I tried patting her. I'm not entirely incompetent with— Oh, that's revolting. Eliza, I'm appalled. We need to discuss standards."

Kit laughed as the baby gave him an indignant look that closely resembled one of Percy's. "Have either of you managed any sleep at all?"

"Well, not recently. She seems to be getting a new tooth and is under the impression that it's my fault."

"They often are," Kit said, and saw a stricken look flicker over Percy's face as he recalled how Kit came by his knowledge of babies. "This one, however, comes from a long line of complainers, so I daresay she came by it honestly."

The baby was getting to the age where she was a bit too heavy and wriggly to hold with one arm, so Kit sat before the fire and let her chew on the collar of his coat.

"Put that kettle on, will you?" Kit asked, then watched as Percy glanced around, as if not entirely clear what a kettle was or where it was supposed to go. "On the hook over the fire," he clarified. "Then come here."

Percy came to sit on the arm of his chair. When Kit tilted his head up and raised his eyebrows, Percy bent down for a kiss. He tasted of tooth powder and smelled of shaving soap, and Kit's heart thrilled at the normalcy of it.

"You could come for supper," Percy said softly. "Collins hired a cook, because apparently he's far too grand to get his food from taverns and chophouses."

Kit was impressed with how well Collins had maneuvered Percy into living in a way that Percy—and, presumably, Collins—would find acceptable. "The baby will need nourishing food to eat with all these teeth you're insisting she grow. Collins is staying on, then?"

Percy sniffed. "He's being quite unreasonable. I told him to go to Marcus, because Marcus doesn't have a valet, and I tell you, Kit, it shows."

As Percy spoke, he pulled the leather cord from Kit's queue and proceeded to plait Kit's hair at the nape of his neck. "Would you like to know something exceptionally droll?" Percy asked. "I haven't stopped being invited to things. If anything, I'm getting more invitations than ever, presumably from people with a taste for scandal and disorder. One imagines I'm invited as a spectacle, but I'm invited nonetheless."

That reminded Kit of something he had been turning over in his mind for the past month. "I wonder," he said, "if you'd like to help me with a project."

"Anything," Percy said.

"I don't know if Rob got to me or if Betty did or if I've just stopped trying to argue with myself. But I loved planning that holdup, Percy. And not just because your father was the target, although that was part of it. God help me, this is probably prideful in a dozen different ways, but I think I can right wrongs. With some information from Scarlett, a proper burglar, a runner, and a fence, I'd have enough to go on. But what I really need is someone to get access to the homes of targets—someone to open a window, leave a door unlocked, draw up the layout of the house."

"I'd be delighted to turn traitor to my class," Percy said easily. "Honestly, I've been wondering when you'd ask."

Percy knew he had promised Kit supper, but when Kit came over that night, he found Percy sitting on the bare floor of the empty sitting room, surrounded by yards of sky-blue silk and staring at a framed portrait.

"Did you do this?" Percy asked. He knew it was obvious he had been crying, and he didn't even care.

Kit knelt beside him. "I thought you might like it, but I'll take it all away if you don't."

"How did you manage it?"

"I very politely explained that you required your bed hangings and your mother's portrait, and the housekeeper wrapped them up immediately."

Percy laughed wetly. "That's all it took?"

"I reckon you were expecting a daring heist, but I took a gamble that the servants would either be fond of you or . . . less than fond of your father, and it worked."

Knowing what Cheveril meant to Kit, Percy could hardly believe that Kit had willingly gone back. He took Kit's hand and kissed it. He was being maudlin. Soft. And he reveled in the freedom to be that way.

"I don't have any supper for you," Percy said. "Because I sent everybody out of the house. Except Eliza, and she's asleep in her cradle and unlikely to inform on us. And you may visit her *later*, Kit. Right now you have other matters to attend to."

"Is that so," Kit said, already pushing Percy back into the blue silk.

"I'm prizefighting tomorrow," Percy said while kissing Kit's jaw. "Want to watch?"

Kit kissed him hard, as if to show him how much he wanted to watch.

It felt unexpectedly intimate to be together in this narrow little house that was Percy's in a way no place ever had been, a place he had chosen because he had chosen Kit. He felt exposed, as if all the weakest parts of him were visible for Kit to see. But it was also comforting to know that Kit would guard his weaknesses as fiercely as Percy would, rather than exploit them. Percy knew he would do the same for Kit. This was what he wanted—the chance to be known for the worst of what he was and to be held dear anyway, the ability to trust a person as more than an ally.

He knew he had found that in Kit and would every day try to

show Kit that he had found the same in Percy. And he knew that they had also found other things—a chance to try to make the right choices, a small but sure haven of comfort, hope where they least expected it.

"Where did you go?" Kit asked, looking down at Percy with an expression so hopelessly fond, Percy had to force himself not to shut his eyes.

"I'm right here," Percy said, and reached up for a kiss.

Cat Sebastian will be back to steal your heart
with Rob and Marian's story
Coming Summer 2022

Acknowledgments

As always, I'm indebted to my editor, Elle Keck, and my critique partner, Margrethe Martin. My agent, Deidre Knight, has been endlessly supportive, not just of this project, but for the past five years. I'm so grateful for the enthusiasm of everyone at Avon who helped produce this book and get it out into the world.

This book was written in the midst of global and personal upheaval and it would never have gotten finished without my family making sure I had the space—both physical and mental—to write, and for that I'm enormously grateful. I wrote half of it in my daughter's bedroom and the other half in my parents' spare room, and they were all extremely good sports about letting me leave coffee cups and sticky notes all over their belongings. Both my sons were instrumental in coming up with inventive ways to do away with bad guys, and to them I apologize for not having the range to write about cannibal sheep.

About the Author

CAT SEBASTIAN lives in a swampy part of the South with her family and pets. Before her kids were born, she practiced law and taught high school and college writing. When she isn't reading or writing, she's doing crossword puzzles, bird watching, and wondering where she put her coffee cup.

MORE ROMANCE FROM CAT SEBASTIAN

THE TURNER SERIES

The Soldier's Scoundrel
Cat Sebastian's debut romance about a former criminal who has never followed the straight and narrow and a soldier who is determined to find law and order in a chaotic world.

The Lawrence Browne Affair
Sebastian returns to her Turner series with a stirring romance about an earl hiding from his future and a swindler haunted by his past.

The Ruin of a Rake
When the most upstanding man in London crosses paths with the ton's most dashing rake, a scandalous love affair will overtake them both.

A Little Light Mischief
Sebastian dives back into her Turner series with the sparkling novella of a lady's maid with a penchant for thievery and the vicar's daughter who falls in love with her.

THE SEDUCING THE SEDGWICKS SERIES

It Takes Two to Tumble
Sebastian begins the Seducing the Sedgwicks series by asking, how do you solve a problem like a vicar in love?

A Gentleman Never Keeps Score
In the second installment of the Seducing the Sedgwicks series, two wounded men brought together by scandal will find a love that neither thought possible.

Two Rogues Make a Right
The Seducing the Sedgwick series concludes with this moving romance of two lifelong friends who are trapped in a small cottage and finally forced to admit their long-held love for each other.

THE REGENCY IMPOSTORS SERIES

Unmasked by the Marquess
Beginning her Regency Impostors series, Sebastian crafts a vivid tale about a serious man and the person who shows him that in love, everything may not be as it seems.

A Duke in Disguise
The Regency Impostors series continues as one reluctant heir and one radical bookseller spark a fire that will burn forever.

A Delicate Deception
The final enchanting romance in the Regency Impostors series finds a reclusive young woman and a wounded man find healing and love in one another's arms.

DISCOVER GREAT AUTHORS, EXCLUSIVE OFFERS, AND MORE AT HC.COM.